The Beggar in the Harem

Impudent Adventures in Old Bukhara

by

Leonid Solovyev

Translated by Tatiana Shebunina

Stillwoods Edition

Stillwoods.Blogspot.Ca

Catalogue Information:
Title: The Beggar in the Harem
Subtitle: Impudent Adventures in Old Bukhara
U.K. Title: Adventures in Bukhara
Author: Leonid Solovyev (often Solovyov)
Translated by Tatiana Shebunina
First published in Russian: 1943
This Edition by: Stillwoods, 2022
ISBN Canada: 978-1-989788-88-2
Blog: Stillwoods.Blogspot.Ca
Storefront: http://www.lulu.com/spotlight/lulubook22

Cautionary Note: This series of books by Stillwoods are intended to make stories available to collectors, readers and researchers. The editor, or rather digitizer has not altered the original publication.

This story may contain language and racial terms that are not appropriate to today. I apologize for them; I know that the author was using his voice to excite and entertain an adventurous audience. These works were published many years ago. Most every work has characters of redeeming ethnicity within.

I hope you enjoy and share these stories; I have.

This edition is dedicated to all those people that have come into Canada from middle and western Asia, and from those troubled countries touching the Eastern Mediterranian.

Your cultures add a further layer to the riches of our melting pot. May you enjoy our riches.

Books by this author include:
Black Sea Sailor
The Beggar in the Harem
The Enchanted Prince
All published as Stillwoods Editons.

Doug Frizzle

This story comes to us from Abu-Omar-Ahmad-ibn-Muhammad, who had it from Muhammad-ibn-Ali-ibn-Rifaa, who quotes Ali-ibn-Abd-al-Aziz, who quotes Abu-Ubayd-al-Kasim-ibn-Selam, who took it down from the mouth of his teachers the last of whom gives for his authority Omar-ibn-al-Khattab and his son Abd-Allah, may Allah's favour abide with them both."

IBN HAZM: *The Turtledove's Necklace.*

I DEDICATE this book to the pure and everlasting memory of my friend Mumin Adilov, who perished from a dastardly bullet on 18 April 1930.

He had many of Khoja Nasreddin's traits—selfless devotion to the people, courage, noble shrewdness and honest astuteness. When I was writing this book, more than once in the quiet of the night I seemed to feel his shade at my side guiding my pen.

He died in the mountain village of Nanay and lies buried in Kanibadam. A short while ago I visited his grave. Children were playing round the mound covered with spring grass and flowers, while he slept the sleep of eternity and did not respond to the call of my heart. . . .

L. S.

Various spellings of the family name exist in English web pages:
Solovyev
Solovyov
Solov'ev
Soloviev
/drf

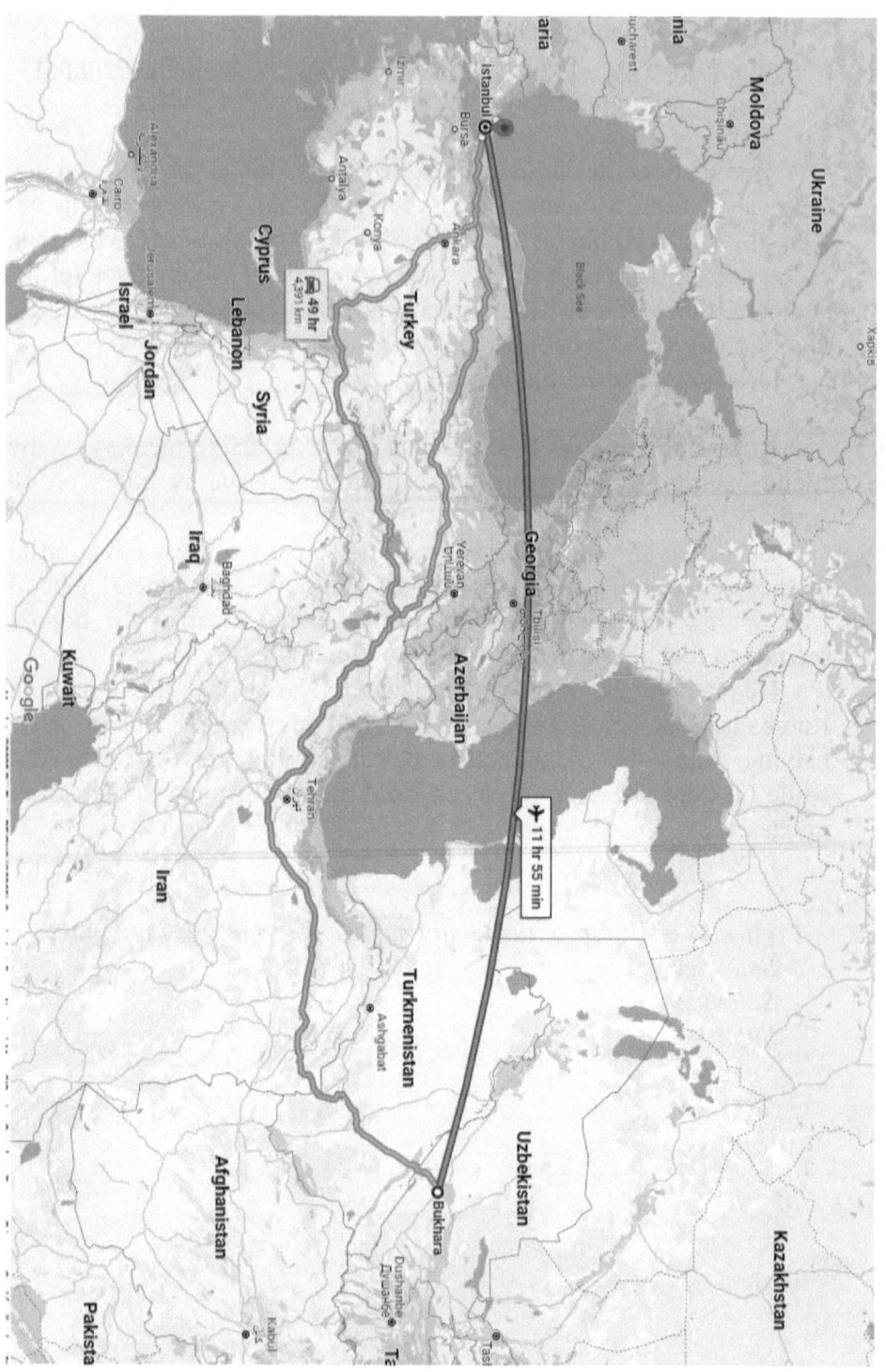

1

KHOJA NASREDDIN'S thirty-fifth birthday found him on the road.

He had spent over ten years in exile, wandering from town to town, from country to country, crossing seas and deserts, and sleeping where night overtook him: on the bare earth by a shepherd's meagre camp-fire, in a crowded caravanserai, where all night long, in the dusty gloom, camels sigh and scratch themselves with a hollow tinkling bells, or in a smoky, sooty tea-house among sprawling water-carriers, beggars, drivers and other poor folk, who at the break of dawn fill the bazaars and the narrow streets of the town with their shrill cries.

Many a night he had spent too on the soft silk cushions of some Persian dignitary's harem, while the master of the house, accompanied by guards, would be scouring the tea-houses and caravanserais for that impious vagabond whom he would impale if he caught him.

A light streak appears in the sky through the latticed window, the stars pale, the breeze heralding the dawn rustles gently and damply among the foliage, and on the window-ledge gay turtle-doves begin to coo and to preen themselves. Khoja Nasreddin says, kissing the languid beauty:

"It is time. Farewell, my matchless pearl. Do not forget me."

"Stay," she pleads, clasping her lovely arms round his neck. "Are you going away for good? Listen, tonight, as soon as it is dark, I shall send the old woman to fetch you again."

"No. I have long forgotten what it is to spend two nights under the same roof. I must be on my way. I am in a hurry."

"On your way? Have you pressing business in some other town? Where are you going?"

"I do not know. But it is light already; the city gates are open and the first caravans are moving out. Do you hear the tinkle of camels' bells? When I hear it, *jinns* seem to possess my feet and I cannot keep still."

"Go, then!" petulantly exclaims the harem beauty, vainly trying to hide the tears which glisten on her long eyelashes. "But at least tell me your name before you go."

"My name? Listen then: you have spent the night with Khoja Nasreddin. I am Khoja Nasreddin, the Disturber of the Peace and the Sower of Discord, a man with a high price on his head; every day town-criers announce it in public places and bazaars. Yesterday they were offering three thousand *tomans*, and I was tempted to sell my own head at such a good price. You laugh, my little star? Well, give me your lips for the last time. I wish I could give you an emerald, but as I have no emerald, take this little white pebble to remember me by."

He pulls on his ragged *khalat*,[1] burnt through in many places by the sparks of camp-fires, and steals away. At the door snores the lazy, stupid eunuch in turban and soft slippers with turned-up toes—negligent guardian of the most precious treasure of the palace. Further on, stretched out on rugs and felts, snore the guards, their heads pillowed on naked daggers. Khoja Nasreddin creeps past them on tiptoe, always safely, as though for the time being rendered invisible.

And once more the stony road rings and smokes under the brisk hooves of his ass. The sun shines upon the world out of a blue sky. Khoja Nasreddin can look up at it without blinking. Dewy fields and barren deserts where camels' bones gleam white among the sand-drifts, green gardens and foaming rivers, bleak hills and smiling pastures hear Khoja Nasreddin's song. On and on he rides without a backward glance, without regret for what he is leaving behind nor fear of what awaits him.

But in the town which he has just left memory of him survives for ever. Mullahs and notables pale with rage at the mere mention of his name. Water-carriers, drivers, weavers, coppersmiths and saddlers foregathering at night in the tea-houses entertain each other with stories of his adventures which always end to his advantage. The languorous harem beauty often gazes at the white pebble and hastens to slip it into a mother-of-pearl casket at the sound of her lord's footsteps.

"Ough!" says the fat dignitary panting and grunting as he struggles out of his brocaded khalat. "This accursed vagabond Khoja Nasreddin has worn us all out. He has stirred up and upset the whole country. Today I received a letter from my old friend, the worthy governor of the province of Khorasan. What do you think? Hardly

---

[1] Long coat.

had this tramp, this Khoja Nasreddin, appeared in his towns than all at once the blacksmiths stopped paying the taxes and the inn-keepers refused to feed the guards without payment. To crown all, this thief, this defiler of Islam, this son of sin, dared enter the governor's harem and seduce his favourite wife! Verily, the world has never yet seen such a miscreant! Pity this worthless beggar did not try to make his way into my harem, for then his head would have been already sticking on a pole in the main square."

The beauty remains silent, smiling wistfully to herself.

Meanwhile the road rings and smokes under the brisk hooves of the ass to the sound of Khoja Nasreddin's singing.

In these ten years he had been everywhere: in Baghdad, Stambul and Tehran, in Bakhche-saray, Echmiadzin and Tiflis, in Damascus and Trebizond. He knew all these cities and many others besides, and everywhere he left an unforgettable memory.

Now he was on his way back to his native town, *Bukhara-yi Sherif,* Noble Bukhara, where he hoped to rest awhile from his endless wanderings under cover of an assumed name.

2

HE crossed the frontier of Bukhara with a large merchant caravan to which he had attached himself, and on the eighth day of the journey glimpsed far ahead in the dusty haze the familiar minarets of the great and famous city. The camel-drivers, exhausted by thirst and heat, raised a hoarse shout, and the camels stepped out faster. The sun was setting and there was need to make haste to enter Bukhara before the city gates were shut. Khoja Nasreddin rode at the tail-end of the caravan, wrapped in a thick and heavy cloud of dust; this was his very own, sacred dust which seemed to him to smell better than the dust of other distant lands. Sneezing and coughing he kept saying to his ass:

"Well, here we are. Home at last! By Allah, success and happiness await us here."

The caravan reached the town wall just as the guards were shutting the gates.

"Wait for us, for Allah's sake!" shouted the chief of the caravan exhibiting from afar a gold coin.

But the gates had already closed, the bolts fell with a clang, and the guards took up their posts at the guns on the towers. A fresh breeze sprang up, the pink gleam died away in the misty sky, the slender crescent of the young moon stood out sharply, and in the twilit stillness there floated out from all the innumerable minarets the high, long-drawn, mournful voices of the muezzins, calling the faithful to evening prayer.

As the merchants and drivers sank to their knees, Khoja Nasreddin quietly drew aside with his ass.

"These merchants have something to thank Allah for," he said, "they have dined today and now they expect to sup. You and I, my faithful ass, have not dined, nor shall we sup. If Allah desires our thanks let him send me a bowl of pilau and you a bundle of clover."

He tethered his ass to a roadside tree and lay down by his side on the bare earth with a stone for pillow. Looking up into the dark transparency of the sky he could see the shining network of the stars. Every constellation was familiar to him. How often in these ten years had he looked up into the open sky! It always seemed to him that these hours of wise and silent contemplation made him richer than the richest, for each has his lot in this world; though the wealthy man may eat off gold dishes, yet he is obliged to spend the night under a roof, and so is unable to savour in the midnight quiet, the feeling of the flight of the earth through the cool blue starry mist.

Meanwhile in the caravanserais and tea-houses clustering outside the crenellated city wall, fires had sprung up under huge cauldrons, and sheep set up a pitiful bleating as they were dragged to the slaughter. Wise in experience, Khoja Nasreddin had selected for his night's rest a spot windward from the tantalizing smell of food so that it should not disturb him. Knowing well the customs of Bukhara he had resolved to save the last of his money to pay the toll at the city gates on the morrow.

For a long time he kept tossing from side to side but sleep would not come. It was not hunger that made him sleepless but the bitter thoughts which beset and tormented him.

He loved his native land, it was his greatest love, this astute and merry fellow with a little black beard on his copper-coloured, sun-tanned face and a roguish twinkle in his clear eyes. And the farther away from Bukhara he wandered in his patched coat, greasy skull-cap and shabby boots, the more strongly he loved it and missed it. In his exile he cherished the memory of the little streets, so narrow that the araba[2] scrapes the mud walls on either side in its passage; of the tall

---

[2] Native cart.

4

minarets with their patterned glazed-brick tops which catch the fiery reflection of sunrise and sunset; of the ancient sacred plane-trees cradling among their branches the dark masses of storks' nests.

He remembered the gay tea-houses over the irrigation ditches in the shade of rustling poplars, the smoke and smell of cooking food in the over-heated cook-shops, the motley bustle of the bazaars; he remembered the hills and streams of his native land, its villages, fields, pastures and deserts, and when in Baghdad or Damascus he recognized a fellow-countryman by the pattern of his skull-cap or the peculiar cut of his robe, Khoja Nasreddin's heart missed a beat and his throat contracted.

On his return he found his country still more unhappy than when he had left it. The old Emir had been buried long ago. Within the last eight years the new Emir had managed to bring Bukhara to the verge of ruin. Khoja Nasreddin saw broken-down bridges, meagre, sun-parched roughly cultivated crops of wheat and barley, dry beds of irrigation ditches cracked by the heat. Fields were going to waste, overgrown with weeds and thorns, gardens withered for lack of water; the peasants had neither bread nor cattle; beggars lined the roads clamouring for alms from others as needy as themselves.

The new Emir had posted detachments of guards in every village with orders to the villagers to feed them at their own expense. He founded many mosques and then ordered the people to finish building them. The new Emir was very pious and never failed to perform a pilgrimage twice a year to the relics of the most holy and peerless Shaikh Baha ed-din, whose tomb was situated in the neighbourhood of Bukhara. To the existing four taxes he had added three more: he introduced tolls at every bridge, raised the taxes on trade and legal dues, and had minted a quantity of debased coin. Crafts were falling into decay, trade was on the decline.

It was a sorry homecoming for Khoja Nasreddin.

. . . Early in the morning the muezzins again sounded their call from all the minarets. The gates opened and the caravan slowly entered the city with a hollow tinkling of bells.

Once through the gates the caravan came to a standstill; the road was barred by the guards. They were very numerous; some were shod and well dressed, others who had not had time yet to fatten in the Emir's service were bare-footed and half-naked. They shouted and pushed each other, quarrelling over the loot that was going to be theirs. At last the tax-collector emerged from a teahouse, obese and sleepy-looking, clothed in a silk khalat with greasy sleeves, bare feet thrust into slippers, and his bloated face bearing all the marks of self-indulgence and vice. He inspected the merchants with a greedy eye and said:

"Welcome, O merchants! May you be successful in your business! And know you that the Emir has ordered that any man who conceals the tiniest portion of his wares shall die under the bastinado."

The merchants, perplexed and alarmed, silently stroked their dyed beards. The tax-collector turned to the guards who were prancing with impatience, and wiggled his thick fingers. At this signal the men threw themselves with whoops and yells upon the camels. Jostling each other in their frantic haste, they slashed the hair-ropes with their swords and noisily ripped open the bales, spilling on to the roadway brocades, silks and velvets, cases of pepper, tea and amber, phials of precious attar of roses and Tibetan drugs.

Horror kept the merchants tongue-tied.

Two minutes later the inspection was over. The guards lined up behind their chief, their coats bulging and swelling. Then began the collection of taxes on the wares and on the right of entry into the city. Khoja Nasreddin had no merchandise and was liable to pay only the entrance tax.

"Where do you come from and for what purpose?" asked the tax-collector.

The scribe dipped a reed-pen into his ink-horn and prepared to take down Khoja Nasreddin's statement in a thick ledger.

"I come from Iran, Your Excellency. Here in Bukhara live some relatives of mine."

"So," said the tax-collector, "you have come to visit your relations. In this case you must pay the visitor's tax."

"But I have not come to visit them," retorted Khoja Nasreddin. "I have come on important business."

"On business!" cried the tax-collector, and his eyes lit up. "Then you have come both on a visit and on business. Pay the visitor's tax, the business tax and make a donation towards the adornment of the mosques to the glory of Allah who has preserved you from robbers on the way."

"I had rather he preserved me now, for I would have found means to avoid the robbers myself," thought Khoja Nasreddin. But he held his tongue, having calculated that every word of this conversation was costing him more than ten tangas. He undid his sash, and under the greedily intent stare of the guards counted out the tax for entry into the city, the guest-tax, the trade-tax and the donation towards the adornment of the mosques. The tax-collector sternly eyed the guards who turned away. The scribe, his nose in the ledger, scratched away with his reed-pen.

Having paid up, Khoja Nasreddin was on the point of leaving, when the tax-collector noticed that he still had some coins left in his sash.

"Stay!" he ordered. "And who is going to pay the tax for your ass? If you are going to visit your relations, it means that your ass is also going to visit his relations."

"You are right, O wise Master," blandly retorted Khoja Nasreddin, undoing his sash once more. "Indeed, my ass must have a great number of relations in Bukhara. Otherwise, by the way things are run here, your Emir would long since have been pushed off his throne, while you, O worthy one, would have been impaled for greed."

Before the tax-collector could collect his wits, Khoja Nasreddin jumped on his ass, set off at a gallop and disappeared down the nearest lane.

"Faster! Faster!" he kept saying. "Hurry, my faithful ass, hurry, or your master will have to pay another tax with his head!"

Khoja Nasreddin's ass was very intelligent. He understood everything. His long ears had caught the noise and outcry at the city gates and the shouting of the guards, so he sped on, heedless of the road, and at such a pace that his master had to cling to the saddle, his arms hugging the animal's neck and his feet tucked up high. Dogs raced after them barking hoarsely, chickens scurried away in all directions, and passers-by pressed against the walls, shaking their heads and staring after them.

In the meantime, at the city gates the guards searched among the crowd looking for the bold freethinker. The merchants smiled and whispered to each other:

"That was an answer worthy of Khoja Nasreddin himself."

Towards noon the whole town had heard the story. Traders in the bazaar whispered it to their customers who passed it on, and all laughed, never failing to remark:

"These words are worthy of Khoja Nasreddin himself."

3

NEITHER relatives nor old friends did he find in Bukhara. He did not even find his father's house where he had been born and had grown to manhood, nor its shady garden where in the clear autumn days yellowing leaves rustled in the wind and ripe fruit thudded on to the ground; where birds whistled in high-pitched song and sun-flecks trembled upon the fragrant grass; where busy bees hummed as they gathered the last tribute of the fading flowers and the stream in the irrigation ditch murmured mysteriously telling the boy its endless unintelligible stories. . . . The site was now a plot of waste land pitted and covered with mounds of rubble, thorny thistles, fire-stained bricks, crumbling remnants of walls and scraps of rotting matting. Not a bird, not a bee did Khoja Nasreddin glimpse. Only from under a heap of stones over which he stumbled there suddenly oozed out a long oily streak which glistened dully in the sunlight and disappeared again under the stones—a snake, lonely and fearsome dweller in deserted places forever abandoned by man.

Khoja Nasreddin stood for a long time silent, with downcast eyes. Grief clutched at his heart.

The sound of a racking cough made him wheel round.

An old man bowed down by poverty and cares was coming along the path across the waste ground. Khoja Nasreddin stopped him.

"Peace be with you, old man, and may Allah send you many years of health and prosperity. Tell me, whose house stood here on this waste land?"

"It was the house of Shir-Mamed the saddler," replied the old man. "I knew him well once. This Shir-Mamed was the father of the famous Khoja Nasreddin, of whom, O wayfarer, you must have surely heard a good deal."

"Yes, I have heard something about him. But tell me, where has this saddler Shir-Mamed, father of the famous Khoja Nasreddin, gone to, and where is his family?"

"Not so loud, my son. There are thousands and thousands of spies in Bukhara. If they were to hear us, we would have no end of trouble. You must have come from afar not to know that in our town it is strictly forbidden to mention Khoja Nasreddin's name. It is enough to

8

get one sent to prison. Come closer and I shall tell you."

Concealing his agitation Khoja Nasreddin bent close.

"It happened in the old Emir's time," began the old man, coughing as he spoke. "Eighteen months after Khoja Nasreddin had been sent into exile a rumour spread in the bazaar that he had illegally and secretly returned and was staying in Bukhara composing mocking songs about the Emir. This rumour reached the Emir's palace. The guards started a search for Khoja Nasreddin but could not find him. Then the Emir ordered the seizure of his father, his two brothers, his uncle and all his distant relatives and friends. They were to be tortured until they revealed the whereabouts of Khoja Nasreddin. Allah be praised for giving them the courage and fortitude to keep silent, so that our Khoja Nasreddin did not fall into the Emir's hands. But his father, the saddler Shir-Mamed, sickened from the torture and soon died. His relatives and friends left Bukhara, fleeing the Emir's wrath, and no one knows where they are. Then the Emir ordered the destruction of their homes, and their gardens were uprooted so that the very memory of Khoja Nasreddin should be blotted out."

"But why were they tortured?" cried Khoja Nasreddin.

Tears ran down his face, but the old man did not see that, for his sight was dim. "Why were they tortured? Khoja Nasreddin was not in Bukhara at the time. I know it full well!"

"None can tell," replied the old man. "Khoja Nasreddin comes and goes when and how he pleases. He is everywhere and nowhere, our incomparable Khoja Nasreddin!"

With these words the old man trudged off groaning and coughing. Khoja Nasreddin buried his face in his hands, and went off to his ass.

He threw his arms round the ass, pressing his wet face against the warm, smelly neck.

"Ah, my good, my true friend," said Khoja Nasreddin. "You see, I have nobody left of my near and dear ones, only you, constant and faithful companion of my wanderings."

As though aware of his master's grief the ass stood still and even stopped chewing a thistle, which remained suspended from his lip.

An hour later Khoja Nasreddin had mastered his grief and the tears had dried on his face.

"Never mind!" he cried with a hearty slap on the ass's back. "Never mind! I have not been forgotten yet in Bukhara. They still know and remember me. We'll manage to find some friends! And we'll compose such a song about the Emir that he'll burst with rage on his throne, and his filthy guts will spatter those finely decorated walls of his palace! Come, my faithful ass, forward!"

4

IT was a quiet hour of the afternoon, and very close. A lazy heat came up from the dusty road, the stones, the mud walls and fences, and the perspiration on Khoja Nasreddin's face dried before he had time to wipe it off.

He recognized with emotion the familiar streets, the tea-houses and minarets. In ten years nothing had changed in Bukhara. Just as always some mangy dogs were asleep by the water-tanks, and a woman, bending gracefully and holding back her veil with a dark-skinned hand tipped with painted nails, plunged a narrow, ringing jug into the dark water.

Where and how to get a meal was the problem. Khoja Nasreddin tightened his sash for the third time since yesterday.

"I must find a way," he said. "Let's stop, my faithful ass, and think. And here, most opportunely, is a tea-house."

Unbridling his ass he let him loose to feed on wisps of clover dropped beside the tie-rail. Then, gathering up the skirts of his khalat he squatted down by the irrigation ditch where the water, thick with clay, bubbled and foamed at the turnings.

"Whither, what for and whence does this water flow? It does not know and does not think about it," Khoja Nasreddin wistfully reflected. "I, too, know neither rest nor home, nor whither I am going. Why did I come to Bukhara? Where shall I go tomorrow? And where am I to get the half-tanga for my dinner? Am I still to be hungry? That accursed tax-collector! He's cleaned me out. What impudence to mention robbers to me!"

At that very moment he caught sight of the man who was the cause of his misfortunes. The tax-collector was riding up to the tea-house. Two guards were leading by the bridle his Arab stallion, a handsome bay with a noble and flashing fire in its dark eyes. Its neck was arched, and as it trod daintily and impatiently on its slender legs it seemed loath to be carrying the bloated carcass of its master.

The guards respectfully helped their chief to dismount. He went into the tea-house. The flustered and obsequious owner showed him to some silk cushions on which he seated himself. Then he brewed a special pot of his finest tea and offered his guest a delicate tea-glass of Chinese workmanship.

"He's getting a grand welcome and at my expense!" thought Khoja Nasreddin.

The tax-collector filled himself with tea and soon fell into a doze on the cushions. The sound of his gurglings, snores and smacking of lips filled the tea-house. The other guests lowered their conversation to a whisper for fear of disturbing his slumbers. The guards sat on either side of him and chased away the pestering flies with leafy twigs. When they were sure that he was fast asleep they exchanged a wink, unbridled the stallion, threw a bundle of clover before it, and picking up a narghile, retired into the dark interior of the tea-house. A moment later Khoja Nasreddin smelt the sweetish scent of hashish. The guards were freely indulging in their favourite vice.

"Well, it is time I was off," decided Khoja Nasreddin, recalling his morning adventure at the city gates and fearing that the guards might recognize him. "But still, where am I to get half a tanga? O almighty Fate, you who have so often come to Khoja Nasreddin's rescue, cast a benevolent eye upon him!"

Just then someone hailed him. "Hey, you there!"

Khoja Nasreddin wheeled round and saw a covered, richly decked wagon drawn up in the road. A man in a large turban and expensive khalat was peering out from between the curtains. Even before this stranger—a wealthy merchant or a dignitary—had uttered his next words, Khoja Nasreddin knew that his prayer had not remained unanswered; as usual, Fate had cast a benevolent eye upon him in his difficulty.

"I like this stallion," said the rich stranger haughtily, looking over Khoja Nasreddin's head to admire the handsome Arab bay. "Tell me, is this stallion for sale?"

"There is no horse in the world which could not be sold," Khoja Nasreddin replied evasively.

"You have probably got a pretty empty pocket," the stranger went on. "Listen to me carefully. I do not know to whom this stallion belongs, from whence it comes nor who was its former master. I am not asking you. Judging by the dust on your clothes you must have come to Bukhara from afar. That is enough for me. Do you understand?"

Khoja Nasreddin nodded. He had understood immediately what the rich stranger was driving at, and even more. What he hoped for now was that some silly fly should not crawl into the tax-collector's nostril or throat and so wake him up. He was less concerned about the guards, for the clouds of thick green smoke which issued from the dark interior showed that they were wholeheartedly indulging in their vice.

"You must realize," the rich stranger continued patronisingly and importantly, "that it is not for you in your tattered khalat to be riding such a horse. It would even be dangerous, for everyone would wonder: 'Where did this beggar get such a fine stallion?' You might easily land in prison."

"You are right, noble master," humbly agreed Khoja Nasreddin. "The horse is certainly far too fine for me. In my tattered khalat I have been riding an ass all my life and dare not even think of mounting such a steed."

His answer met with the rich stranger's approval.

"It is well that, poor as you are, you should not be blinded by pride. The poor man must be humble and modest, for beautiful flowers are natural to the noble almond-tree and not to the miserable thorn-bush of the steppe. Now answer me: do you want this purse? It contains exactly three hundred tangas in silver."

"Do I want it?" cried Khoja Nasreddin, now on tenterhooks because a stupid fly had managed to crawl into the tax-collector's nostril making him sneeze and stir. "I should think so! Who would refuse three hundred tangas in silver? Why, it is just like finding a purse on the road!"

"It looks as though you had found something quite different on the road," said the rich stranger with a knowing smile, "but I am prepared to exchange this silver for what you found on the road. Here are your three hundred tangas."

He handed the heavy purse to Khoja Nasreddin and made a sign to his servant, who stood scratching his back with his whip and silently taking in the conversation. As the servant went up to the stallion Khoja Nasreddin noted from the grin on his flat pock-marked face and his shifty eyes that he must be as thorough a rascal as his master.

"Three rogues on one road are at least one too many. It is time I made myself scarce," he decided.

Extolling the piety and generosity of the rich stranger, he jumped on his ass and gave him such a thump with his heels that the animal, for all its natural indolence, started off at a gallop.

When Khoja Nasreddin looked back he saw the servant tying the bay Arab to the wagon. When he looked again, the rich stranger and the tax-collector were clawing at each other's beards while the guards made vain efforts to separate them.

The wise man takes no part in other men's quarrels. Khoja Nasreddin wove his way in and out of by-streets until he felt safe from pursuit. He pulled in his ass to a slower gait.

"Wait, wait," he began, "there is no hurry now. . . ."

Suddenly he heard quite close the rapid and alarming beat of hooves. "Oho! Forward, my faithful ass! Forward! Get me out of here!" he shouted, but too late; from behind a corner a horseman sprang out into the road.

It was the pockmarked servant. He was riding a horse unharnessed from the wagon. Swinging his legs he dashed past Khoja Nasreddin and brought his mount to a sudden halt, setting it across the road.

"Let me pass, good fellow," meekly pleaded Khoja Nasreddin. "On such narrow roads one should ride lengthwise, not crosswise."

"Aha!" replied the servant with malicious glee. "Now there will be no escaping the dungeon for you! Do you know that this dignitary, the stallion's owner, has pulled out half my master's beard and that my master has made his nose bleed? Tomorrow you will be taken before the Emir's tribunal. Truly, fellow, your lot is a bitter one!"

"What's that you are saying?" exclaimed Khoja Nasreddin. "What has made these respectable persons quarrel so bitterly? And why have you stopped me? I can be no judge in their dispute. Let them settle it between themselves as best they can."

"Hold your tongue!" said the servant. "Turn back. You will have to answer for that stallion."

"What stallion?"

"You dare to ask? Why, the one for which you received a purse of silver from my master."

"By Allah, you are mistaken," replied Khoja Nasreddin. "The stallion does not enter into this business. Judge for yourself. You heard the whole conversation. Your master, a pious and generous man, wishing to help a poor fellow, asked me whether I would like three hundred silver tangas, and I said that of course I would. Then he gave me three hundred tangas, may Allah prolong the days of his life. But before he gave me the money, he tested my modesty and humility in order to ascertain whether I deserved the reward. He said: 'I do not ask whose stallion this is nor where it comes from.'

"You see, he wished to know whether out of false pride I would claim to be its owner. I kept silent, and the generous, pious man was pleased. Then he said that such a stallion would be too good for me and I agreed with him, at which he was also pleased. Then he said that I had found on the road that which could be exchanged for silver, thus hinting at my zeal and firmness in Islam, which I have acquired in my travels to the Holy Places. And after all this he rewarded me, intending by this pious deed to facilitate his future entrance into paradise over the bridge which is lighter than a hair and narrower than the edge of a sword, as the holy Koran tells us. In my very first prayer I shall tell Allah of your master's pious deed so that he may put up railings for him on this bridge."

The servant listened thoughtfully to this long speech, scratching his back with his whip. At the end he said with a sly grin which disturbed Khoja Nasreddin:

"You are right, O traveller! How is it that I did not realize at once that your conversation with my master had such a virtuous meaning? But as you have decided to help my master to cross the bridge to the other world, it would be safer if it had railings on both sides. I, too, would gladly pray for my master so that Allah should put up railings on the other side."

"Then pray!" cried Khoja Nasreddin. "Who hinders you? You are even bound in duty to do so. Does not the Koran instruct slaves and servants to pray daily for their masters without asking for any special reward?"

"Turn back your ass!" the servant shouted roughly, kneeing his mount and pressing Khoja Nasreddin against the wall. "Now then, hurry up, do not make me lose any more time."

"Wait," Khoja Nasreddin interrupted hastily. "I have not finished. I was going to recite a prayer of three hundred words according to the number of tangas received. But now I think that a prayer of two hundred and fifty words might suffice. The railings on my side will be only slightly thinner and shorter. As for you, you will recite a prayer of fifty words, and the all-wise Allah will know how to make a railing for your side out of the same wood."

"What?" said the servant. "Why should my railing be five times shorter than yours?"

"But it will be in the most dangerous part," Khoja Nasreddin hastened to add.

"No," the servant said firmly. "I don't agree to such short railings. It would mean that part of the bridge would be without railings. I tremble at the very thought of the danger that would threaten my master. In my opinion we must each say a prayer of one hundred and fifty words each so that the railings on both sides shall be of the same length. Let them be thin, but at least both sides will be guarded. And if you do not agree, then it means that you have evil designs upon my master and wish him to fall off the bridge. Then I shall summon help and you will take the shortest cut to the dungeon."

"Thin railings!" cried Khoja Nasreddin enraged and feeling as though the purse was stirring in his sash. "From what you say it would be good enough to have railings made of twigs! Don't you understand that the railings must be thicker and stronger on one side so that your master will have something to clutch if he loses his footing and starts to fall?"

"Verily truth falls from your mouth!" cried the servant gleefully. "Let the railing be thicker on my side and I shall not spare myself and will recite a prayer of two hundred words."

"Perhaps you would like to make it three hundred?" Khoja Nasreddin said with venom.

When they finally parted Khoja Nasreddin's purse was lighter by a half. They had agreed at last that the bridge leading into paradise should be guarded for the man's master by railings of equal strength and thickness on both sides.

"Farewell, traveller," said the servant. "You and I have indeed performed a pious deed today."

"Farewell, most kind, loyal and virtuous servant, so full of anxiety for the salvation of your master's soul. I should like to add that you will soon be a match for Khoja Nasreddin himself."

"What makes you mention him?" asked the servant, pricking up his ears.

"Nothing. . . . It just occurred to me," replied Khoja Nasreddin, thinking to himself: "Oho, this fellow is no simpleton."

"Maybe you are a distant relative of his?" asked the servant. "Or perhaps you know a member of his family?"

"No, I have never met him. And I do not know any of Khoja Nasreddin's relations."

"Listen, I will tell you a secret." The servant bent down from his saddle. "I am a relation of his. His cousin, in fact. We spent our childhood together."

Khoja Nasreddin's suspicions became a certitude and he held his tongue. The servant leaned still closer.

"His father, two brothers and an uncle have died. You have probably heard that, eh, traveller?"

But Khoja Nasreddin still remained silent.

"Such cruelty on the part of the Emir!" hypocritically exclaimed the servant.

But Khoja Nasreddin still kept silent.

"All the viziers of Bukhara are fools!" said the servant unexpectedly. He was agog with impatience and greed, for the Treasury paid handsome rewards for the apprehension of freethinkers. But Khoja Nasreddin remained stubbornly silent.

"And our illustrious Emir is also a fool!" said the man. "And it is not at all certain that Allah even exists!"

But Khoja Nasreddin did not open his mouth, although a stinging answer was on the tip of his tongue. The servant, bitterly disappointed, shouted out an oath, struck his horse and in two bounds disappeared round the corner. All grew quiet. Only the dust raised by the horse's hooves hung like a golden mist in the still air pierced by hot, slanting rays.

"Well, so I have found myself a relative," Khoja Nasreddin thought and smiled to himself. "The old man did not lie to me. Spies are as thick as flies in Bukhara, and it will pay to be careful. As the old proverb says: 'the guilty tongue is chopped off with the head'."

Thus he rode on for a long time, alternately brooding over the loss of half the contents of his purse, and grinning over the memory of the fight between the tax-collector and the haughty stranger.

5

WHEN Khoja Nasreddin reached the other end of the town he stopped, handed his ass to the care of a tea-house owner and hurried without loss of time to an eating-house.

It was crowded, full of smoke and the smell of cooking food. The stoves glowed hotly, and the flames lit up the sweating-backs of the cooks who worked stripped to the waist. They bustled, shouted, jostled each other and boxed the ears of the kitchen-boys who dashed about wild-eyed, adding to the general crush, noise and confusion. Huge kettles bubbled under dancing wooden lids; thick steam gathered near the ceiling where clouds of flies were buzzing. In the smoky haze butter hissed and puttered furiously, the sides of red-hot braziers shone and the fat which fell from the spits on to the coals burned with a blue and smoky flame. Here they were cooking pilau, roasting shishliks, boiling tripe and baking pies stuffed with onion, pepper, meat and sheep's-tail fat which melted in the oven and boiled in tiny bubbles as it seeped out of the pastry.

With great difficulty Khoja Nasreddin found himself a seat into which he had to squeeze so tightly that those whom he pressed with his back and sides grunted audibly. But no offence was taken, no one said a word to him, neither did he grumble. He had always liked the hot crowding of these bazaar eating-houses, all this discordant din, the jokes, the laughter, the shouting, the jostling, the vigorous snorting, chewing and champing of hundreds of men who have no time after a day of heavy toil to pick and choose among the dishes: powerful jaws grind anything—tendons and gristle alike—while the tough-lined belly accepts anything, so long as it is cheap and plentiful!

Khoja Nasreddin could put away a good deal. He ate at one sitting three bowls of noodles, three bowls of rice and two dozen samsa-pasties on top of it all. It took something of an effort to finish the samsa, which he did, true to his rule never to leave anything in the bowl when it had already been paid for.

At last he started towards the door, and when, after working hard with his elbows, he finally emerged into the open air, he was bathed in sweat. His arms and legs felt weak and soft as though he had just left the hands of a hefty bath-attendant. Heavy with the food and heat he walked with dragging steps to the tea-house where he had left his ass. He ordered tea and stretched out luxuriously on the felts. His eyelids drooped and slow and pleasant thoughts floated through his mind:

"I have a pretty sum of money just now. It would be a good idea to invest it in a workshop—a saddlery or a pottery. I know both these trades. It is about time I stopped wandering. Am I worse or more stupid than other men? Can't I have a kind, beautiful wife? Can't I have a son whom I could dandle in my arms? By the beard of the Prophet, the noisy little fellow will grow up into a famous rascal, and I shall not fail to pass on my wisdom to him! Yes, my mind is made up. Khoja Nasreddin gives up his restless life. To begin with I must buy a potter's business or a saddler's. . . ."

He began to count. A good workshop would cost at least three hundred tangas whereas he had only one hundred and fifty. He cursed the pock-marked servant. "May Allah curse that robber with blindness. He took away from me just what I needed to make a start!"

Once again Fate came to his rescue. "Twenty tangas!' somebody called out suddenly. Then came the sound of dice falling on to a copper tray.

On the edge of the porch and quite close to the tie-rail where the ass was tethered there sat a close circle of men. The owner of the teahouse stood behind them craning over their heads.

"Gambling!" guessed Khoja Nasreddin, raising himself on his elbow. "As sure as my name is Khoja Nasreddin, they're gambling! I must have a look, if only from a distance. I won't gamble, I'm not such a fool. But why shouldn't a wise man watch fools?"

He rose and went up to the gamblers.

"Foolish men," he whispered to the owner of the teahouse. "They risk their last coin in the hope of gain. Has not the Prophet prohibited gambling for money? Allah be praised, I am free from this fatal passion. . . . But what luck that red-haired gambler has! He has won for the fourth time running. . . . Look, look—he has won for the fifth time! O the senseless fool! He is lured by the false vision of wealth, whereas poverty has already dug a pit in his path. What? He has won for the sixth time? I have never seen such luck. Look, he is staking again. Truly, there is no limit to human folly! He cannot possibly win without a break! This is how men perish who put their faith in false luck! This red-haired fellow should be given a lesson. If he wins for the seventh time, I shall stake against him, even though in my heart I am against all gambling. Were I the Emir, I should long ago have forbidden it!"

The red-haired gambler threw the dice and won for the seventh time in succession.

Khoja Nasreddin stepped resolutely forward, shouldered the players aside and squatted down in the circle.

"I want to play with you," he said to the lucky winner, taking up the dice and examining them on all sides with an experienced eye.

"How much?" asked the red-haired one hoarsely. Tremors passed over his body. He was in a hurry to make the best of his ephemeral luck.

Khoja Nasreddin took out his purse, put back into his pocket twenty-five tangas for emergencies, and emptied out the rest. The silver tinkled and rang on the copper tray. The gamblers greeted the stake with an eager buzzing. A game for high stakes was going to start.

The red-haired man took up the dice and shook them for a long time, hesitating over his throw. Everyone held his breath, even the ass stretched out his muzzle *and* cocked his ears. The only sound was the clicking of the dice in the gambler's fist. This dry clicking sent a yearning weakness through Khoja Nasreddin's limbs and belly At last the red-haired one made his cast. The other players craned forward, then fell back as one man, heaving a great sigh as though with one breast. The gambler paled and groaned through clenched teeth. The dice showed three-spots—a certain loss, for the deuce turns up as seldom as the double six. Any other number would be to Khoja Nasreddin's advantage.

Shaking the dice in his fist he mentally thanked Fate for being so kind to him on this day. But he had forgotten that Fate is whimsical and fickle and easily betrays him who importunes it. Now it decided to give Khoja Nasreddin a lesson for his self-assurance, choosing for its weapon his ass, or rather the ass's tail adorned at the end with prickles and burrs. Turning his back upon the gamblers the ass swung his tail which brushed against his master's hand. The dice tumbled out, and instantly the red-haired gambler threw himself upon the tray with a hoarse shout, covering the stakes with his body.

Khoja Nasreddin had thrown two ones.

He sat for a long time silently moving his lips. The world tottered and swam before his staring eyes and a strange ringing filled his ears.

Suddenly he sprang up, seized a stick and began to belabour the ass, chasing him round the tie-rail.

"Accursed ass! O son of sin! O stinking brute and disgrace of all living creatures!" shouted Khoja Nasreddin. "Is it not enough that you should gamble with your master's money, that you must needs lose it? May your rascally hide peel! May almighty Allah put a pit in your path so that you break your legs! When will you die and so let me be rid of the sight of such an abominable face!"

The ass brayed. The gamblers shouted with laughter, and loudest of all the red-haired one who was now sure of his good luck.

"Let us play again," he said when Khoja Nasreddin, tired and out of breath, had thrown away the stick. "Come, a few more throws. You still have twenty-five tangas."

So saying, he thrust out his left foot and slightly waggled it, thus showing his contempt for Khoja Nasreddin.

"Why not?" replied the latter, thinking that now the hundred and twenty-five tangas had been lost it did not matter what happened to the last twenty-five.

He threw the dice carelessly and won.

"The whole lot!" proposed the red-haired one throwing down his lost stake on to the tray.

Khoja Nasreddin won again.

The red-haired one could not believe that luck had turned its back upon him.

"The whole lot!"

Seven times in succession he said it, and every time he lost. The tray was full of money. The gamblers sat very still, their flaming eyes alone betrayed the inner fire which consumed them.

"You cannot win every time unless the devil is helping you!" cried the red-haired one. "You must lose some time! Here on the tray are one thousand and six hundred tangas of yours. Once more will you stake the whole lot? Here is the money I was going to use tomorrow to buy goods in the bazaar for my shop. I stake this money against yours!"

He produced a small purse full of gold—rupees, tillas and tomans.

"Put your gold on the tray!" cried Khoja Nasreddin flushed with excitement.

Never had this tea-house seen such high stakes. The owner forgot all about his boiling kettles. The gamblers panted heavily. The red-haired one threw the dice first screwing up his eyes because he was afraid to look.

"Eleven!" all cried in chorus. Khoja Nasreddin realized that he had as good as lost: only a double six could save him.

"Eleven! Eleven!" repeated the red-haired gambler in unrestrained delight. "Look—I have got eleven! You have lost! You have lost!"

Khoja Nasreddin went cold all over. He took up the dice and prepared to cast them, when suddenly he stayed his hand.

"Turn round!" he said to his ass. "You have managed to lose against three pips. Now try to win over eleven. Otherwise I'll take you at once to the knacker's."

Seizing the ass's tail with his left hand, he struck with it his right hand which held the dice.

A great shout from all the men shook the tea-house. The owner clutched at his heart and sank helplessly to the ground, unable to stand the strain.

The dice showed a double six.

The red-haired gambler's eyes popped out of their sockets and glazed in his blood-drained face. He got up slowly and tottered away crying: "Woe is me! **Woe** is me!"

It is said that since that day the red-haired one has been seen no more in the town. He fled into the desert and there all hairy and terrible to see, wandered among the sands and thorn-bushes, ceaselessly crying: "O woe! Woe is me!" until at last the jackals made an end of him. But no one lamented him, for he had been a cruel and an unjust man, and had done much harm by ruining trusting simpletons.

As for Khoja Nasreddin, he stowed his newly won riches into his saddle-bags, hugged his ass, giving him a hearty kiss on his warm muzzle, and treated him to some nice fresh bread-cakes, greatly to the astonishment of the worthy animal, who only a few minutes previously had been treated to something quite different.

6

MINDFUL of the wise rule to keep away from people who know where you keep your money, Khoja Nasreddin did not loiter at the tea-house and started off for the marketplace. He kept looking back from time to time to see whether he was being followed, for the faces of the gamblers and of the tea-house owner did not bear the stamp of virtue.

It was a happy going. Now he would be able to buy any workshop, two workshops, three workshops. This he made up his mind to do.

"I shall buy four workshops: a pottery, a saddlery, a tailor's shop and a cobbler's shop. In each I shall set two workmen on the job, and all I shall have to do is to collect the money. In two years' time I shall become rich. I shall buy a house with fountains in the garden. I shall hang up gold cages with singing birds everywhere, and I shall have two, perhaps three, wives and three sons by each of them. . . ."

He let himself be carried away by the sweet river of day-dreams. Meanwhile the ass, no longer feeling the bridle, took advantage of his master's reverie. As they came up to a little bridge, instead of crossing over it like all other asses, he turned aside and taking a run jumped straight over the ditch.

". . . And when my children grow up I shall call them together and tell them . . ." ran Khoja Nasreddin's thoughts. "But why am I flying through the air? Has Allah turned me into an angel and given me wings?"

The next moment he saw so many stars that he realized he had no wings. Catapulted out of his saddle he had landed on the road half a dozen yards ahead of his mount.

When he had picked himself up, groaning and covered with dust, the ass came up to him, pricking up his ears in friendly fashion and with the most innocent expression on his face, as though inviting his master to get back into the saddle.

"O you, you who have been sent to me as a punishment not only for my own sins, but for the sins of my father, grandfather and great-grandfather, for according to the justice of Islam it would be unjust to punish a man so heavily for his own sins!" began Khoja Nasreddin, his voice trembling with anger. "O you, you miserable offspring of a spider and hyena! O you . . ."

But here he broke off on catching sight of a group of people sitting not far off in the shade of a half-ruined wall.

The imprecations died on Khoja Nasreddin's lips. He realized that a man who had got himself into such a ridiculous and undignified position in the presence of onlookers should himself laugh loudest at his own discomfiture. He winked at the seated group and grinned broadly, showing all his white teeth.

"Oho!" he said gaily in a loud voice. "What a fine flight I made! Tell me, how many somersaults did I turn? I had no time to count them myself. You old rascal!" he went on, slapping the ass good-naturedly although he felt more like giving him a good hiding. "He's full of ranks! That's the kind of fellow he is! No sooner do I look away than he's up to his tricks!"

Khoja Nasreddin broke into a merry laugh but to his surprise no one joined him. The people sat still with bowed heads and gloomy faces, and the women who were holding babies in their arms wept quietly.

"Something is amiss," thought Khoja Nasreddin.

He approached the group and addressed a grey-haired man with an emaciated face.

"Tell me, venerable old man, what has happened? Why do I see no smiles and hear no laughter, and why are these women weeping? Why are you sitting by the roadside in the dust and heat? Would it not be better to sit in the cool shelter of your homes?"

"Sitting at home is good for the one who has a home," replied the old man sadly. "Do not question me, O passer-by. Great is our trouble, and in no way can you help us. For myself, old and decrepit as I am, I pray God sends me death quickly."

"How can you say such things?" Khoja Nasreddin said reproachfully. "Men should never think like that. Tell me your trouble and do not judge by my poor appearance. Perhaps I may be able to help you."

"My tale will be brief. Only an hour ago Jafar the Usurer passed along our street with two of the Emir's guards. I owe him money and tomorrow the debt falls due. So they have turned me out of the house where I have spent all my life. I have no family, no place where I can rest my head. . . . And all my property—my house, garden, cattle and vineyards will be sold tomorrow by Jafar."

The old man's eyes filled with tears and his voice trembled.

"And do you owe him much?" asked Khoja Nasreddin.

"A great deal, O traveller! I owe him two hundred and fifty tangas!"

"Two hundred and fifty tangas!" exclaimed Khoja Nasreddin. "And a man desires death because of a miserable two hundred and fifty tangas! There, there quiet—you," he added, turning to the ass and untying the saddle-bags. "Now then, my venerable friend, here are two hundred and fifty tangas. Give them back to the usurer, kick him out of your house and spend the remainder of your days in peace and happiness."

At the sound of the clinking silver, the whole group came to life. The old man, unable to utter a word, looked up gratefully at Khoja

Nasreddin with tear-filled eyes.

"You see? And yet you would not tell me your troubles," said Khoja Nasreddin, counting out the last coin and thinking at the same time: "Never mind, instead of eight workmen I shall hire only seven, and that will be plenty."

Suddenly a woman seated next to the old man fell at Khoja Nasreddin's feet and weeping loudly held out her child to him.

"Look!" she said between sobs. "He is ill. His lips are parched and his face is burning. My poor little boy will die on the road, for I too have been turned out of my house."

Khoja Nasreddin looked at the thin pale face of the child, at its transparent hands, then at the faces of the group of seated people. And the sight of these faces seamed with wrinkles, lined with suffering and with eyes dimmed by ceaseless weeping made him feel as though a hot knife had been plunged into his heart. A sudden spasm clutched at his throat. Pity and anger sent a hot wave of blood to his face. He turned away.

"I am a widow," the woman continued. "My husband died six months ago. He owed the usurer two hundred tangas. According to the law, the debt fell upon me."

"Certainly the boy is sick," said Khoja Nasreddin. "Here are two hundred tangas. Go home quickly and put a cool bandage on his head. And here are fifty more tangas. Go, call a physician and buy some medicine." To himself he thought: "I can very well manage with six workmen."

But just then a great big stone-hewer fell at his feet. On the morrow his whole family was to be sold into slavery for a debt to Jafar of four hundred tangas.

"Five workmen will be plenty," thought Khoja Nasreddin as once more he began untying his saddlebag. No sooner had he tied it up again than two other women fell on their knees before him. The tales they told were so pitiful that Khoja Nasreddin did not hesitate to give them enough to pay off the usurer. Then, realizing that the money left over would hardly suffice to keep three workmen, he decided it was no longer worth while bothering about workshops, and generously shared out his money among the other debtors of Jafar the Usurer.

No more than five hundred tangas were left in the saddle-bag. Only then did Khoja Nasreddin catch sight of another man sitting by himself. He had not asked for help but his distress was plain to see.

Hey you, listen!" Khoja Nasreddin called out. "Why are you sitting here if you are not in debt to the usurer?"

"I am in debt," the man answered hoarsely. "Tomorrow I go in chains to the slave-market."

"Why have you kept silent?"

"O generous and kind traveller! I know not who you are. Maybe you are the saint Baha ed-din arisen from his tomb to help the poor, or Harun ar-Rashid in person. I have not sought your help because you have already spent a great deal and my debt is heaviest of all—five hundred tangas. And I was afraid that if you gave me such a sum there would not be sufficient for the old men and the women."

"You are an upright and noble man, and you have a conscience," said Khoja Nasreddin greatly moved. "But I too am upright and noble. I too have a conscience, and I swear you shall not go tomorrow to the slave-market. Hold out your coat."

He emptied out his saddle-bag to the last coin. Then the man, holding up the skirt of his khalat with his left hand, embraced Khoja Nasreddin with his right and pressed his face wet with tears to his breast.

"You certainly flew off your ass in fine fashion," said the great big bearded stone-hewer suddenly bursting-into a roar of laughter. At this, all the others burst out laughing—the men in rough deep voices, the women in their high-pitched ones, while the children smiled and stretched out their hands to Khoja Nasreddin who laughed louder than any of them.

"Oh-ho-ho!" he laughed, doubled up with mirth. "You don't know what sort of an ass he is! He's an accursed ass!"

"No! No!" said the woman with the sick child. "Do not speak like that of your ass. He is the cleverest, the noblest, the most precious ass in the world. There never has been and never will be another ass like him. I would like nothing better than to look after him all my life, give him the choicest grain to eat, never burden him with work, curry him and comb his tail. For if this incomparable ass, who like a rose has nought but virtues, had not jumped over the ditch and thrown you from the saddle, you, O traveller, who came to us like the sun in the darkness—you would have ridden past without even seeing us and we would never have dared to stop you."

"She is right," said the old man importantly. "We owe much of our salvation to this ass. Verily he is an ornament in the world and shines like a jewel among all other asses."

Then all of them loudly praised the ass and vied with each other in offering him cakes, roasted corn, dried apricots and peaches. The ass swished his tail at the pestering flies and serenely and gravely accepted the offerings, though not without an uneasy glance at the whip which Khoja Nasreddin was stealthily shaking at him.

The day was wearing on, shadows lengthened. Red-legged storks, crying and flapping their wings, were returning to their nests where the fledglings stretched their greedy gaping beaks towards them.

Khoja Nasreddin took his leave. All bowed and thanked him.

"We thank you. You have understood our troubles."

"How could I fail to understand;" he replied. "Only today I lost four workshops where eight skilled workmen were working for me, and a house with a garden where fountains played and song-birds in golden cages hung on the trees. How could I fail to understand you!"

The old man said in his toothless mumble:

"I have nothing to offer you as a gift of thanks, O traveller. Here is the only thing which I took with me when I left my house. It is *a* Koran, the holy book. *Take* it, and may it be a guiding light for you in this world "

Khoja Nasreddin had little use for holy books but, unwilling to hurt the old man's feelings, he took the Koran put it away in his saddle-bag and jumped into the saddle.

"Your name? Your name?" cried the others in one voice. "Tell us your name so that we may know whom to thank in our prayers."

"Why do you need to know my name? True virtue needs no fame. As for prayers, Allah has many angels to inform him of pious deeds. If the angels are lazy and careless and sleep on soft clouds instead of counting the pious and impious deeds on earth, then your prayers will be of no avail, for Allah would be foolish to believe people on their word alone without demanding confirmation from trustworthy persons."

While he was speaking one of the women suddenly let out a stifled gasp. So did another woman. Then the old man started and stared at Khoja Nasreddin. But the latter was in a hurry and took no notice.

"Good-bye! May peace and happiness abide with you." Followed by blessings he disappeared at the turn of the road.

The others remained silent. One single thought shone in their eyes. The silence was broken by the old man. He said solemnly and with feeling:

"Only one man in the whole world could perform such a deed. Yes, and only one man in the world can speak thus, and only one man in the world carries within him a soul whose light and warmth light up and warm the poor and oppressed, and this man is our —"

"Hold your tongue!" hastily interrupted another man. "Have you forgotten that walls have ears, stones have eyes and hundreds of dogs would take up his trail?"

"You are right," added a third man. "We must hold our tongues, for at present it is as though he were walking on a tight-rope. The slightest push might prove his undoing."

"I will let them tear out my tongue rather than say his name aloud," said the woman with the sick child.

"I too will be silent," cried the second woman. "I would rather die than unwittingly present him with a rope."

So spoke all save the mighty bearded stone-hewer, who was not quick-witted. He could not understand from what he had heard why dogs should take up the traveller's trail if he was neither a butcher nor a seller of boiled tripe. Again, if the traveller was a tight-rope walker, why could not his name be spoken aloud? And why was the woman prepared to die rather than present her benefactor with a rope so necessary to his trade? By this time the stone-hewer was completely bewildered. He snorted loudly, took a deep breath and decided to think no more about it for fear of losing his reason.

Meanwhile Khoja Nasreddin had covered quite a distance, but he still had before his eyes the emaciated faces of those poor people. He kept recalling the sick child, its feverish cheeks and parched lips. He thought of the grey-haired old man who had been turned out of his house, and a great anger rose from the depth of his heart.

He could no longer stay in the saddle. He jumped down and walked beside his ass, kicking the stones out of his way.

"Just you wait, master usurer, just wait!" he muttered, and a sinister glare burned in his black eyes. "One of these days we shall meet and then your lot will be bitter. As for you, Emir," he went on, "tremble and grow pale, for I, Khoja Nasreddin, am in Bukhara! O vile and monstrous leeches that suck the very life-blood of my unhappy people! O grasping greedy hyenas! O stinking jackals! You will not prosper for ever, nor will the people for ever suffer! And as for you, Jafar the Usurer, may my name be eternally covered with shame if I do not settle accounts with you for all the sorrow which you bring to the poor."

7

EVEN Khoja Nasreddin, who had gone through much in his life, found his first day in his homeland too restless and too full of incident. He was weary and wished to find some secluded spot where he could rest.

"No!" he sighed, catching sight of a multitude of people crowding round a pond. "It looks as if there'll be no rest for me today! Something seems to have happened here." The pond was at some little distance from the road and Khoja Nasreddin could easily have passed it, but he was not the man to miss an opportunity of mixing in a dispute, a row or a tussle.

The ass, who during the long years of their association had become well acquainted with his master's ways, turned towards the pond of his own accord.

"What's the matter?" shouted Khoja Nasreddin, steering his ass into the thick of the crowd. "Has somebody been murdered? Anyone robbed? Make way there! Make way!"

After pushing his way through the crowd to the edge of the pond, which was covered with green slime, he came upon an extraordinary sight. A few feet from the bank a man was drowning. From time to time he came up to the surface only to sink again, sending up large bubbles.

A number of people kept bustling about on the bank stretching out their hands to the drowning man and trying to seize him by his clothes, but he was just out of reach.

"Give us your hand!" they shouted. "Here! Give it here!"

The drowning man did not seem to hear what they were saying and did not stretch out his hand, but went on alternately bobbing up and going down again. As he went down to the bottom slow waves spread over the pond and gently lapped the bank.

"Strange!" thought Khoja Nasreddin observing the scene. "Very strange. What can be the reason for this? Why doesn't he stretch out his hand? Maybe he is an expert diver and is doing it for a bet, but in that case why does he wear a khalat?"

He almost lost himself in speculation. Meanwhile the drowning man went down at least four times, each time remaining a little longer under the surface.

"Very strange," repeated Khoja Nasreddin to himself, dismounting. "Wait here," he told his ass, "while I go to take a closer look."

By now the drowning man had gone down again. This time he did not reappear for so long that some of the people on the bank began to recite prayers for the dead. Suddenly he reappeared.

"Here! Here!" cried the men. "Give us your hand," and they stretched out their hands towards him, but he only gave them a blank stare and again went soundlessly, smoothly to the bottom.

"Oh, you stupid fellows!" cried Khoja Nasreddin. "Surely you could see by his expensive khalat and silk turban that this man is either a mullah or a wealthy dignitary? And haven't you learnt enough of the ways of mullahs and dignitaries to know how to pull them out of the water?"

"Pull him out yourself and be quick about it, that is if you know how!" shouted voices in the crowd. "Go on, save him! He has come up again! Go on, pull him out!"

"Wait," answered Khoja Nasreddin. "I haven't finished my speech yet. When, may I ask, have you ever seen a mullah or a dignitary give anything to anyone? Remember, O ignoramuses, that mullahs and dignitaries never, never give anything away; they only take. Therefore, they should be rescued scientifically, that is according to the peculiarities of their own nature. Now watch me."

"But it is too late!" cried voices in the crowd. "He won't come up again."

"Do you think the water spirits will accept a mullah or a dignitary so easily? You are wrong. The water spirits will do their utmost to be rid of him."

Khoja Nasreddin squatted down and waited patiently. He watched the bubbles come up from the bottom and float to the bank, pushed forward by a light breeze.

At last a dark shape came up slowly from the depths. The drowning man appeared on the surface—for the last time, had it not been for Khoja Nasreddin.

"Here, take this!" shouted Khoja Nasreddin. "Take this!"

The drowning man clutched convulsively at the outstretched hand. Khoja Nasreddin winced at the pain of his grip.

It took a long time to unclasp the fingers of the rescued man.

For some moments he lay motionless, covered with weeds and evil-smelling slime which concealed his features. Then water spouted from his mouth, his nose and ears.

"My pouch! Where is my pouch?" he moaned, and would not rest until he felt the pouch at his side. Then slowly he shook off the weeds and wiped his face with the skirt of his khalat. Khoja Nasreddin recoiled. This face with its flat, broken nose, flaring nostrils and one blind eye was hideous. Also, the man was hunch-backed.

"Who is my rescuer?" he asked in a grating voice looking around at the crowd with his one good eye.

"Here he is!" roared the crowd, and pushed Khoja Nasreddin forward.

"Come here, I am going to reward you." The man plunged his hand into his squelching pouch and brought out a handful of wet silver. "Although there is nothing very wonderful or extraordinary in your having pulled me out. I might have got out by myself," he added querulously.

While he was talking, and whether from weakness or some other reason, his hand opened slowly and the coins slipped through his fingers back into the pouch with a gentle clink. Only one solitary coin remained in his hand —half a tanga. Sighing deeply he offered the coin to Khoja Nasreddin.

"Here, take this money and go buy yourself a bowl of pilau in the bazaar."

"This isn't enough to buy a bowl of pilau," said Khoja Nasreddin.

"Never mind. Buy some rice without meat."

"Now," said Khoja Nasreddin to the bystanders, "you see, I rescued him in a truly scientific manner."

And he went off to his ass.

On the way he was stopped by a man—tall, lean, sinewy, of sullen and unfriendly appearance. His arms were black with soot and coal and he had a blacksmith's hammer in his belt.

"What is it, blacksmith?" asked Khoja Nasreddin.

"Look here," said the smith measuring him up and down with a hostile eye, "do you realize what man that was you rescued? Yes, and at the last minute, after which no one could have saved him? Do you know how many tears will be shed because of what you have done? Do you know how many people will lose their homes, their fields and their vineyards or will be sent to the slave-market, and from there in chains along the Khiva highroad?"

Khoja Nasreddin stared at him in astonishment.

"I don't understand you, blacksmith! Is it worthy of a man and a Muslim to pass by a drowning man without giving him a helping hand?"

"So you think that one should rescue all the poisonous snakes, all the hyenas and vipers?" cried the smith. Then something seemed to dawn upon him, for he added: "But are you a local man?"

"No, I have come from afar."

"Then you don't know that the man you have rescued is an evil-doer and a blood-sucker, and that one man out of three in Bukhara groans and weeps because of him!"

A dreadful thought flashed through Khoja Nasreddin's mind.

"Blacksmith!" he faltered, fearing to hear his guess confirmed. "Tell me the man's name."

"You have saved Jafar the Usurer, may he be damned in this and in the future life, and may festering sores plague his tribe to the fourteenth generation!" replied the smith.

"What?" cried Khoja Nasreddin. "What are you saying, blacksmith! O woe is me! Woe! Woe! O shame on my head! Have my two hands dragged this snake out of the water? Truly, there is no atoning for such a sin! O woe! O shame! O calamity!"

His remorse touched the smith who unbent a little.

"Calm yourself, traveller, there is nothing to be done about it now. Why did you ride up to the pond just then? Why didn't your ass baulk and linger on the road? The usurer would have just had time to drown."

"That ass!" said Khoja Nasreddin. "If he lingers on the road it is only to empty the money out of my saddlebags. He finds they are too heavy when they are full. But when it is a question of my disgracing myself by rescuing a usurer, you may be sure the ass will bring me to the spot in good time!"

"Yes," agreed the smith, "but the deed cannot be undone. One cannot push the usurer back into the pond."

Khoja Nasreddin's spirits revived.

"I may have performed an evil deed, but I shall put it right! Listen, blacksmith, I swear that Jafar the Usurer shall be drowned by me. I swear by my father's beard. Yes, he shall be drowned by me and in this very same pond! Remember my oath, blacksmith, for I have never spoken in vain. The usurer is to drown! And when you hear about it in the bazaar, then know I have atoned for my guilt before the citizens of Noble Bukhara!"

8

TWILIGHT was falling gently on the town like a cool and fragrant mist when Khoja Nasreddin reached the marketplace.

Cheerful fires were kindling in the tea-houses, and soon the entire market-place was circled by lights. An important market was to be held on the morrow. One by one caravans of camels came slowly padding by. As one of the caravans disappeared into the darkness, the rhythmic, clear and melancholy tinkling of its bells lingered in the air. And when at last the sound had faded into the distance, more bells would clang and moan as another caravan came into the square.

This went on and on, as though the very night itself were ringing, quivering and moaning softly, overflowing with sounds brought from the ends of the earth. Invisible bells from India and Persia, Arabia, Afghanistan and Egypt rang out in wistful song. Khoja Nasreddin listened, and felt that he could have listened for ever. In a near-by tea-house a tambourine was booming and humming and was answered by the strings of a *dutar*. An invisible singer lifted his tense clear voice up to the very stars. He sang about his beloved and complained of her.

To the accompaniment of this song Khoja Nasreddin went off in search of a night's lodging.

"I have half a tanga for myself and my ass," he said to the owner of a tea-house.

"You may spend the night here for half a tanga," said the man. "But you won't get a blanket."

"And where can I tether my ass?"

"Why should I worry about your ass?"

There was no tie-rail near the tea-house. Khoja Nasreddin saw a hook which protruded from beneath the raised porch, and without troubling to look to what the hook was fixed, tied his ass to it. Once inside the tea-house he immediately lay down, for he was very tired.

He was dozing when suddenly he heard his name. He half-opened his eyes.

Close by, seated in a little circle and drinking tea were some men who had come to the market—a camel-driver, a shepherd and two artisans. One of them was saying in a low voice:

"They also tell this of Khoja Nasreddin. One day when in Baghdad, he was walking in the bazaar. Suddenly he heard noise and shouting in a tavern. Our Khoja Nasreddin, as you know, is very inquisitive, so he went to look inside. There he saw a fat, red-faced inn-keeper holding a beggar by the scruff of his neck and shaking him. He was demanding money from him but the beggar refused to pay. 'What's all this noise?' asked our Khoja Nasreddin. 'What are you quarrelling about?' 'This tramp,' shouted the inn-keeper, 'this scurvy, cheating beggar, may his bowels rot, came into my eating-house, took a piece of bread from the breast of his khalat, held it for a long time over the brazier where I was roasting a succulent shishlik, and waited until the bread had absorbed the smell of the roast meat and was doubly soft and tasty; then he devoured the bread. And now, may his teeth fall out and his hide peel off, he refuses to pay!' 'Is it true?' asked our Khoja Nasreddin sternly. The beggar was too frightened to utter a word. 'It is wrong, you know,' said Khoja Nasreddin, 'it is wrong to make use of other people's property without paying.' 'Do you hear, you wretch, do you hear what this respectable and worthy man is saying?' said the inn-keeper, very pleased. 'Have you any money?' Khoja Nasreddin asked the beggar. The beggar took his last coppers from his pocket and handed them to Khoja Nasreddin. The inn-keeper stretched out his greasy paw for the money. 'Wait, O worthy one,' said Khoja Nasreddin. 'Lend me your ear first.' And for quite a while he jingled the coins in his fist at the inn-keeper's ear. Then he handed back the money to the beggar and said: 'Go in peace, my poor fellow!' 'What!' shouted the inn-keeper. 'But I haven't been paid!' 'He has paid you in full,' replied Khoja Nasreddin, 'and now you are quits. He smelt your *shishlik* and you heard his money ring.' "

The audience burst out laughing. One of the men hurriedly warned the others:

"Not so loud, or they will soon guess we are talking about Khoja Nasreddin."

"How do they know?" thought Khoja Nasreddin smiling to himself. "True, this did not happen in Baghdad but in Stambul. Still, how do they know?"

Then a second man, in shepherd's dress and a coloured turban showing him to be from Badakhshan, told his tale in a low voice.

"They also say that one day Khoja Nasreddin was passing a mullah's kitchen-garden. The mullah was gathering some pumpkins into a sack. From greed he had filled the sack so full that he could not lift it, let alone carry it. So there he stood wondering how to get the sack home. He saw a passer-by and was delighted. 'Listen, my son, can you carry this sack to my house?' Khoja Nasreddin had no money at the time. 'How much will you pay me?' he asked the mullah. 'O my son, why do you ask for money? While you are on the way and carrying the sack I will reveal three wisdoms to you and this will bring you happiness for life.' 'I should very much like to know what those wisdoms are,' thought our Khoja Nasreddin.

"Curiosity seized him. He lifted the sack on to his shoulders and started off. The path was up-hill and skirted a precipice. Khoja Nasreddin halted to take breath. The mullah said, looking important and mysterious: 'Listen to the first wisdom, for there has been no greater wisdom in all the world since the time of Adam. If you come to comprehend the full depth of its meaning, it will be as much as possessing the secret meaning of the letters *Alif, Lam, Mim* with which Muhammad, our Prophet and teacher, opens the second *sura* of the Koran.

" 'Listen carefully: if anyone tells you that it is better to walk than to ride, do not believe him. Remember my words, O my son, and ponder over them ceaselessly by day and by night, and then you will comprehend the wisdom they contain. But this wisdom is nothing compared to the second which I will disclose to you over there by that tree. Look, over there, ahead of us.' 'All right!' thinks our Khoja Nasreddin. 'You wait a bit, my fine mullah.' Dripping with sweat he dragged the sack up to the tree.

"The mullah raised a finger. 'Open your ears and listen, for the second wisdom contains the entire Koran and half of the Shariat and also a quarter of the Tarikat. He who comprehends it will never err from the path of virtue and will never leave the road of truth. Therefore, my son, endeavour to understand this wisdom and rejoice at receiving it for nothing. The second wisdom says: if anyone tells you that the poor man has an easier life than the rich man, do not believe him. But this second wisdom is nothing compared with the third, the shining light of which can only be likened to the blinding radiance of the sun and the depth of which can only be likened to the depth of the Ocean. I shall disclose this third wisdom to you at the gate of my house. Let us hasten, for I am already rested.'

"'Wait, mullah!' said Khoja Nasreddin. 'I already know your third wisdom. You are going to tell me at the gate of your house that a clever man can always make a stupid man carry a heavy sackful of pumpkins for nothing.' The astounded mullah recoiled. Khoja Nasreddin had guessed right.

"'Now, mullah, you listen to my one and only wisdom which is worth all of yours,' went on Khoja Nasreddin. 'And my wisdom, I swear by the Prophet, is so blinding and so profound that it contains the entire Islam with the Koran, the Shariat, the Tarikat and all the other books, and also the entire Buddhist creed, and the entire Christian creed, and the entire Jewish creed. There never was and never will be at any time a more irrefutable wisdom than the one which I shall now disclose to you, O mullah, my master and teacher in the true faith! But prepare yourself so that this wisdom does not overcome you, for it may easily cause a man to lose his mind—so amazing is it, so striking and so immeasurable. Steel your mind, mullah, and listen: if anyone tells you that these pumpkins did not smash—spit in the face of that man, call him a liar and turn him out of your house!'

"With these words Khoja Nasreddin lifted the sack and dropped it over the steep precipice. The pumpkins tumbled out of the sack and went bounding and bursting noisily over the stones. 'Oh woe! Woe!' wailed the mullah. 'What a loss! What ruin!' And he went on yelling and lamenting and scratching his face, and behaving like a madman.

"'You see,' said Khoja Nasreddin, 'I warned you! I told you my wisdom might make you go out of your mind!' "

The audience rocked with laughter.

Lying in his corner on the dusty, flea-infested felt mat Khoja Nasreddin thought to himself:

"So they have heard this one too? But how? There were only two of us on that path—the mullah and myself, and I never told a soul. Perhaps the mullah told the story when he found out who had been carrying his pumpkins."

Then the third man started with his tale:

"One day Khoja Nasreddin was returning from the town to the Turkish village where he was then living. Feeling tired, he lay down on the bank of a stream, and, without being aware of it, fell asleep to the pleasant gurgle of the water, fanned by the fragrant breath of the spring breeze. And he dreamt that he had died. 'If I am dead,' he decided, 'then I must neither move, nor open my eyes.' So he remained lying quite still on the soft grass. He found that being dead was after all not so bad. There you lie without any of the fuss and worry which pursue us relentlessly throughout our mortal earthly existence.

"Some travellers who were passing by caught sight of Khoja Nasreddin. 'Look!' said one. 'It is a Muslim.' 'He is dead,' added another. 'We must carry him to the nearest village.'

"This was the village that Khoja Nasreddin was going to. The men cut down several saplings, made a stretcher out of them and laid Khoja Nasreddin upon it. They carried him for a long time, while he lay motionless with closed eyes, as becomes a man who is dead and whose soul is already knocking at the gates of Paradise.

"Suddenly the stretcher came to a halt. The wayfarers were arguing about the ford. One suggested they should go to the right; another to the left; while a third proposed going straight across the river. Khoja Nasreddin peeped out of one eye and saw that the men were standing before the deepest, swiftest and most dangerous part of the river, where many careless people had been drowned. 'I don't care about myself,' thought Khoja Nasreddin, 'for I am dead and it doesn't matter whether I lie in a grave or at the bottom of the river. But these travellers must be warned because they might lose their lives through being kind to me. Not to warn them would be sheer ingratitude on my part.'

"He raised himself on the stretcher and pointing towards the ford said in a weak voice: 'When I was alive, O travellers, I always crossed the river near to those poplars there.' Then he closed his eyes again. The travellers thanked Khoja Nasreddin and went on carrying the stretcher and loudly reciting prayers for the salvation of his soul."

While the audience and the story-teller himself were laughing and digging their elbows into each other's sides, Khoja Nasreddin grumbled:

"They've got it all wrong. First of all, I never dreamt I had died. I'm not such a fool as to be unable to distinguish between myself dead and myself alive. Why, I even remember that a flea was biting me at the time and I fervently wished I could scratch myself. Surely that is clear proof that I was alive? Had it been otherwise I would certainly not have felt the flea-bites. It was only because I was tired and did not want to walk, while the travellers were strong, and it meant nothing to them to go slightly out of their way and carry me to the village. But when they decided to cross the river where its depth is three times the height of a man, I stopped them, though of course I was thinking of their families, and not of mine, for I do not possess one. And immediately I tasted the bitter fruit of ingratitude; for instead of thanking me for my timely warning, they tumbled me out of the stretcher and beat me with their fists. They would have beaten me severely had it not been for my swift legs. Extraordinary how people manage to distort the truth!"

Meanwhile a fourth man began his tale.

"They also tell this of Khoja Nasreddin. Once he lived for about half a year in a village where he gained much fame by his ready tongue and quick wit—"

Khoja Nasreddin pricked up his ears. Where had he heard this voice—not loud, but distinct and slightly hoarse. And quite recently too . . . Perhaps this very day . . . However he tried, he could not remember.

The man went on:

"One day the governor of the province sent one of his elephants to the village where Khoja Nasreddin was living. It was to be fed and cared for by the inhabitants. The elephant was a great eater. In twenty-four hours he ate fifty measures of barley, fifty measures of sorghum, fifty measures of maize and one hundred bundles of hay. Within a fortnight the villagers had given to the elephant all their reserves. They were utterly ruined and were filled with despair. Finally they decided to send Khoja Nasreddin to the governor to beg that the elephant be taken away.

"So they sought out Khoja Nasreddin who agreed to do what they asked. He saddled his ass, which, as the whole world knows, is comparable by its obstinacy, evil temper and laziness to a jackal, a viper and a frog rolled into one, and having saddled it he set off to find the governor, without neglecting to make an agreement with the villagers about payment for his services. Actually he exacted such a large sum that many of them were obliged to sell their houses and became beggars thanks to Khoja Nasreddin."

"Hm!" came from the corner where Khoja Nasreddin was tossing and turning on his felt mat in an effort to hold back the fury which was choking him.

The man went on:

"And so Khoja Nasreddin arrived at the palace. He stood for a long time among the crowd of servants and dependents waiting for the illustrious governor to deign to turn upon him his luminous gaze which sheds happiness upon some and destruction upon others. And when the governor deigned to favour Khoja Nasreddin by turning his countenance towards him, such were Khoja Nasreddin's fear and amazement on beholding this magnificence that his knees trembled like a jackal's tail and his blood ran slow in his veins. He was bathed in sweat and became paler than chalk."

"Hm!" came from the corner, but the story-teller went on without paying heed to the interruption.

" 'What do you want?' the governor asked in noble and resounding tones resembling the roar of a lion. Fear rendered Khoja Nasreddin tongue-tied. His voice squeaked like the yap of a stinking hyena. 'O noble lord!' said Khoja Nasreddin. 'O light of our province, its sun and its moon, dispenser of happiness and joy to all who live in our province! Hear this your miserable slave, unworthy to wipe the threshold of your palace with his beard. You have, O most resplendent one, conferred on our village the favour of sending one of your elephants to be fed and cared for by the villagers. So we are a little worried. . . .'

"The governor frowned ominously. Khoja Nasreddin bowed before him like a reed before the storm. 'What worries you?' asked the governor. 'Speak up. Or has your tongue dried up in your filthy and miserable throat?' 'A . . . we . . . we . . .' mumbled the cowardly Khoja Nasreddin. 'We are worried, O most resplendent lord, that the elephant is feeling lonely by himself. The poor creature is very unhappy, and all the villagers have become woebegone and melancholy at the sight of its misery. So they have sent me to you, O noblest of the noble, whose person adorns the earth, to ask you to confer yet another favour upon us by sending a cow-elephant to keep him company.' The governor was greatly pleased by this request and ordered it to be immediately carried out. To mark his pleasure he permitted Khoja Nasreddin to kiss his boot, which Khoja Nasreddin did with such assiduity that the governor's boot lost colour while Khoja Nasreddin's lips became black—"

Here the story-teller was interrupted by the thundering voice of Khoja Nasreddin in person:

"You lie!" cried Khoja Nasreddin. "It is your lips, you dirty, mangy dog, and your tongue, and all your inside which are black from the licking of the great ones' boots! Khoja Nasreddin has never and nowhere bowed before the great. You slander Khoja Nasreddin. Do not listen to him, O Muslims! Turn him out!"

He rushed forward to deal with the calumniator, but was suddenly brought to a standstill on recognizing the flat, pock-marked face and the yellow shifty eyes. This was the servant who had argued with him in the alley about the length of the rails on the bridge to paradise.

"Aha!" cried Khoja Nasreddin. "I know you, you spy! Tell me, how much do they pay you for informing, how much do they pay you a head for every man whom you betray? I know you, Emir's spy and informer!"

The spy who until then had remained motionless suddenly clapped his hands and shouted in a high-pitched voice:

"Guard, here!"

Khoja Nasreddin heard the running footsteps of the guard, the rattle of spears and the ringing of shields in the dark. Without losing an instant he jumped to one side and knocked down the pock-marked spy who barred his way.

But now he heard the tramping of guards coming from the other side of the square. In whichever direction he darted, he was brought up against the guards. For a moment he thought escape was impossible.

"Woe is me! I am lost!" he cried loudly. "Farewell, my faithful ass!"

But here there occurred an unexpected and amazing event which to this day is remembered in Bukhara and will never be forgotten, so great were the tumult and destruction.

On hearing the sad cries of his master, the ass started out towards him but in his wake an enormous drum came bumping from under the porch. Khoja Nasreddin had unwittingly tethered his ass in the dark to the iron hook of this drum which the owner of the tea-house used to beat to attract customers to his establishment on great festivals. The drum hit a stone and boomed; the ass looked back and the drum boomed again. Then the ass, imagining that evil spirits, having done away with his master, were now after his own grey hide, brayed in terror, raised his tail and dashed across the square.

At this particular moment the last fifty camels of a caravan bringing a load of crockery and sheet-copper were moving into the square. At sight of the terrible braying, bounding and booming creature which charged at them in the dark, the terrified camels scattered, shedding crockery and clanging copper.

A moment later the entire market-place and the adjoining streets were filled with a great panic and unheard of confusion. The thundering, ringing, banging, yelling, barking, howling, crashing and smashing merged into a hellish din. Everyone was bewildered. Hundreds of camels, horses and asses tearing away from their tethers dashed about in the dark, thundering among the scattered sheet-copper, while the drivers shouted and ran about brandishing torches.

People awakened by the unholy noise jumped up and ran half-naked hither and thither, crashing into each other and filling the night with cries of grief and despair, for they thought that the end of the world had come. Cocks crowed and flapped their wings. The tumult grew, and spread all over the great town to its very outskirts. Finally the guns on the city-wall boomed out, for the town-guard imagined that enemies had broken into Bukhara; and the guns in the palace grounds boomed too, for the palace-guard imagined that a revolt had broken out. From all the innumerable minarets came the plaintive, alarmed calls of the muezzins. Confusion in the dark was complete, and none knew whither to run or what to do.

And in the very centre of this dark chaos Khoja Nasreddin ran about, nimbly avoiding the maddened horses and camels, pursuing his ass by the sound of the drum. He did not catch him until the rope at last broke and the drum rolled aside under the feet of the camels who, in a mad rush to avoid it, tore down with a crash awnings, sheds, tea-houses and booths.

It would have taken Khoja Nasreddin a long time to find his ass had they not accidentally come face to face. The ass was covered with lather and trembling all over.

"Come, come quickly, it is a bit too noisy for us here," said Khoja Nasreddin dragging his ass after him. "It is astonishing how much havoc one little ass can make in a big town if a drum is tied to him. See what you have done! True, you have saved me from the guards, but nevertheless I am sorry for the poor citizens of Bukhara. It will take them till the morning to straighten out the mess. Where can we find a quiet and peaceful spot?"

Khoja Nasreddin decided to spend the night in a cemetery, rightly arguing that whatever the disturbance, the dead would certainly not be rushing about, shouting and yelling, and brandishing torches.

Thus Khoja Nasreddin, the Disturber of the Peace and Sower of Discord, ended the first day of his return to his native town in a manner worthy of his title. He tethered his ass to a tombstone and making himself comfortable on a grave, soon dropped off to sleep. Meanwhile in the town the din, noise, shouting, banging, ringing, booming of guns and general confusion went on for a long time.

9

AT the break of dawn when the stars dimmed and faint outlines began to stand out of the darkness, many hundreds of sweepers, dustmen, carpenters and clay-treaders came into the market-square and set to work with a will. They straightened out the fallen awnings, mended the bridges, stopped up the gaps in the fences and cleared away all the splinters and broken pots, so that the first rays of the sun found no trace of the night's disturbance in Bukhara.

The market opened.

After a good night's rest beside the tombstone, Khoja Nasreddin rode into the square. It was already humming with activity and movement and overflowed with a colourful crowd of many tongues and races. "Make way! Make way!" cried Khoja Nasreddin hardly able to hear himself among the general shouting of merchants, water-carriers, barbers, wandering dervishes, beggars and bazaar tooth-drawers who brandished the rusty and terrifying tools of their trade. Multi-coloured khalats, turbans, horse-blankets and carpets; Chinese, Arabic, Mongolian and many other different tongues mingled in a swaying, jostling and buzzing crowd.

Dust rose obscuring the sky, while an endless human stream kept pouring into the square to spread out their wares and add their voices to the general din. Potters beat ringing tattoos with little sticks on their pots, catching passers-by by the skirts of their khalats and begging them to listen to the clearness of the tone and so be tempted to buy. In the coppersmiths' row the blaze of copper was blinding and the air rang out with the tapping of tiny hammers with which the coppersmiths hammered out patterns on trays and jugs, while they loudly extolled their own skill and decried that of their neighbours. Jewellers melted silver in small crucibles, stretched gold and polished precious Indian gems on leather discs.

At times the light breeze carried a heavy wave of fragrance from the perfumers' row where attar of roses, ambergris, musk and various spices were being sold. On one side there stretched the endless figured, flowered and motley carpet-row exhibiting Persian, Damascus and Tekke rugs, Kashghar woven carpets, coloured horse-blankets, both cheap and high-priced for ordinary mounts or noble steeds. Khoja Nasreddin rode past the silk row, the saddlers', the armourers' and dyers' rows, the slave-market and the wool-carders' yard.

And all this was only the beginning of the bazaar, for hundreds of other different rows stretched ahead. The deeper Khoja Nasreddin on his ass penetrated into the crowd, the more deafening became the shouting, arguing, yelling and bargaining around him. Yes, this was the same bazaar, the famous and unmatched bazaar of Bukhara, such as neither Damascus, nor even Baghdad itself possessed.

At last he came to the end of the rows and saw before him the Emir's palace surrounded by a high crenellated and embrasured wall. The four corner towers were skilfully faced with coloured mosaic over which Arab and Persian craftsmen had toiled for many years.

Outside the gates of the palace a motley camp was pitched. In the shade of tattered awnings people, exhausted by the heat, sat or lay on reed mats—some alone, others with their families. Women nursed babies, cooked food in pots, mended torn khalats and quilts. Half-naked children scampered about shouting, fighting and tumbling, and with utter disrespect turning towards the palace that part of their anatomy which is not supposed to be exposed. The men slept or pottered about, or else talked among themselves in groups seated around teapots.

"Oho! These people have been here for more than one day!" thought Khoja Nasreddin.

Two men, one bald, the other bearded, attracted his attention. They lay on the bare ground, each under his awning. A white goat, so thin that its ribs seemed about to burst through its hide, was tethered to a poplar peg between the two. It bleated piteously and nibbled at the peg which was already half eaten away.

Being naturally inquisitive Khoja Nasreddin could not refrain from asking a question.

"Peace be with you, citizens of Noble Bukhara! Tell me, since when have you joined the gypsy community?"

"Do not mock us, O traveller!" replied the bearded man. "We are no gypsies but as good Muslims as yourself."

"Then why do you not stay at home if you are good Muslims? What are you waiting for at the palace gate?"

"We are waiting for the just and gracious judgment of the Emir, our sovereign Lord and Master, whose radiance eclipses that of the sun."

"So!" said Khoja Nasreddin with unconcealed irony. "And have you been waiting long for the just and gracious judgment of the Emir, your sovereign Lord and Master, whose radiance eclipses that of the sun?"

"We have been waiting more than five weeks, O traveller," put in the bald man. "This bearded quibbler, may Allah chastise him, may the devil spread his tail on his bed—this bearded quibbler is my elder brother. Our father died and left us a small property. We have divided everything except this goat. Let the Emir decide to whom it should belong."

"But where is the rest of the property which you have inherited?"

"We have turned everything into money. One has to pay the public scribes who write the petitions and the clerks who receive them, and the guards, and many others."

The bald man suddenly jumped up and ran to meet a dirty, barefooted dervish in a pointed cap with a black hollow gourd at his side.

"Pray for me, holy man! Pray that the judgment be given in my favour!"

The dervish took the money and started to pray. As soon as he had pronounced the concluding words of the prayer the bald man threw another coin into his gourd to make him start all over again.

The bearded man raised himself uneasily and ran his eyes over the crowd. After a lengthy search he saw a second dervish, still more dirty and ragged and therefore more holy. This dervish demanded an exorbitant sum. The bearded man wanted to bargain but the dervish fumbled under his cap and brought out a handful of good-sized lice, at which the bearded man, thus persuaded of his holiness, accepted his price. With a triumphant glance at his younger brother, he counted out the money.

The dervish knelt down and started to pray loudly, drowning with his bass the thin tones of the first dervish. The bald man becoming uneasy added a few coins to his dervish, the bearded one did the same with his, and the two dervishes in their efforts to outdo each other set up such a yelling and shouting that Allah must have ordered the angels to shut the windows of his heavenly abode for fear of going deaf. The goat, nibbling at the wooden peg, bleated piteously and continuously.

The bald brother threw it half a bundle of clover, at which the bearded one yelled.

"Take your dirty stinking clover away from my goat!"

He kicked the clover away and set a pot of bran before the animal.

"No!" shouted the bald brother angrily. "My goat shall not eat your bran!"

The pot joined the clover; it broke and the bran mingled with the dust of the road, while the brothers grappled furiously, rolling on the ground and exchanging blows and curses.

"Two fools are fighting, two swindlers are praying and meanwhile the goat has died of hunger," said Khoja Nasreddin shaking his head. "Hey you, virtuous and loving brothers, look here— Allah has settled your dispute in his own way by taking the goat from you."

The brothers, coming to their senses, let go of each other and stood with blood-streaked faces gazing for a long time at the dead goat. At last the bald one said:

"It should be skinned."

"I'll do that!" quickly replied the bearded brother.

"Why you?" asked the other, his bald pate reddening with fury.

"The goat is mine and so is the hide."

"No, it is mine!"

Before Khoja Nasreddin could put in a word the brothers were again rolling on the ground in a shapeless grunting tangle. For an instant a heavy fist showed grasping a tuft of black hair from which Khoja Nasreddin concluded that the elder brother had lost a goodly portion of his beard.

With a hopeless gesture he rode on.

Coming towards him was a blacksmith with a pair of pincers thrust into his belt—the same blacksmith who had spoken to Khoja Nasreddin the day before at the

"Good day, blacksmith," cried Khoja Nasreddin joyfully. "Here we meet again, though I have not had time yet to fulfil my promise. What are you doing here, blacksmith? Have you also come to seek the Emir's justice?"

"What good can come from such justice?" the smith said gloomily. "I have come with a complaint from the blacksmiths' row. We have been given fifteen guards whom we were supposed to feed for three months. Now a year has passed and we are still keeping them and suffering much loss in consequence."

"And I have come from the dyers' row," put in a man with stains of dye on his hands and whose face had taken on a greenish hue from the poisonous fumes which he inhaled every day from sunrise till sunset. "I have come with a similar complaint. We have been given twenty-five guards to feed. Our trade is ruined and our profits have dwindled. Perhaps the Emir will take pity on us and deliver us from this unbearable burden."

"Why have you taken such a dislike to the poor guards?" cried Khoja Nasreddin. "Truly, they are not the worst or greediest inhabitants of Bukhara. You keep without complaining the Emir, his viziers and dignitaries. You feed two thousand mullahs and six thousand dervishes. Then why should the unfortunate guards go hungry? Don't you know the proverb: where one jackal has found food for himself, ten others immediately assemble. I do not understand your dissatisfaction, O blacksmith and dyer!"

"Not so loud," said the smith looking around.

The dyer threw Khoja Nasreddin a reproachful glance.

"You are a dangerous man, O traveller, and your words are deprived of virtue. But our Emir is wise and generous—"

He broke off for suddenly there was a blaring of trumpets and a rolling of drums. The whole motley camp came into movement, as the brass-bound palace gates opened ponderously.

"The Emir! The Emir!" came from all sides and the people crowded towards the palace to gaze at their ruler. Khoja Nasreddin took up a convenient position in the first rows.

First came the heralds who ran out of the gates crying: "Make way for the Emir! Make way for the Most Serene Emir! Make way for the Commander of the Faithful!" These were followed by the guards who hit out with their sticks right and left at the heads and backs of the curious who had crowded in too close. A broad passage opened in the crowd, and out came the musicians with drums and flutes, tambourines and *karanay*. Next came the suite clad in silk and gold, with curved sabres in velvet sheaths studded with precious stones. Then two elephants with tall plumes on their heads were led out. Finally there appeared a richly ornamented litter in which the great Emir in person reposed under a heavy baldaquin of cloth of gold.

A subdued roar rose from the crowd at this sight as though a gust of wind had swept the square, and the people prostrated themselves on the ground in conformity with the Emir's order, which commanded all loyal subjects to regard their ruler with servility and not otherwise than with upturned gaze. In front of the litter ran servants spreading out carpets in its path. To the right of the litter walked the palace fly-swatter carrying a fan of horses' tails on his shoulder, and to the left gravely and importantly strode the Emir's pipe-bearer carrying a golden Turkish narghile.

The rear of the procession was made up by the guard in brass helmets armed with shields, spears, cross-bows and naked swords. Last of all came two small cannon. The pageant was lit up by the bright noonday sun which sparkled in the jewels, shone on the gold and silver ornaments, hotly mirrored itself in the brass shields and helmets and glistened on the white steel of the bare blades. . . . But in the enormous prostrated crowd there shone neither jewels, nor gold, nor silver, nor even copper —nothing gladdened the heart by flaming and shining in the sun; there were only rags, poverty and hunger. And when the sumptuous Emir's procession moved through the sea of dirty, ignorant, downtrodden and ragged people it was as though a thin golden thread was being drawn through a sordid rag.

The high carpeted dais from which the Emir was to dispense his favours to his devoted people was already surrounded on all sides by guards, while below on the execution ground the executioners were busily making ready to carry out the Emir's will, testing the flexibility of rods and the strength of sticks, soaking in vats many-tailed raw-hide whips, erecting gallows, sharpening axes and fixing pales into the ground. The man in charge was the chief of the palace guard, Arslan-bek, whose ferocity had rendered him notorious far beyond the frontiers of Bukhara. He was handsome, with thick body and black hair. His beard covered his chest and reached down to his belly, and his voice was like the roar of a camel.

He was generously distributing blows and kicks, when all of a sudden he bent low and quivered with servility.

Slowly swaying, the litter mounted the dais and the Emir, pushing aside the curtains of the baldaquin, showed his countenance to the people.

10

The Most Serene Emir was not so very handsome after all. His face, which the court poets always likened to a silver full moon, looked more like an over-ripe flabby melon. Supported by his viziers he stepped out of the litter to take his seat on the gilded throne, and Khoja Nasreddin saw that, contrary to the assertions of the court poets, the Emir's figure did not resemble a slender cypress. His body was fat and heavy, his arms were short and his legs were so bowed that not even his khalat could hide their ugliness.

The viziers took up their positions on his right, the mullahs and dignitaries on his left, the scribes settled lower down with their books and ink-horns, while the court poets formed a semicircle behind the throne, fixing their devout gaze on the back of the Emir's neck. The palace fly-swatter waved his fan. The narghile-bearer placed the golden mouthpiece between his master's lips. The vast crowd surrounding the dais held their breath. Khoja Nasreddin raised himself in his stirrups, stretched out his neck and became all ears.

The Emir sleepily nodded his head. The guard divided, making way for the two brothers, the bald one and the bearded one, whose turn had at last come. They crawled on their knees up to the dais and kissed the carpet which hung to the ground.

"Get up!" said the Grand Vizier Bakhtiyar.

The brothers rose without daring to shake the dust from their khalats. Fear tied their tongues so that their speech was mumbling and incoherent. But being a vizier of great experience Bakhtiyar understood the situation at a glance.

"Where is your goat?" he interrupted the brothers impatiently.

The bald brother replied:

"It is dead, O high-born Vizier! Allah has taken it to himself. But which of us is to have the hide?"

Bakhtiyar turned to the Emir.

"What is to be the decision, O Wisest of Rulers?"

The Emir yawned and closed his eyes with an air of complete indifference. Bakhtiyar respectfully bowed his head under its heavy white turban.

"O Master! I read the decision on your countenance. Listen," he said, turning to the brothers.

They sank to their knees ready to thank the Emir for his wisdom, justice and mercy. Bakhtiyar pronounced the verdict and the scribes scratched away with their pens as they wrote down his words in the huge registers.

"The Commander of the Faithful and Sun of the Universe, our Great Emir, may Allah's blessing rest upon him, has deigned to decide that if the goat has been taken to Allah, then in all justice the hide should belong to Allah's vice-regent on earth, that is to the Great Emir himself, by reason of which the goat should be skinned, the hide dried and tanned, brought to the palace and delivered to the Royal Treasury."

The disconcerted brothers exchanged swift glances, a light murmur passed over the crowd. Bakhtiyar went on in a loud and clear voice:

"Besides which, the suitors should be made to pay legal costs to the amount of two hundred tangas, a palace tax to the amount of one hundred and fifty tangas, the tax for the upkeep of the scribes to the amount of fifty tangas and also make a donation for the adornment of the mosques—all this to be exacted immediately in cash, or in clothing, or in any other kind of property."

Hardly had he finished speaking when on a sign from Arslan-bek, the guards threw themselves upon the two brothers, unwound their sashes, turned their pockets inside out, tore off their khalats, pulled off their boots and sent them away bare-foot and half-naked.

The whole affair took barely a minute. As soon as the verdict had been announced the court sages and poets burst into a chorus of panegyrics:

"O wise Emir! O wisest of the wise! O wise with the wisdom of the wise! O Emir wisest above all the wise!" They went on like this for a long time, craning their necks towards the throne, each trying hard to make his voice reach the Emir above the others. Meanwhile the crowd around the dais kept silent, eyeing the two brothers with compassion.

"Never mind," said Khoja Nasreddin in pious tones to the unfortunate brothers who were loudly weeping in each other's arms. "After all you haven't been wasting your time sitting in the square for six weeks. You have received a just and merciful verdict, for everybody knows there is none so wise or more merciful in all the world than our Emir, and if anyone doubts it..." here he looked round at his neighbours in the crowd—"it wouldn't take long to call the guards. And they? Why, they would deliver the impious doubter into the hands of the executioners, who will easily show him the error of his ways. O brothers, go home in peace. If ever you squabble over a fowl, come again to the Emir's tribunal, only first remember to sell your houses, your vineyards and fields; otherwise you'll be unable to pay the taxes and that will mean loss to the Emir's treasury, the very thought of which ought to be unbearable to a loyal subject."

"It would have been better for us to have died with our goat," cried the brothers shedding bitter tears.

"Do you think they haven't enough fools in heaven?" asked Khoja Nasreddin. "Reliable men tell me that nowadays both heaven and hell are brimful of fools and won't take any more. Brothers, I foresee immortality for you . . . and be quick in getting away from here, for the guards are beginning to look this way, and unlike yourselves I cannot count upon remaining immortal." The brothers went away loudly sobbing, scratching their faces and sprinkling the yellow road-dust onto their heads.

Then the blacksmith came before the Emir. He stated his complaint in a hoarse and sullen voice. The Grand Vizier Bakhtiyar turned towards the Emir:

"What is your decision, O Master?"

The Emir was asleep and snoring softly, with his mouth open. Bakhtiyar was quite unabashed.

"O Master! I read the decision on your noble countenance."

He announced solemnly:

"In the name of Allah, the Merciful and Compassionate: the Commander of the Faithful and our Master, the Emir, in his incessant concern for his subjects, has manifested his great favour and kindness towards them by giving them the honour of keeping and feeding the faithful guards in his service. By this privilege he has granted to the citizens of Noble Bukhara the honourable opportunity of showing daily and hourly their gratitude to their Emir. Such an honour is not bestowed upon the inhabitants of other countries neighbouring on ours. Despite this, the blacksmiths have not distinguished themselves by their piety. On the contrary, the blacksmith Yusuf, disregarding the torments of the other world and the hair-woven bridge reserved for sinners, has insolently opened his mouth to express ingratitude. Further, he has had the temerity to bring his complaint to the feet of our Lord and Master, the Most Serene Emir, whose radiance eclipses the very sun.

"Because of this our Most Serene Emir has graciously pronounced the following judgment: the smith Yusuf is to receive two hundred lashes of the whip. This will no doubt inspire him with penitence without which he would wait in vain for the gates of paradise to open to him. As for the blacksmiths' row, the Serene Emir manifests anew his favour and condescension by ordering that they be sent a further twenty guards to be kept and fed. Thus they will not be deprived of the happy opportunity of extolling daily and hourly the wisdom and mercy of our Emir. Such is his decision and may Allah prolong his days for the good of all his loyal subjects."

The chorus of court flatterers again came to life and droned praises to the Emir. Meanwhile the guards seized the smith Yusuf and dragged him to the place of execution where the executioners, grinning hideously, were already testing the weight of their heavy whips.

The smith stretched himself face down on a mat. The whip whistled and fell, and the smith's back was dyed with blood.

The executioners beat him cruelly. They tore his skin in strips and cut his flesh to the bone. But never a cry, never a groan did he utter. When he stood up there was a black froth on his lips; during the punishment he had bitten the earth so as not to scream.

"This smith is not one to forget," said Khoja Nasreddin. "He will remember to the end of his days the Emir's kindness. What are you waiting for, dyer? Go, it is your turn now."

The dyer spat and left the crowd without a backward glance.

The Grand Vizier quickly dispatched other cases, out of each of which he never failed to draw profit for the Emir's treasury, an aptitude which distinguished him from among the other dignitaries.

The executioners worked without respite. Screams and yells sounded from their direction. The Grand Vizier sent many fresh sinners to the executioners. A long queue waited: old men, women and even a ten-year old boy who was convicted of insolently and mutinously wetting the ground in front of the Emir's palace. He trembled and cried, smearing the tears on his face. Khoja Nasreddin's heart was full of pity and indignation as he gazed at him.

"Truly this boy is a dangerous criminal," he said aloud.

And one cannot praise sufficiently the Emir's foresight for guarding his throne against similar enemies. For such are more dangerous since they hide potentially evil thoughts under the tenderness of their years. Only today I saw another criminal, far worse and terrible even than this one. This second criminal—would you believe it!— behaved worse than the first, and what is more, right under the very wall of the palace! Any punishment would have been too light for such impertinence. He ought to have been impaled! I fear, though, that the pale would have passed through him like a spit through a chicken, for he was only four years old. However, as I have said, his age cannot be taken as an excuse. My heart is sorrowful at the thought of the terrible vices which have woven their nests in our Bukhara. Nevertheless, let us trust that with the help of the Emir's executioners and his guards such vices will soon be uprooted and replaced by virtues!"

Thus he spoke in the manner of a mullah delivering a sermon. Both his tone and his words sounded well-meaning, but those who had ears heard and understood, and they smiled secretly and bitterly in their beards.

11

SUDDENLY Khoja Nasreddin saw that the crowd had thinned out. Many had hurried away, some even had taken to their heels.

"Are the guards coming after me?" he thought uneasily.

He understood the reason as soon as he saw the approaching usurer. Behind him, surrounded by guards, walked a decrepit grey-bearded old man in an earth-stained khalat, and a veiled woman, or rather a young girl, as Khoja Nasreddin's practised eye deduced from her gait.

"And where are Zakir, Jura, Said and Sadik?" croaked the usurer surveying the people out of his one good eye. The other eye was dull and motionless and covered with a white film. "They were here just now, I saw them from a distance. Their debts are due soon, and it is useless for them to run away and hide."

And he limped on under his hump.

People began to talk among themselves:

"Look, the old spider is dragging the potter Niyaz and his daughter before the Emir."

"He wouldn't give the potter even a day's grace."

"Curse him! My debt falls due in a fortnight."

"And mine in a week."

"Look how everybody runs and hides when he comes as though he were bringing leprosy or cholera!"

"The usurer is worse than a leper!"

Khoja Nasreddin's soul was torn with remorse. He repeated his oath:

"I shall drown him in that very same pond!"

Arslan-bek allowed the usurer to come up out of turn. After him came the potter and his daughter. They fell on their knees and kissed the fringe of the carpet.

"Peace be unto you, worthy Jafar," the Grand Vizier said affably. "What business brings you here? State your business to the Great Emir."

"O great Sovereign! My Lord!" said Jafar addressing himself to the Emir who nodded somnolently only to resume his snores and snuffles. "I come to crave your justice. This man, Niyaz by name and potter by trade, owes me one hundred tangas and another three hundred tangas of interest on this debt. The debt fell due this morning, but the potter has paid me nothing. Give us your judgment, O wise Emir, Sun of the Universe."

The scribes entered the usurer's complaint in their books. Then the Grand Vizier turned to the potter: "Potter, answer the Great Emir. Do you recognize this debt? Perhaps you contest the day and hour?"

"No," replied the potter in a feeble voice. "No, most wise and just Vizier, I contest nothing—neither the debt, nor the day, nor the hour. I ask only for one month's respite and throw myself upon the mercy and generosity of our Emir."

"Allow me, O Master, to announce the verdict which I have read on your countenance," said Bakhtiyar. "In the name of Allah the Merciful and Compassionate, according to the law, whoever does not pay his debt in time becomes with his family the slave of his creditor, and remains in slavery until he has paid the debt with interest for the whole time, including the time spent in servitude."

The potter's head drooped lower and lower and suddenly began to tremble. Many in the crowd turned away stifling heavy sighs. The girl's shoulders quivered; she was weeping under her veil.

Khoja Nasreddin repeated to himself for the hundredth time:

"He shall drown, this merciless tormentor of the poor!"

"But our Master's mercy and generosity are boundless," continued Bakhtiyar raising his voice.

A hush fell over the crowd. The old potter lifted his head and hope lit up his face.

"Though the debt is now due, the Emir grants the potter Niyaz a respite—one hour. If at the end of this hour the potter Niyaz neglects the precepts of the faith and does not pay the entire debt with interest, the law will be fulfilled, as already said. Go, potter, and may the Emir's mercy abide with you henceforth."

Bakhtiyar finished, and the chorus of flatterers thronging behind the throne took up its drone:

"O just Emir, eclipsing with his justice justice itself! O merciful and wise Emir! O generous Emir! O adornment of the earth and glory of heaven, our Serene Emir!" This time the flatterers outdid themselves by singing their praises so loudly that the Emir woke up and angrily ordered them to hold their tongues. They fell silent. The people in the square were also silent. Suddenly a powerful, ear-splitting braying broke the general silence.

It was Khoja Nasreddin's ass. Whether he was tired of standing in one spot, or had caught sight of a long-eared brother whom he wished to greet—the fact was that he brayed, tail uplifted, muzzle stretched out, yellow teeth bared. He brayed deafeningly, uncontrollably, and if he stopped for an instant it was only to take a breath, open his jaws still wider and bray and screech still louder.

The Emir stopped his ears. The guards threw themselves into the crowd. But Khoja Nasreddin was already far away. He pulled and tugged his baulking ass and loudly scolded him:

"What makes you so happy, accursed ass? Can't you praise the mercy and generosity of our Emir without so much noise? Perhaps you hope to become chief court flatterer by such efforts?"

The crowd roared with laughter at his words, made way to let him pass through and again closed their ranks before the guards could overtake him. If they had caught Khoja Nasreddin they would have lashed him for this insolent disturbance of the peace and they would have confiscated his ass.

12

"JUDGMENT has been given and my power over you is now

unbounded," said Jafar the Usurer to the potter Niyaz and his daughter Guljan after the three had left the place where justice had been dispensed. "My beauty, ever since I saw you by chance I have lost all peace of mind. I cannot sleep. Show me your face quickly. Today, in exactly an hour's time you will enter my house. If you are kind to me, I shall give your father light work, and good food. If you are stubborn, then by the light of my eyes, I shall feed him on raw beans, make him carry stones and sell him to the Khivans who, as you well know, treat their slaves cruelly. Do not be stubborn, show me your face, O lovely Guljan!"

His crooked, sensual fingers slightly lifted her veil. She threw off his hand with an angry gesture. Guljan's face remained uncovered only for an instant but it was enough for Khoja Nasreddin who was passing by on his ass. The beauty of the girl was so breathtaking that Khoja Nasreddin nearly lost his senses. The world grew dim before his eyes, his heart stopped beating, he paled, staggered in the saddle and covered his eyes with his hand in utter confusion.

Love had struck him instantly, like a thunderbolt.

It took him some time to recover.

"And this lame, hunch-backed, one-eyed ape dares aspire to a beauty the like of whom has never yet been seen in this world!" he cried to himself. "Why, O why did I drag him out of the water yesterday? Now my deed has indeed turned against me! But we shall see, we shall see, you dirty usurer! You are not yet master of the potter and his daughter. They have still an hour's grace, and Khoja Nasreddin can do more in an hour than another man in a whole year."

Meanwhile the usurer took a wooden sundial from his pocket and marked the hour.

"Wait for me, potter, here under this tree. I shall return in an hour's time. And do not try to hide, for I shall find you even at the bottom of the sea and shall deal with you as with a fugitive slave. And you, fair Guljan, think over my words: your father's fate depends on how you treat me."

And with a satisfied smile on his hideous face he set off to the jewellers' row to buy ornaments for his new concubine.

The potter, bowed down with grief, remained with his daughter in the shade of the roadside tree.

Khoja Nasreddin approached them.

"Potter, I have heard the judgment. You are in great trouble, but perhaps I may be able to help you."

"No, kind man," replied the potter hopelessly. "I see from your patched clothes that you are not rich, and I have to find four hundred tangas! I have no wealthy friends, they are all poor, ruined by levies and taxes."

"I, too, have no rich friends in Bukhara," said Khoja Nasreddin, "but all the same I'll try to raise the money."

"Raise four hundred tangas in one hour!" The old man shook his head and smiled bitterly. "Surely you mock me, stranger. Only Khoja Nasreddin could succeed in such an undertaking."

"O stranger, save us, save us!" cried Guljan throwing her arms round her father.

Khoja Nasreddin looked at her and saw that her hands were perfect. She gave him a long glance and through her veil he could see the liquid radiance of her eyes filled with prayer and hope. His blood raced, running through his veins like a flame, his love grew a thousandfold. He said to the potter:

"Stay here, old man, and wait for me. May I be the most despised and lowest of men if I do not find four hundred tangas before the usurer's return."

He jumped on his ass and disappeared among the bazaar crowd.

13

IT was much quieter now and less crowded than in the morning, when during those busiest hours everyone was running, shouting and hurrying for fear of missing his chance. It was close upon noon and the people, seeking to avoid the heat, were going off to the tea-houses quietly to take stock of their gains and losses. The sun flooded the square with a hot light, the shadows lay short and sharp, as though etched on the hard earth. Beggars sheltered in all the quiet corners, while sparrows hopped around them picking up crumbs and chirping merrily.

"In Allah's name, good man, give us something," droned the beggars showing to Khoja Nasreddin their deformities and ulcers.

He answered crossly:

"Keep your hands off. I am as poor as you are and I am looking for someone who will give me four hundred tangas."

The beggars, thinking he was taunting them, showered curses on his head, but Khoja Nasreddin was too busy with his thoughts to answer them.

In the row of the tea-houses his choice fell upon the largest and most crowded of those where there were neither costly carpets, nor silk cushions. He entered and pulled his ass up the steps behind him instead of leaving him at the tie-rail.

An astonished silence greeted him. This did not disturb him in the least. Out of his saddle-bag he took the Koran, given him the day before by the old man. He opened the book, and laid it in front of the ass.

He did this without haste and unsmilingly, as though it were the most natural thing in the world. The men assembled in the tea-house began to exchange glances.

The ass stamped his hoof resoundingly on the wooden floor.

"Already?" asked Khoja Nasreddin turning over the leaf. "You are making remarkable progress."

At this point the paunchy, good-humoured owner rose from his seat and came towards Khoja Nasreddin.

"See here, good man, is this the proper place for your ass? And why have you laid the sacred book in front of him?"

"I am teaching this ass theology," replied Khoja Nasreddin calmly. "We have reached the end of the Koran and will soon pass on to the Shariat."

Murmurs and whispers ran over the tea-house. Many stood up to see better. The owner's eyes opened wide, his mouth fell agape. Never in his life had he seen such a wonder. At this moment the ass stamped again.

"Good," approved Khoja Nasreddin turning over the leaf. "Very good. A little more and you will be able to take the place of the chief doctor of law in the Mir-Arab Madrasa. The only thing he can't do is to turn over the pages for himself, and one has to help him. Allah has given him a quick intelligence and a remarkable memory. But he forgot to give him fingers," added Khoja Nasreddin for the benefit of the tea-house owner.

The guests left their tea-pots and gathered close. In a few moments a crowd had collected around Khoja Nasreddin.

"This is no ordinary ass," he explained. "He belongs to the Emir in person. One day the Emir called me and asked: 'Can you teach my favourite ass theology, so that he should know as much as I do?' They showed me the ass, I tested his abilities and replied: 'O most Serene

Emir! This remarkable ass possesses an intelligence not inferior to that of any of your viziers, or even your own. I undertake to teach him theology and he will know as much as you, and even more, but it will take twenty years. The Emir ordered the treasury to pay me five thousand tangas in gold and said: 'Take the ass and teach him, but I swear by Allah that if at the end of twenty years he does not know theology and cannot recite the Koran by heart, I shall cut off your head.' "

"Then you had better say farewell to your head!" exclaimed the tea-house owner. "Who ever saw an ass learn theology and recite the Koran!"

"There are quite a few such asses in Bukhara," replied Khoja Nasreddin. "I must add that five thousand tangas in gold and a good ass are not come by every day. And do not deplore the loss of my head, for in twenty years' time one of us is sure to die—either myself, the Emir, or the ass. Then it will be too late to discover which of the three is the best doctor of law!"

The tea-house rocked with a burst of thunderous laughter. The owner fell down convulsed on the felts and laughed until his face streamed with tears. He was a very merry, a very jolly man, this tea-house owner.

"Did you hear that?" he shouted, wheezing and choking. "Then it will be too late to discover who is the best doctor of law!" And assuredly he would have burst with mirth if a sudden thought had not struck him.

"Wait! Wait!" He waved his arms calling for attention. "Who are you? Where do you come from, you who teach theology? Could you possibly be Khoja Nasreddin in person?"

"Would that be so remarkable? You have guessed right, I am Khoja Nasreddin. I greet you, citizens of Noble Bukhara!"

For a long minute all remained as though spellbound. Suddenly a triumphant voice broke the silence:

"Khoja Nasreddin!"

"Khoja Nasreddin! Khoja Nasreddin!" the others caught up one by one. The cry spread to the other teahouses and then to the entire bazaar—all over the place it rang out, boomed and echoed:

"Khoja Nasreddin! Khoja Nasreddin!"

Men came running to the tea-house from all sides— Uzbeks, Tajiks, Persians, Turcomans, Turks, Georgians, Armenians, Tatars—

and once there they welcomed with loud cries their well-beloved Khoja Nasreddin, the famous gay-hearted and astute Khoja Nasreddin.

The crowd swelled.

From somewhere there appeared a sack of oats, a bundle of clover and a pail of clean water which were set before the ass.

"Welcome, Khoja Nasreddin!" came from the crowd. "Where have you been wandering? Come, tell us, Khoja Nasreddin!"

He came forward to the edge of the porch and bowed low to the crowd.

"I greet you, citizens of Bukhara! For ten years I have been parted from you, and now my heart rejoices at the reunion. You ask me to tell you something—I had rather sing it!"

He caught up a large earthen pot, threw the water out of it and striking it with his fist like a tambourine, loudly intoned:

Ring earthen pot, sing earthen pot,
Give worthy praise to the Emir!
And tell the world our happy lot
Under our generous Emir.

The earthen pot now hums and rings
And in an angry voice it sings.
It sends a hoarse and angry call
On every side to one and all.

Hear what the pot has got to tell:
"The potter Niyaz here does dwell.
He works the clay and pots he turns,
But little is it that he earns.
He could not save from what he got
Enough to fill a tiny pot.

"Jafar the Hunchback does not sleep
His brimming pots of gold to keep.
The Emir's treasury too has gold
Hoarded in quantities untold.
The palace guards too do not sleep
Those large and brimming pots to keep.

"One day to old Niyaz came grief
Stealing upon him like a thief.
Guards came and seized him to be brought
For judgment to the Emir's court.
Dragging his hump behind him came
Jafar of evil face and fame."

How long injustice must we bear?
Tell, earthen pot, to all who hear!
For truthful is your tongue of clay—
The potter's crime, what is it, say?

The earthen pot rings loud and high
And truthfully it does reply:
"It is the poor old potter's fault
That in a net he has been caught.
The spider's web has got him fast,
The spider's slave he'll be at last."

Before the lord Niyaz appears
And to his feet he clings in tears.
He says: " 'Tis known to all mankind
That our Emir is great and kind.
May he then graciously impart
Some solace to my humble heart."
The Emir says: "Weep not, poor man,
I grant thee grace—a whole hour's span!
For it is known to all mankind
That I am generous and kind."
How long injustice must we bear?
Tell, earthen pot, to all who hear!

The earthern pot sings loud and high
And truthfully it does reply:
"Truly a madman he would be
Who justice would expect to see
From the Emir whose price, we know,
Is very low, is very low!
He's but a sack of trash and rot

With for a head an earthen pot!"

Say, pot, how long have we to bear
With the misrule of our Emir?
When will the people sorely tried
At last in happiness abide?

The pot sings loud, the pot rings high,
And truthfully it does reply:
"The Emir's power is strong withal,
And yet some day he'll have to fall.
Your days of sorrow will depart.
The years go by. There'll come the day
When in due time he'll break apart
And crumble like this pot of clay!"

Raising the pot high over his head Khoja Nasreddin dashed it to the ground where it shattered into hundreds of fragments. Straining to cover the noise of the crowd Khoja Nasreddin shouted:

"Then let us all help to rescue the potter Niyaz from the usurer and the Emir's clemency! You know Khoja Nasreddin! Loans are never lost with him! Who will lend me four hundred tangas for a short term?"

A bare-footed water-carrier stepped forward:

"Khoja Nasreddin, how can we have money? We pay heavy taxes. But I have a sash. It's nearly new. It might bring in something."

And he threw his sash at Khoja Nasreddin's feet. The crowd buzzed and seethed. Skull-caps, slippers, sashes, kerchiefs and even khalats came flying to Khoja Nasreddin's feet. Every man held it as an honour to help Khoja Nasreddin. The fat tea-house owner brought out his two best tea-pots and a copper tray, eyeing the others proudly, for he had given generously. The pile of gifts kept growing, Khoja Nasreddin shouted at the top of his voice:

"Enough! Enough, O generous citizens of Bukhara! Enough, do you hear me? Saddler, take back your saddle —it is enough, I tell you! What? are you trying to turn your Khoja Nasreddin into an old clothes man? Now I shall begin the sale. Here is the water-carrier's sash. He who buys it will never know thirst. Come along, I am selling cheap! Here are some old patched slippers. They have certainly walked at least twice to Mecca. He who wears them will feel as though he were making a pilgrimage! Here are knives, khalats, slippers! Come on, I am selling cheaply without any bargaining. Time is too precious!"

But the Grand Vizier Bakhtiyar in his incessant care for the loyal subjects had taken great pains to order things in Bukhara so that not a copper should linger in the inhabitants' pockets, but should find its way immediately into the Emir's treasury. In vain did Khoja Nasreddin loudly extol the quality of his wares—there were no buyers.

14

Just then Jafar the Usurer happened to be passing by. His pouch was weighed down with gold and silver trinkets which he had bought for Guljan in the jewellers' row. Although the hour's grace was nearly gone and the usurer was hurrying along, spurred on by sensual impatience, greed took the upper hand when he heard Khoja Nasreddin advertising a cheap-sale.

At the sight of the usurer the crowd rapidly melted away, for out of every three men one was in his debt.

Jafar recognized Khoja Nasreddin.

"So it is you, who pulled me out of the water yesterday? Are you trading here? Where did you get so much stuff to sell?"

"Don't you remember giving me half a tanga yesterday, worthy Jafar?" replied Khoja Nasreddin. "I made the money work and luck has favoured my trade."

"And you have managed to get all these goods in one morning?" cried the usurer in astonishment. "My money has benefited you indeed! How much do you want for the whole lot?"

"Six hundred tangas."

"You are mad! You ought to be ashamed to ask such a sum from your benefactor! Don't you owe your prosperity to me? Two hundred tangas—that is my price."

"Five hundred," retorted Khoja Nasreddin. "Out of respect for you, worthy Jafar—five hundred tangas!"

"O ungrateful one! Once again, is it not to me that you owe your prosperity?"

"And you, O usurer, don't you owe your life to me?" countered Khoja Nasreddin losing patience. "It is true that you gave me only half a tanga for rescuing you, but your life isn't worth more than that so I am not offended. If you are here to buy, name the proper price."

"Three hundred!"

Khoja Nasreddin said nothing.

The usurer paused, appraising the goods with an experienced eye, and having satisfied himself that all these khalats, slippers and skullcaps would fetch at least seven hundred tangas, decided to raise his offer.

"Three hundred and fifty."

"Four hundred."

"Three hundred and seventy-five."

"Four hundred."

Khoja Nasreddin was adamant. Several times the usurer made as though to leave, returning again to add another tanga, until at last he gave in. They struck the bargain. Groaning and complaining, the usurer counted out the money.

"By Allah, I am paying double what the stuff is worth. But such is my nature to incur great losses out of sheer kindness."

"This coin is counterfeit," interrupted Khoja Nasreddin returning one of the coins. "And there are not four hundred tangas here. There are only three hundred and eighty. Your sight is poor, worthy Jafar."

The usurer was obliged to add another twenty tangas and replace the false coin. This done, he hired a porter for a quarter of a tanga, and having loaded him up, ordered him to follow. The unfortunate porter nearly sank down under the weight of the load.

"We are going the same way," said Khoja Nasreddin.

He could hardly wait for the sight of Guljan and kept hurrying ahead. The usurer's lameness hindered him and he trailed behind.

"Whither are you hurrying?" asked the usurer wiping the sweat away with his sleeve.

"To the same spot as yourself," replied Khoja Nasreddin with a sly twinkle in his black eyes. "You and I, worthy Jafar, are going to the same spot on the same business."

"But you do not know my business," said the usurer. "If you did, you would envy me."

The hidden meaning of these words was not lost on Khoja Nasreddin and he answered with a gay laugh:

"But if you, O usurer, knew my business, you would envy me ten times as much."

Jafar frowned, sensing the impertinence of the reply.

"You make too free with your tongue. Men like you should stand in fear when speaking with one like myself. There are few men in Bukhara whom I could envy. I am rich, and my wishes know no obstacles. I have wished for the most beautiful maiden in Bukhara and today she will be mine."

Just then a man selling cherries from a flat basket which he carried on his head came past them. Khoja Nasreddin picked a long-stalked cherry from the basket and showed it to the usurer.

"Hear me out, worthy Jafar. They say that one day a jackal saw a cherry high up in a tree. And he said to himself: 'I shall not rest until I have eaten that cherry.' So he started to climb up the tree, and he climbed for two hours, tearing himself badly on the twigs. Suddenly, just as he was preparing to enjoy himself and had opened his mouth wide, a falcon flew up, seized the cherry and carried it off. After this the jackal climbed back for another two hours, tearing himself still worse. He shed bitter tears and kept saying: 'Why ever did I climb to get that cherry, for it is well known that cherries do not grow on trees for jackals.' "

"You are foolish," said the usurer scornfully. "I see no sense in your fable."

"Profound meaning is not realized all at once," retorted Khoja Nasreddin.

The cherry hung behind his ear, its stalk tucked under his skull-cap.

The road turned. Beyond the turning the potter and his daughter sat on the stones.

The potter stood up. His eyes, in which the light of hope had lingered, dulled, for he thought that the stranger had been unable to raise the money. Guljan turned away with a little moan.

"Father, we are lost!" she said with such pain in her voice that even a stone would have been moved to tears. But the usurer's heart was harder than any stone. Only cruel triumph and lust showed in his face as he said:

"The time is up, potter. Henceforth you are my slave, and your daughter is my slave and concubine."

Wishing to wound and humiliate Khoja Nasreddin he unveiled the girl's face with an air of ownership.

"See, is she not beautiful? Today I shall sleep with her. Tell me now who must envy whom?"

"She is beautiful indeed," said Khoja Nasreddin. "But have you got the potter's receipt?"

"Of course. How can one do business without receipts? All men are cheats and thieves. Here is the receipt, with a record of the debt and the date of repayment. The potter has printed his thumb at the bottom."

He showed the receipt to Khoja Nasreddin.

"The receipt is in order," confirmed the latter. "Now receive your money according to this receipt. Stay awhile, O worthy ones, and be witnesses," he added, turning to some passers-by.

He tore the receipt in two, then again four times across, scattering the pieces to the wind. Then he untied his sash and returned to the usurer all the money which he had just received from him.

The potter and his daughter seemed as though turned to stone with amazement and joy, the usurer—with fury. The witnesses winked at one another, laughing and enjoying the discomfiture of the hated usurer.

Khoja Nasreddin took the cherry from behind his ear, put it in his mouth and winking at the usurer smacked his lips.

A slow shudder passed along the usurer's ugly body; his hands clawed, his one good eye bulged angrily, his hump trembled.

The potter and Guljan begged:

"O stranger! Tell us your name so that we may know whom to name in our prayers."

"Yes!" the usurer spluttered. "Tell us your name so that I may know whom to curse!"

Khoja Nasreddin's face shone. He replied in a clear and strong voice:

"In Baghdad and in Tehran, in Stambul and in Bukhara— everywhere I am known by one name—Khoja Nasreddin!"

The usurer recoiled blanching:

"Khoja Nasreddin!"

And he darted away in terror hustling his porter before him.

As for the others, they welcomed him crying: "Khoja Nasreddin! Khoja Nasreddin!" Guljan's eyes shone under her veil. The potter only mumbled and gesticulated helplessly, still unable to recover himself.

15

The Emir's court of justice was still busy. The executioners had been replaced several times. The number of unfortunates waiting for the bastinado was still growing. Two victims were squirming on pales, a third lay beheaded on the blood-soaked earth. But the cries and groans did not reach the ears of the dozing Emir for they were drowned by the chorus of court flatterers who had become quite hoarse with their efforts. In their praises they were careful to include the Grand Vizier, the other ministers and Arslan-bek. They even remembered the fly-swatter and the narghile-bearer, for they rightly judged that it is safest to try to please everyone: some because they might be useful, others so that they should not become dangerous.

For some time Arslan-bek had been listening uneasily to a strange hum of noises that came from the distance. He called up two of his most able and experienced spies:

"Go and find out why the people are so excited. Go and report immediately to me."

The spies left, one disguised as a beggar, the other as a dervish. But before they had time to return the usurer came running. He was pale and his feet stumbled. He kept tripping over the skirts of his khalat.

"What has happened, worthy Jafar?" Arslan-bek inquired anxiously.

"Woe to us!" groaned the usurer through trembling lips. "O much respected Arslan-bek, a great misfortune has befallen us. Khoja Nasreddin is in our town. I have just seen him and spoken to him."

Arslan-bek's eyes bulged and stared. The dais steps sagged under his weight as he ran up and bent down to the ear of his somnolent master.

The Emir started up on the throne as though he had been pricked.

"You lie!" he cried. His features contorted with fear and rage. "It isn't true! The Caliph of Baghdad wrote to me a short while ago that he had beheaded him! The Sultan of Turkey wrote that he had impaled him! The Shah of Persia wrote to me in his own hand that he had hanged him! The Khan of Khiva declared publicly last year that he had skinned him alive! How could this accursed Khoja Nasreddin have escaped unharmed from the hands of four monarchs?"

The viziers and dignitaries paled at the mention of Khoja Nasreddin's name. The fly-swatter started and dropped his swat; the narghile-bearer choked with the smoke and started coughing; the flattering tongues of the poets clove to their palates from fear.

"He is here," repeated Arslan-bek.

"You lie!" shouted the Emir, heavily striking him on the cheek with his royal hand. "You lie! But if he is really here, how could he have entered Bukhara, and what is the use of your guard and yourself? Then it is he who caused all that uproar in the bazaar last night! He wanted to raise the people against me while you slept and heard nothing!"

And the Emir struck Arslan-bek again. The latter bowed low, kissing the Emir's hand as it fell.

"O Master, he is here, in Bukhara. Do you not hear?" The distant rumble grew and spread like an approaching earthquake. And then the crowd surrounding the court of justice, caught up by the general excitement, began to rear in its turn, at first indistinctly and low, then louder and stronger until the Emir felt the dais and his gilded throne shake under him. Suddenly out of the buzz and roar of voices there emerged a name, to be repeated and echoed many times from end to end:

"Khoja Nasreddin!"

"Khoja Nasreddin!"

The guards ran to the guns with smoking torches. The Emir's face worked with emotion.

"Put an end to this!" he screamed. "Back to the palace!"

And gathering up the skirts of his brocaded robe he scuttled back to the palace, followed by the stumbling, running servants with the empty litter. Panic-stricken, jostling in their efforts to get ahead of each other, losing their slippers and not bothering to stop to pick them up, the viziers, executioners, musicians, guards, the flyswatter and the narghile-carrier ran for their lives. The elephants alone proceeded with their former dignity, for although they too belonged to the Emir's retinue they had no reason to fear the people.

The ponderous brass-bound gates of the palace clanged shut behind the Emir and his court.

In the meantime the market-place packed to overflowing, buzzed, rumbled and seethed, echoing and reechoing the name of Khoja Nasreddin.

1

FROM time immemorial the potters of Bukhara had settled down near the eastern gates of the city, around a large clay hillock, and no better site could they have chosen clay was near at hand, while water was generously supplied by an irrigation ditch which ran at the foot of the city wall. The grandfathers, great-grandfathers and great-great-grandfathers of the potters had reduced the hillock to half its size. They built their dwellings of clay, they shaped their pots of clay and into the clay they themselves were laid mourned by their relations. Often enough some potter, having shaped a pot or jug, dried it in the sun and baked it in the fire, must have wondered at the clear, strong ring of the vessel, never suspecting that some distant ancestor, anxious for the welfare of his descendant and the sale of his wares, had ennobled the clay by a particle of his own dust, so making it ring like pure silver.

Here, in the shade of mighty, ancient plane-trees, on the very brink of the irrigation ditch stood the house of Niyaz the Potter. The leaves rustled in the wind, the water murmured, and in the tiny garden the songs of the fair Guljan rang out from morning to night.

Khoja Nasreddin refused to take up his abode in Niyaz's house.

"No, Niyaz," he said. "I might get caught in your house. I shall spend the nights not far from here in a safe place which I have found. In the day-time I shall come here and help you with your work."

And he did as he had said. Every morning before sunrise he would come to Niyaz and sit down next to the old man at the potter's bench. There was no trade in the world with which Khoja Nasreddin was not familiar. He knew the potter's trade well, and the pots he turned out were smooth, had a clear ring and would keep water ice-cold in the hottest weather. Formerly the old man, whose eyesight had been failing lately, could hardly manage to turn out five or six pots a day, whereas now long rows of pots—thirty, forty and sometimes even fifty —were drying in the sunshine. On market days the old man would bring home a full purse, and at nightfall the savoury smell of a meat pilau spread from his house along the whole street. The neighbours were happy for the old man's sake and said:

"At last good fortune has come to Niyaz and poverty has left him, please God, for ever!"

"They say he has hired another workman to help him. They also say the workman is the potter of potters."

"Yes, I heard that too. One day I looked in on Niyaz to see his workman. But just as I entered the garden gate the workman got up, went away, and did not show himself again."

"Yes, the old man hides his workman. He must be afraid that one of us will entice such a skilled worker away from him, queer fellow! As though we potters had no conscience. As if we would try to spoil the luck of an old man who has at last found happiness."

Thus the neighbours settled the question among themselves. Not one of them suspected that old Niyaz's workman was none other than Khoja Nasreddin himself. All firmly believed that Khoja Nasreddin had long since left Bukhara. He himself had started the rumour so as to baffle the spies and cool their zeal in the search. That he had attained his aim was proved by the fact that some ten days later the supplementary barriers were taken down at all the city gates and night rounds no longer disturbed the inhabitants of Bukhara by the glare of torches and the clash of arms.

One day old Niyaz, after grunting uneasily for a long time with his eyes on Khoja Nasreddin, ended by saying: "You have saved me from slavery, Khoja Nasreddin, and my daughter from dishonour. You work with me and turn out ten times as much as I do. Here are three hundred and fifty tangas of clear profit which I have made from selling pots since you began to help me. Take the money, it is yours by right."

Khoja Nasreddin stopped his wheel and fixed his astonished gaze on the old man.

"Surely you must be ill, O worthy Niyaz! You make such strange speeches! You are the master here and I am your workman. If you give me a tithe of the profit, say, thirty-five tangas, I shall be more than satisfied."

Taking Niyaz's worn purse he counted out thirty-five tangas which he put in his sash, returning the rest to the old man. But the latter stubbornly refused to take back the money.

"That's not right, Khoja Nasreddin. This money belongs to you! If you won't take all, at least take half of it."

Khoja Nasreddin lost his temper.

"Put away your purse, worthy Niyaz, and please do not upset the usage of the world. What would happen if all the masters were to go halves with their workmen? There would be neither masters nor workmen in this world, neither rich nor poor, neither guards nor Emirs. Just think: how could Allah put up with such disorder? He would immediately send another Great Flood! Take your purse and hide it well, otherwise your mad ideas may bring down Allah's wrath upon mankind and thus destroy the entire human race."

Having spoken Khoja Nasreddin set his wheel spinning again.

"This will be an excellent pot!" he said slapping the wet clay with his hands. "It rings like the head of our Emir! I shall have to take this pot to the palace. Let them keep it there in case the Emir happens to lose his head."

"Look out, Khoja Nasreddin. One day you may lose your own head for saying such things."

"Oho! Do you think it is so easy to chop off the head of Khoja Nasreddin?

"I, Khoja Nasreddin, ever free have I been,
And I say, 'tis no lie, that I never shall die:
Let the Emir prepare a sharp axe and declare
That I rob and I fleece and disturb the world's peace!
I, Khoja Nasreddin, ever free have I been,
And I say, 'tis no lie, that I never shall die:
I shall live, I shall sing and the sunshine admire,
And shall shout to the world: 'Let the Emir expire!'
Yes, the Sultan has said he will chop off my head,
'Tis a noose with the Shah, and the stake in Khiva!
I, Khoja Nasreddin, always free have I been,
And I say, 'tis no lie, that I never shall die!
Though a tramp poor and bare, I have never a care.
Well beloved by mankind, Fate to me has been kind.
Of Sultan or Emir, or the Khan I've no fear!
I, Khoja Nasreddin, ever free have I been
And I'll say, 'tis no lie, that I never shall die!"

Guljan's laughing face peeped out through the vine-leaves behind Niyaz's back. Khoja Nasreddin broke off in the middle of his song to exchange gay and mysterious signs with her.

"What are you looking at?" asked Niyaz. "What do you see there?"

"I see a bird of paradise, the loveliest in the world!"

The old man turned round laboriously but Guljan had already disappeared among the foliage and only her silvery laughter sounded in the distance. For a long time the old man screwed up his feeble eyes, shading them with his hand from the bright sunshine, but all he could see was a sparrow hopping from branch to branch.

"Do be sensible, Khoja Nasreddin! What kind of bird of paradise is that? It is only a sparrow!"

Khoja Nasreddin laughed heartily while Niyaz shook his head, unable to understand the reason for such gaiety.

At night after supper, when Khoja Nasreddin had left, Niyaz went up on the roof and settled down for the night, fanned by a warm gentle breeze. Soon he was snoring. Then a light cough came from behind the low fence. Khoja Nasreddin was back again.

"He is asleep," whispered Guljan.

In one leap he cleared the fence.

They moved into the shadow of the poplars. The trees seemed to be gently dozing, wrapped in their long green robes. The moon stood high in the clear sky and its light turned everything into a misty blue. The water-course murmured, lit up here and there by spangles of light before it was lost in the shadows.

Guljan stood before Khoja Nasreddin in the full light of the moon, herself radiant as a full moon, slender and supple and framed by her long plaits. He spoke very low: "I love you, queen of my soul, you are my first and only love. I am your slave, willing to carry out your slightest wish. My whole life has been just waiting for you. And now I have found you, I shall never forget you. I cannot live without you!"

"I am sure you are not saying this for the first time," she said jealously.

"I?" he cried indignantly. "Oh, Guljan! How can you say such a thing?"

He seemed so sincere that she believed him. Relenting she sat down beside him on the bench of packed earth. He pressed his lips to hers for so long that she was breathless.

"Listen," she said after a pause. "It is our custom, you know, to give a present to a girl you kiss, and here you have been kissing me every night for more than a week and you haven't even given me a pin."

"Only because I hadn't any money," he replied. "But today your father paid me and tomorrow, Guljan, I shall bring you a fine present. What would you like? Beads or a kerchief? Or perhaps a ring set with an amethyst?"

"I don't really care," she whispered. "I don't really care, my dear Khoja Nasreddin, so long as it is a present from you. I loved you since the moment when you came up to us that day in the market place, and I loved you still more when you drove away that wicked usurer Jafar."

The dark water murmured; the stars twinkled brightly in the clear sky. Khoja Nasreddin pressed closer to the girl, stretched out his hand and covered her warm breast with the palm of his hand. He held his breath, entranced. Suddenly he saw sparks and his cheek tingled from a resounding slap. He recoiled, shielding himself with his elbow. Guljan rose angrily.

"I thought I heard the sound of a slap," he said mildly. "Must one fight when one can talk?"

"Talk!" interrupted Guljan. "It is bad enough that I have been so lost to all shame as to unveil before you. Why do you stretch out your long arms where you shouldn't?"

"And who, pray, has decided where arms should be stretched or not?" retorted Khoja Nasreddin much abashed. "Now if you had read the books of the most wise Ibn Tufayl—"

"Thank God," she interrupted heatedly, "thank God I haven't read such lewd writings! I guard my honour as a decent girl should!"

She turned from him and walked away. The steps creaked under her light tread, and soon a light showed through the chinks of the balcony shutters.

"I have hurt her feelings," thought Khoja Nasreddin. "I was a fool. Never mind, at least I know what her temper is like. If she can slap me like that, it means she'll slap any other fellow's face and will make a faithful wife. Yes, I'll be content to be slapped by her ten times ten before we are married if after the wedding she is as generous with her slaps towards other men."

He tiptoed up to the balcony and called softly: "Guljan!"

No answer.

"Guljan!"

Fragrance and darkness and silence. Khoja Nasreddin was sad. In a low voice so as not to wake up the old man, he started to sing:

> *"Your eye-lashes have stolen my heart.*
> *You condemn me yet steal with your eye-lashes.*
> *Now you ask payment for stealing my heart!*
> *O wonder of wonders! Who ever has heard*
> *Of thieves being paid by their victim!*
> *Then make me a present of two or three kisses.*
> *No, that is not enough.*
> *There are kisses like bitter waters:*
> *The more you drink of them, the greater your thirst.*
> *You have shut the door in my face—*
> *O had rather my blood had been spilt on the ground!*
> *Where shall I now find sleep and solace?*
> *Perhaps you will tell me?*
> *So great is my yearning for your eyes*
> *Which wound me with their arrows!*
> *So great is my yearning for your locks*
> *Fragrant like musk!"*

Thus he sang, and though Guljan neither showed herself, nor made answer, he knew that she was listening intently. He knew no woman could remain unmoved by such a song. He was right. The shutter opened slightly.

"Come!" Guljan whispered. "Only come quietly so as not to waken my father."

He mounted the steps and sat down at her side. The wick floating in the earthen cup full of melted mutton fat sputtered and burnt until daybreak. They talked and could not talk enough. In a word all was as it should be and as it is described by the most wise Abu Muhammad Ali ibn Hazm in his book *The Turtledove's Necklace,* in the chapter on the nature of love. "Love—may Allah glorify it!—starts by being a sport, but ends by being an important matter. Its qualities are too exalted to be described and its true substance can be comprehended only with difficulty. As for the reason why in most cases love is inspired by a handsome appearance, this is easy to understand, for the soul is beautiful, is attracted by everything beautiful and inclined towards perfect forms. On seeing such a form the soul examines it, and if beyond the surface something akin to itself is descried, a union takes place, and then true love is born. . . . Truly the external form miraculously unites the remote particles of the soul!"

2

ON the roof the old man stirred, wheezing and coughing, and called out sleepily to Guljan to bring him a drink of water. She pushed Khoja Nasreddin towards the door. He fled down the stairs hardly touching the steps with his feet and jumped over the fence. A little later, having washed himself in the nearest irrigation ditch and wiped himself with the skirt of his khalat he was knocking on the wicket gate.

"Good morning, Khoja Nasreddin," the old man welcomed him from the roof. "How early you have been getting up these last few days. When do you have time for sleep? Now we shall drink our tea before settling down to work."

At noon Khoja Nasreddin left the old man and set out for the bazaar to buy a present for Guljan. He took his usual precaution of wearing a coloured Badakhshan turban and a false beard. Thus disguised he was unrecognizable and could safely walk about among the stalls and in the tea-houses without fear of spies.

He chose a coral necklace whose colour reminded him of the lips of his beloved. The jeweller proved an amenable man and it took only an hour of noisy bargaining and wrangling for the necklace to become Khoja Nasreddin's property for the sum of thirty tangas.

On his way back Khoja Nasreddin noticed a large crowd near the bazaar mosque. People were pressing close and craning over each other's shoulders. As he drew near Khoja Nasreddin heard a harsh, strident voice saying: "See for yourselves, O true believers! He is paralysed and has been lying without moving for ten years. His limbs are cold and lifeless. See, he doesn't even open his eyes. He came from afar to our town. Kind relatives and friends brought him here to try out the only remaining remedy. In a week's time, on the day of the festival commemorating the most holy and incomparable Baha ed-din he will be laid on the steps of the tomb. Thus the blind, the halt and the bedridden have been cured, and more than once. Let us then pray, O true believers, that the holy Shaikh may have mercy and grant recovery to this unfortunate man."

The assembled people recited a prayer, after which the same strident voice resumed:

"See for yourselves, O true believers! He has lain without

moving for ten years!"

Khoja Nasreddin pushed his way through the crowd, stood up on tiptoe and saw a tall, raw-boned mullah with small evil eyes and a short sparse beard. He was shouting and pointing his finger at a stretcher at his feet on which lay the paralysed man.

"Look, O Muslims! Look, how pitiful, how unfortunate he is! But in a week's time the holy Baha ed-din will grant him recovery and he will be restored to life!" The paralysed man was lying there, his eyes closed, and a sad, piteous expression on his face. Khoja Nasreddin gasped in surprise. He could recognize this pock-marked face and flat nose among a thousand. The man had apparently been paralysed for a long time for his face had become much plumper from idleness and inactivity.

From that day, whenever Khoja Nasreddin passed this particular mosque he always found the same raw-boned mullah and the paralysed man whose doleful pock-marked face grew fatter and greasier from day to day.

At last came the day of the festival commemorating the holy Shaikh. According to tradition he had died in May at noon, and although the day had been clear without a cloud in the sky, the sun had darkened at the hour of his death, the earth had trembled and many houses where sinners lived were destroyed, burying the sinners under their ruins. This was the story told by the mullahs in the mosques as they called upon the Muslims not to fail to visit the Shaikh's tomb and render honour to his remains so as not to be mistaken for unbelievers and share the fate of those other sinners.

It was still dark when the pilgrims started on their way, and when the sun rose the great place around the tomb was overflowing with people. More were still coming along the roads. All walked barefoot according to ancient custom. Here, among others, were men who had come from afar—particularly pious people and others who had committed some heinous sin and hoped to gain forgiveness. Husbands brought their barren wives, mothers carried sick children, old men hobbled along on crutches, lepers gathered at a distance from where they hopefully gazed at the white dome of the tomb.

The service did not begin for a long time. They were waiting for the Emir. The populace stood tightly pressed together in the scorching heat of the sun, not daring to sit down. Their eyes burned with a greedy, hungry flame. Having lost faith in earthly happiness they waited for a miracle to happen today, and started at every loudly spoken word. The feelings of tense expectation had become intolerable, and already two dervishes had been seized with convulsions, biting the earth and foaming at the mouth. The crowd seethed, on all sides women shrieked and wept. Suddenly there came a low roar from thousands of throats:

"The Emir! The Emir!"

The palace guards plied their sticks to clear a passage through the throng and along this broad path came the Emir on his pilgrimage, barefoot, his head bowed, rapt in pious meditation and impervious to earthly sounds. His retinue followed silently at his heels, while the servants hurried to and fro rolling up carpets and carrying them forward.

Tears gathered in many eyes at this touching spectacle. The Emir walked up the earthen mound at the foot of the tomb. A prayer-rug was spread before him and, aided by his viziers who supported him on either side, he sank to his knees. The white-robed mullahs formed themselves into a semicircle and began to chant, raising their arms towards the heat-misted sky.

The service went on endlessly, interspersed by sermons. Khoja Nasreddin slipped unnoticed out of the crowd and made his way towards a small isolated shed where the blind, the halt and the bedridden, to whom recovery on this day had been promised, awaited their turn.

The doors of the shed were wide open. The curious looked in and exchanged remarks. The mullahs who were on duty here held large copper trays for offerings. The senior mullah was saying:

". . . and since then the blessing of the most holy Shaikh Baha ed-din dwells eternally and immutably upon holy Bukhara and its sun-like Emirs. And every year on this day holy Baha ed-din grants us, God's humble servants, the power to perform miracles. All these blind, halt, possessed and bedridden men await recovery, and we hope with the aid of holy Baha ed-din to free them from their sufferings."

As though in reply to these words, weeping, howling and gnashing of teeth came from the shed. Raising his voice the mullah went on:

"Give generously, O true believers, for the adornment of the mosques, and your gifts will be acknowledged by Allah!"

Khoja Nasreddin peeped into the shed. The pockmarked fat-faced servant lay on his stretcher near to the door. Beyond him in the gloom a multitude of men could be seen propped on crutches, swathed in bandages or lying on stretchers. Suddenly from the direction of the tomb came the voice of the chief mullah who had just ended his sermon:

"The blind one! Bring the blind one to me!"

Pushing Khoja Nasreddin out of the way, the mullahs dived into the stuffy dark interior of the shed and led out a blind man in beggar's rags. He walked feeling before him with his out-stretched hands and stumbling over the stones.

He approached the chief mullah, fell on his face before him and pressed his lips to the steps of the tomb. The chief mullah laid his hands on his head—and instantly he was cured.

"I can see! I can see!" he cried out in a high-pitched, quavering voice. "O most holy Baha ed-din! I can see! I can see! O great and wonderful miracle!"

The crowd of worshippers pressed around him with a deep murmur of voices. Many came up to him and asked:

"Tell me, which arm have I raised—the right or the left?"

He answered correctly and all were satisfied that he had indeed recovered his sight. Then a whole army of mullahs carrying copper trays made its way into the crowd calling out:

"O faithful believers! With your own eyes you have witnessed a miracle. Give something towards the adornment of the mosques!"

The Emir was the first to throw a handful of gold coins on to the tray. He was followed by the viziers and dignitaries who each threw a gold coin. Then the crowd started to give generously of silver and copper. The trays were soon filled and the mullahs were obliged to change them three times.

As soon as the flow of donations slackened, a lame man was brought out of the shed. No sooner had he touched the steps of the tomb than he too was instantly cured and discarding his crutches broke out into a dance, kicking up his legs. And again the mullahs armed with empty trays moved among the crowd calling out:

"Give, O true believers!"

A white-bearded mullah came up to Khoja Nasreddin who stood absorbed in thought, his eyes fixed on the walls of the shed.

"O true believer! You have witnessed a great miracle. Give and your gift will be acknowledged by Allah!"

Loudly, so that all near him should hear, Khoja Nasreddin replied:

"You call this a miracle and ask me for money. To begin with I have no money, and secondly, are you aware, O mullah, that I too am a great saint and can perform an even greater miracle?"

"You are a blasphemer!" shouted the mullah angrily.

"Do not heed him, O Muslims! The devil speaks through his mouth!"

Khoja Nasreddin turned to the crowd.

"The mullah does not believe that I can perform miracles. I shall give him proof of what I have said. In this shed are assembled blind, lame, sick and bedridden men and I undertake to cure them all at once without even touching them. I shall say but a few words and they will all be cured. They will scatter abroad, running so fast that not even the fleetest Arab steeds will be able to overtake them."

The walls of the shed were thin and the earth of which they were built was deeply cracked in many places.

Khoja Nasreddin selected a place in the wall surrounded by many cracks and pressed heavily against it with his shoulder. The earth gave way. There was a slight but sinister rustle. He pushed harder and a large piece of the wall caved in with a loud thud. Thick dust rose from the dark yawning opening.

"Earthquake! Run! Help!" wildly yelled Khoja Nasreddin, pushing in another piece of the wall.

For a moment all was still within the hut. Then a hullabaloo broke out. The pock-marked paralysed servant was the first to lunge towards the door but his stretcher stuck fast in the opening barring the way for the others. The blind, the halt and the bedridden shoved each other, shouting and howling. When Khoja Nasreddin brought down a third piece of the wall, in one mighty rush they pushed out the pock-marked man together with the door and the jambs, and forgetful of their disablements scattered in all directions.

The crowd hooted, whistled, laughed and booed. Khoja Nasreddin made himself heard above the general din:

"You see, Muslims, I was right in saying that they could be cured with a few words!"

Losing interest in the sermons, people came running from all sides, and on learning what had happened roared with laughter and passed the tale on. In less than no time the whole crowd of worshippers had heard what had happened at the shed, and when the chief mullah raised his hand to demand silence, the crowd replied by oaths, shouts and whistles.

And again, as on that memorable day in the marketplace, the crowd buzzed, roared and echoed:

"Khoja Nasreddin! He has come back! He is here, our Khoja Nasreddin!"

Pursued by hoots and jeers the mullahs dropped their trays and hurriedly left the crowd. By this time Khoja Nasreddin was far away. He concealed his coloured turban and false beard under his khalat, for he had now no reason to fear meeting any spies, who had work enough in the neighbourhood of the tomb.

He failed to observe, however, that he was being followed by Jafar the Usurer who took cover behind corners of houses and roadside trees.

In a deserted alley Khoja Nasreddin came up to the wall, drew himself up with his hands, coughed softly and immediately there came the sound of light footsteps and a woman's voice.

"Is it you, my beloved?"

From his hiding-place behind a tree the usurer had no difficulty in recognizing the voice of the fair Guljan. Then he heard whispers, smothered laughter and the sound of kissing.

"So you took her away from me for yourself!" thought the usurer, torn by cruel jealousy.

After taking leave of Guljan, Khoja Nasreddin went off so fast that the usurer could not keep up with him and soon lost him in a maze of narrow alleys.

"Now I shall not receive the reward for his capture," thought Jafar the Usurer disconsolately. "But never mind! Beware, Khoja Nasreddin, I shall have my revenge yet!"

3

THE Emir's treasury had suffered a severe loss. Less than a tenth of the usual amount collected in former years had been taken at the tomb of the holy Baha ed-din. And to make things worse seeds of bold freethinking had again been sown in the minds of the people. Spies reported that the news of what had happened at the tomb had reached the remotest corners of the state and had already borne fruit. In three villages the inhabitants had refused to complete the building of the mosques and in a fourth they had ignominiously driven out their mullah.

The Emir ordered the Grand Vizier Bakhtiyar to convoke the divan or State Council. The divan assembled in the palace garden, a wonderful garden, one of the most beautiful in the world. Rare fruits ripened here on magnificent spreading trees: apricots of many kinds, plums, figs, bitter oranges and many other varieties which it would be impossible to enumerate. Roses, violets, stocks, lavender and anemones blossomed in great clusters and filled the air with heavenly fragrance enamoured narcissi gazed at smiling daisies. Fountains splashed, schools of goldfish darted about in marble basins, and everywhere hung silver cages in which exotic birds twittered, whistled and sang.

But the viziers, dignitaries and sages passed by indifferently, deaf and blind to all this magic beauty, for their thoughts were exclusively centred on their personal aggrandisement, on warding off the blows of their enemies and on dealing blows to them in their turn, so that there was no room for anything else in their hard, shrivelled hearts. If all of a sudden all the flowers in the world had withered and all the birds of creation stopped singing, they would not have noticed for they were too preoccupied with their ambitious and greedy schemes.

They came with lack-lustre eyes and pursed bloodless lips, shuffling their leather slippers along the sanded paths, and entered a summer-house smothered in the thick dark foliage of sweet basil. Here, placing their turquoise-studded staffs against the wall, they seated themselves on silk cushions. Bowing their heads burdened with enormous white turbans they awaited their master in silence.

When he entered with heavy step, his brow clouded with gloomy thoughts, all rose, bowed nearly to the ground and remained thus until he made a slight sign. Then according to etiquette they fell on their knees and threw back the weight of their bodies on to their heels, touching the carpet with their fingers. Each of them was trying to guess upon whose head the wrath of the Emir would fall today and what advantage could be gained therefrom.

The court poets ranged themselves in a semicircle in their accustomed order behind the Emir, coughing gently to clear their throats.

The most able of these, who bore the title of "King of Poets", was running through in his mind the verses which he had composed that very morning and which he proposed to recite to the Emir as though in a fit of supernatural inspiration.

The palace fly-swatter and the Emir's narghile-bearer took up their appointed positions.

"Who rules in Bukhara?" began the Emir in a low voice which sent a shudder through his audience. "Who rules in Bukhara, we ask you—we or this accursed and impious Khoja Nasreddin?" Here he almost choked. Then mastering his rage he ended menacingly: "The Emir is listening to you! Speak!"

The horse-tail swat waved over his head. The courtiers were silent, terror-stricken. The viziers furtively nudged each other.

"He has wrought havoc in the entire state," resumed the Emir. "Three times he has contrived to disturb the peace of our capital. He has robbed us of sleep and rest and has deprived our treasury of lawful revenue. He openly calls the people to rebellion and mutiny! How should we deal with this evil-doer, we ask you?"

The viziers, dignitaries and sages replied in unison:

"Undoubtedly he deserves the most terrible punishment, O Centre of the Universe and Asylum of Peace!"

"Then why is he still alive?" inquired the Emir. "Or is it for us, your ruler, whose very name you ought to pronounce with awe and reverence and not otherwise than prostrated on the ground—which I must say from laziness, impertinence and negligence you fail to do— is it for us, I repeat, to go in person into the bazaar to catch him while you indulge in gluttony and debauchery in your harems, recalling your duties towards us only on pay days? What is your answer, O Bakhtiyar?"

On hearing Bakhtiyar's name, the others heaved a sigh of relief and a malicious smile touched the lips of Arslan-bek with whom he had a long-standing feud. Bakhtiyar folded his hands on his stomach and bowed to the ground before the Emir.

"May Allah guard our great Emir from trials and misfortunes!" he began. "The loyalty and services of this humble slave, who is but a mote in the rays of the Emir's greatness, are known to the Emir. Before my appointment to the dignity of Grand Vizier the State Treasury was always empty. But I introduced a number of taxes, I instituted the tax to be paid on securing appointments, I have taxed everything which could be taxed, and now no man dares even sneeze without paying for it to the Treasury.

"Moreover I have reduced by half the salaries of the lesser government servants and guards, charging the inhabitants of Bukhara with their keep, and thus saving, O Master, quite an appreciable sum for the Treasury. But I have not mentioned all my services yet, through my efforts miracles are again taking place at the tomb of the holy Baha ed-din and attracting thousands of pilgrims to the tomb. Thus the Treasury of our Sovereign, before whom the other monarchs of the world are nothing but dust, has every year been filled to overflowing with donations, and the revenue has multiplied many times—"

"Where is this revenue?" interrupted the Emir. "It has been taken away from us by Khoja Nasreddin. We are not asking you about your services, we have heard all about them more than once. Better tell us how to lay hands on Khoja Nasreddin."

"O Master!" replied Bakhtiyar. "The duties of the Grand Vizier do not include the apprehension of criminals. In our state this is the business of the worthy Arslan-bek, chief of the palace guard and of the army."

Having spoken he again made obeisance before the Emir with a triumphant and malignant glance at Arslan-bek.

"Speak!" commanded the Emir.

Arslan-bek rose, giving Bakhtiyar an ugly look. He sighed deeply and his black beard rose and fell on his paunch.

"May Allah guard our sun-like Sovereign from trials and misfortunes, and from sickness and sorrow! My services are well known to the Emir. When the Khan of Khiva made war upon Bukhara, the Emir, Centre of the Universe and Shadow of Allah upon the earth, graciously entrusted to me the command of the army of Bukhara. I succeeded in repulsing the foe without bloodshed so that it all ended to our advantage.

"What I did was to order the destruction of all the towns and villages from the frontier of Khiva to a distance of many days' march within our borders, to destroy all the crops and gardens, all the roads and bridges. When the Khivans entered our land and found only a desert devoid of gardens and lifeless, they said to themselves: 'We shall not go on to Bukhara for there is no food or loot to be found there.' They turned back and left, tricked and dishonoured. And our Sovereign the Emir graciously recognized that the devastation of the land by its own army was such a wise and useful measure that he commanded nothing to be restored and ordered the towns, villages, fields and roads to be left in their ruined state so that henceforth alien tribes would not dare to set foot on our soil. Thus did I defeat the Khivans. Besides this I trained many thousands of spies in Bukhara"

"Hold your tongue, braggart!" cried the Emir. "Why then have your spies not caught Khoja Nasreddin?"

Embarrassment kept Arslan-bek silent for a long time. Finally he was obliged to admit:

"O Master, I have tried every means but my brain is helpless against this evil-doer and infidel. I think, O Master, that advice should be sought from the sages."

"By our ancestors! You all deserve to hang from the city wall!" exploded the Emir, in his irritation giving a sharp blow to his narghile-bearer who had chosen the wrong moment to be within reach of the royal hand. "Speak," he commanded the oldest of the sages who was famous for the length of his beard which he could wind twice round his waist.

The sage rose, recited a prayer and stroked his famous beard bit by bit, drawing it with his right hand through the fingers of the left.

"May Allah prolong the lustrous days of the Monarch for the good and the happiness of the people!" he said. "As the above-named malefactor and rebel Khoja Nasreddin is nevertheless only human, it can be concluded that his body is built like that of other human beings, that is, it consists of two hundred and forty bones and three hundred and sixty sinews, which command the lungs, the liver, the heart, the pancreas and the gall. The fundamental sinew is, as the wise teach us, the sinew of the heart from which radiate all the others, and this is an incontrovertible and sacred truth opposed to the heretical teaching of the godless Abu-Iskhak who dares falsely to affirm that the foundation of man's life is the sinew of the lungs.

"In accordance with the writings of the most wise Avicenna, the Greek doctor Hippocrates, as well as of Averroes of Cordoba, on the fruit of whose meditations we feed even now, and also in accordance with the teachings of al-Kindi, al-Farabi and Fakhr ar-Razi, I say and dare to affirm that Allah created Adam by combining four elements— water, earth, fire and air, ordering things thus: that yellow gall possesses the nature of fire, which we actually observe, for it is hot and dry; black gall—the nature of the earth, for it is cold and dry; saliva—the nature of water, for it is cold and moist, and finally blood

—the nature of air, for it is hot and moist. If a man be deprived of any of these liquids contained in his body, this man inevitably dies, from which I deduce, O Illustrious Master, that this impious disturber of the peace, Khoja Nasreddin, should be deprived of his blood, which should preferably be done by separating his head from his body, for together with the blood which flows out, life evaporates from the body of the man, never to return. Such is my advice, O Illustrious Sovereign and Asylum of the World!"

The Emir heard him out attentively, and without making any comment made a barely perceptible sign with his eyebrows to the second sage, whose beard was no match to that of the first but whose turban was far greater in size and magnificence. The weight of the turban had in the course of long years bent his neck sideways and downwards which gave him the appearance of a man fixedly looking upwards through a narrow slit. After making obeisance to the Emir he said:

"O Great Sovereign, matching the sun by his splendour! I cannot agree with this method of disposing of Khoja Nasreddin, for it is well known that not only blood is necessary for the life of man but also air, and if a man's throat be compressed by a rope and thus air be prevented from reaching his lungs, that man inevitably dies and cannot again revive—"

"So!" said the Emir in an ominously low voice. "You are perfectly right, O wisest of the wise, and your advice is undoubtedly precious to us. Indeed, how could we get rid of Khoja Nasreddin if you had not given us such invaluable advice?"

He stopped, unable to overcome the anger and rage which filled him. His cheeks quivered, his nostrils flared and lightning blazed in his eyes. But the court flatterers —philosophers and poets—who stood ranged in a semicircle at the Emir's back, could not see the face of their lord and therefore missed the angry sarcasm with which he had addressed the sages. Taking his words at their face value they thought that the sages had indeed acquitted themselves well and would therefore enjoy the Emir's favour and generosity, so that their good will should be immediately sought for better advantage.

"O most wise! O pearls adorning the crown of our Illustrious Sovereign! O wise men excelling in wisdom, wisdom itself and endowed with the wisdom of the most wise!"

So they poured out their eulogies, vying with each other in

refinement and zeal and unaware that the Emir had turned round and was eyeing them convulsed with rage, while a sinister silence had fallen.

"O luminaries of science and vessels of wisdom!" they intoned, closing their eyes in a rapture of passionate servility.

Suddenly the King of Poets caught the Emir's glance and started as though he had swallowed his own flattering tongue. After him all the others fell silent and quaked, realizing the mistake caused by their excessive zeal.

"O rascals! O knaves!" cried the enraged Emir. "Do you think we ourself do not know that if a man's head be cut off or if he be choked with a rope he will not come to life again? But to do this one must first catch the man, whereas you, rascals, idlers, rogues and fools, have not said one word of how it should be done! All the viziers, dignitaries and poets here present will be deprived of their salaries until Khoja Nasreddin is found. And let it be proclaimed that a reward of three thousand tangas shall be given to the man who catches him! We also warn you that having realized your slothfulness, stupidity and negligence we have invited into our service a new sage from Baghdad whose name is Maulana Husain, and who until now has been in the service of the Commander of the Faithful, the Caliph of Baghdad. He is on his way and will arrive soon. Then woe to you, O flatteners of mattresses, devourers of food and fillers of bottomless pockets!. . . Drive them out!" he shouted to the guards in mounting wrath. "Drive them all out of here! Drive them out!"

Throwing themselves on the dumbfounded courtiers the guards seized them without regard or respect and dragged them to the door whence they sent them tumbling down the steps. At the foot of the steps other guards caught hold of them, and beat, thumped, slapped and kicked them on their way. The courtiers fled, trying to overtake each other. The white-haired sage fell down entangled in his own beard; the second sage stumbled over him and fell down, his head in a rose-bush. There he remained lying, stunned by his fall, and still appearing because of his crooked neck to be looking up through a narrow slit.

4

THE Emir remained as black as thunder to the end of the day. On the following morning the terror-stricken courtiers again observed the dark seal of anger on his countenance.

Vain were all efforts to divert or amuse him. In vain did the dancers flourish their tambourines as they swayed before him in a cloud of fragrant incense, swinging their full hips, showing the pearly lustre of their teeth and baring, as though by accident, their creamy breasts. He did not raise his eyes and his face worked angrily, driving fear into the courtiers' hearts. Vain were the tricks of the court fools, acrobats, jugglers and Indian fakirs who charm snakes with the wail of reed-pipes.

The courtiers whispered among themselves:

"O accursed Khoja Nasreddin! O son of sin! What calamities he has brought down upon us!"

And they turned their hopeful gaze towards Arslan-bek.

He called the most able spies together in the guardroom, including the pock-marked one so miraculously cured by Khoja Nasreddin.

"Know you all," said Arslan-bek, "that by command of our most illustrious Emir your pay is stopped until that rascal Khoja Nasreddin is caught. If you don't succeed in tracing him, you are to lose not only your pay but also your heads. I shall see to that! On the other hand, the one who shows the greatest zeal and captures Khoja Nasreddin will receive a reward of three thousand tangas and promotion. He shall be appointed the chief spy."

The spies set out without loss of time disguised as dervishes, beggars, water-carriers and merchants. Meanwhile the pock-marked one, who was more cunning than the others, armed himself with a rug, beans, a chaplet and some ancient books. He took up his stand in the bazaar at the corner of the jewellers' and perfumers' rows. Here in the guise of a fortune-teller he intended to worm out information from the women.

An hour later hundreds of criers appeared in the market square calling upon all Muslims to hearken to them. They proclaimed the Emir's order: Khoja Nasreddin was declared an enemy of the Emir and a defiler of the faith. All intercourse with him was prohibited, especially giving him shelter, for which offence the penalty was instant death. On the other hand, whoever handed him over to the Emir's guard was promised a reward of three thousand tangas and other favours.

The tea-house owners, copper-smiths, blacksmiths, weavers,

water-carriers and drivers whispered among themselves:

"The Emir will have long to wait!"

"Our Khoja Nasreddin is not one to be caught napping!"

"No money can tempt the people of Bukhara to betray their Khoja Nasreddin."

But Jafar the Usurer, performing his daily round of the bazaar to torment his debtors, thought otherwise.

"Three thousand tangas!" he reflected ruefully. "Yesterday this money was nearly in my pocket! Khoja Nasreddin will visit the girl again, but I cannot catch him single-handed. Also if I share the information with another, he will snatch the reward from me! No, I must act otherwise."

He made his way to the palace.

He knocked for a long time. The doors remained shut. The guards did not hear him, for they were heatedly discussing plans for the capture of Khoja Nasreddin.

"O valiant warriors! Are you all asleep in there?" yelled the usurer in desperation. He rattled the iron ring, but it was some time before there came a sound of footsteps followed by the clang of drawn bolts. The wicket-gate opened.

After listening to the usurer Arslan-bek shook his head.

"Worthy Jafar, I do not advise you to show yourself to the Emir today. He is wrathful and gloomy."

"But I have a wonderful remedy to dispel his gloom," retorted the usurer. "O worthy Arslan-bek, support of the throne and subduer of enemies! My business brooks no delay. Go tell the Emir that I have come to dispel his sorrow."

The Emir received him ungraciously.

"Speak, Jafar, but if your news does not gladden my heart, you shall be given forthwith two hundred sticks."

"O mighty Sovereign whose splendour eclipses all other monarchs, past, present and future!" said the usurer. "It is known to me, your worthless slave, that in our town there dwells a maiden whom I dare to proclaim in the face of truth the beauty of beauties. . . ."

The Emir roused himself and raised his head.

"O Master!" the emboldened usurer continued. "I have no words, worthy to extol her beauty. She is tall, lovely, slender and well proportioned. She has a luminous brow and damask cheeks, her eyes are like those of a gazelle and her eyebrows like the crescent moon! Her cheeks are like anemones, her mouth like the seal of Solomon, her lips are like corals, her teeth like pearls, her breast is like marble adorned with twin cherries and her shoulders—"

The Emir checked his flow of eloquence:

"If she is indeed such as you say, then she is worthy of entering our harem. Who is she?"

"She is of humble extraction, O Master. She is the daughter of a potter whose worthless name I would not dare to mention for fear of insulting the ears of my Sovereign. I can show where she lives, but will there be a reward for the Emir's devoted slave?"

The Emir nodded to Bakhtiyar and a purse fell to the usurer's feet. Jafar caught it up with greedy haste.

"If she proves to be as your praises describe her, you will receive as much again," said the Emir.

"The generosity of our Worthy Lord be praised!" cried the usurer "But let him hasten, for I know this gentle doe is being hunted."

The Emir's brows met and a deep furrow appeared over the bridge of his nose.

"By whom?"

"By Khoja Nasreddin," replied the usurer.

"Again Khoja Nasreddin! Khoja Nasreddin even in this! He is everywhere . . . while you"—here the Emir turned so abruptly towards his viziers that his throne rocked—"you do nothing but bring disgrace upon Our Majesty. Hey, Arslan-bek! See to it. This girl is to be brought at once to the palace. If you fail, the executioner will meet you on your way back."

Within a few minutes a large detachment of guards set out from the palace gates. Their weapons clanged and their shields shone in the sun. At their head walked Arslan-bek. A golden badge, sign of his high office, was pinned to his brocaded khalat. Beside the guards, limping and hobbling grotesquely, walked the usurer. From time to time he fell behind and had to catch up with them at a halting trot. The people stepped aside and followed the procession with hostile glances, trying to guess what new villainy they were up to.

5

KHOJA NASREDDIN had just finished his ninth pot. He set it in the sun and scooped up a large lump of clay out of the trough for the next, the tenth pot.

Suddenly there came a loud and peremptory knocking at the gate. Neighbours, who often called on Niyaz to borrow an onion or a pinch of salt, did not knock like that. Khoja Nasreddin and Niyaz exchanged anxious glances as the gate rattled again under a rain of heavy blows. This time Khoja Nasreddin's keen ear caught the clang of metal.

"Guards," he whispered to Niyaz.

"Run!" urged the old man.

Khoja Nasreddin jumped over the garden wall while Niyaz took his time in opening the gate to allow him to get farther away. As the old man threw back the latch some thrushes rose out of the vineyard and scattered in all directions. But old Niyaz had no wings. He could not fly away. He paled, trembled and bent low before Arslan-bek.

"A great honour has fallen on your house, potter," said Arslan-bek. "The Centre of the Universe and Shadow of Allah on earth, our Lord and Master, may his blessed I days be prolonged, the Great Emir in person has graciously deigned to remember your humble name. It has come to his knowledge that a beautiful rose blossoms in your garden and he wishes to adorn his palace with this rose. Where is your daughter?"

The potter's grey head shook and the world went dark before his eyes. Dully he heard his daughter's brief cry as the guards dragged her out of the house into the yard. The old man's knees gave way. He fell to the ground on his face and neither saw nor heard anything more.

"He has fainted from the excess of his joy," said Arslan-bek to his guards. "Leave him. When he recovers his senses he can come to the palace to pour out his boundless gratitude before the Emir. On our way!"

Meanwhile Khoja Nasreddin had circled through back alleys and had returned to the street from the other end. From the shelter of some bushes he could see Niyaz's gate, two guards and a third man whom he recognized as Jafar the Usurer.

"Aha, you lame cur! So it is you who brought the guards here to arrest me!" thought Khoja Nasreddin not suspecting the true state of affairs. "Very good, search carefully! But you'll have to go away empty-handed."

But they did not go away empty-handed! Khoja Nasreddin froze with horror when he saw them bring his beloved out of the gate. She struggled and cried heartbreakingly but the guards held her fast and surrounded her with a double circle of shields.

It was noon on a hot June day but an icy shiver swept over Khoja Nasreddin. The guards were approaching, for their way lay past his hiding-place. His mind clouded. He drew a curved knife out of its sheath and hugged the ground. Arslan-bek with his shining golden badge led the group. The knife would have struck deep into his fat neck under his beard, had not a heavy hand suddenly fallen upon Khoja Nasreddin's shoulder and pinned him to the ground. He started up and recoiled, raising his armed hand to strike, but let it drop on recognizing the familiar soot-smudged face of Yusuf the Blacksmith.

"Lie still!" muttered the blacksmith. "Lie still! You are mad. There are twenty of them well armed, while you are alone and ill-armed. You will perish without helping her. Lie still, I tell you!"

He held him down until the group had disappeared around the bend of the road.

"Why, o why did you hold me back?" cried Khoja Nasreddin. "Better far if I were lying dead now!"

"To raise a hand against a lion or a fist against a sword are not the deeds of wise men," sternly retorted the blacksmith. "I followed the guards from the bazaar. I came just in time to prevent your foolhardy action. You must not die for her but struggle and save her. It is more worthy even if more difficult. Lose no time in sorrowful meditation. Go and act. They have swords, shields and spears, but Allah has given you powerful weapons—a sharp brain and cunning in which you are unequalled."

Thus he spoke. His words were manly and as strong as the iron he had been forging all his life. As Khoja Nasreddin listened his faltering heart became as hard as iron.

"Thank you, blacksmith," he said. "Never have I lived more bitter moments than these, but it would be unworthy to give way to despair. I shall go, and I promise you I shall use my weapons to good purpose."

He stepped out from the bushes into the road. At this moment the usurer came out of a near-by house. He had stayed behind to remind one of the potters of a debt which was about to fall due. Khoja Nasreddin and he met face to face. The usurer blanched, scuttled back, banged the door shut and shot the bolt.

"Beware, Jafar, O offspring of the echidna!" cried Khoja

Nasreddin. "I saw, I heard, I know everything!"

After a moment's silence the usurer called out:

"The jackal did not get the cherry. Neither did the falcon. The cherry fell to the lion!"

"That remains to be seen," retorted Khoja Nasreddin. "Mark my words, Jafar! I dragged you from the water, but I swear I shall drown you in that very same pond. Slime will cover your body. The weeds will choke you."

Without waiting for an answer Khoja Nasreddin walked away. He passed Niyaz's house without stopping lest the usurer was spying and should later denounce the old man. At the end of the street he made sure he was not being followed, then ran swiftly across a piece of waste ground overgrown with weeds, jumped a wall and came back to the house.

The old man was still lying face down on the ground. Near him a handful of silver coins left by Arslan-bek shone dully. The old man lifted his tear-stained and dust-caked face. His lips moved, but he could not speak. Then he caught sight of a kerchief dropped by his daughter and beat his grey head against the hard earth and tore his beard.

It was some time before Khoja Nasreddin could somewhat quieten him. At last he succeeded in making him get up. He helped him to a bench.

"Listen, old man," he said. "You are not alone in your grief. Perhaps you know I loved her and that she loved me? Did you know we had agreed to marry? I was only waiting for a chance to collect enough money to pay you a rich dowry."

"What do I care about dowries?" sobbed the old man. "Would I have crossed my little dove in any of her wishes? Alas, it is too late now to speak of such things. She is lost. By now she is in the harem. . . . O woe! O dishonour!" he wailed. "I must go to the palace. Yes, I shall fall at the Emir's feet, and beg, and cry, and wail, and if only the heart in his breast is not made of stone. . ."

He started up and tottered towards the gate.

"Stop!" said Khoja Nasreddin. "You forget that Emirs are not made like other men. They have no hearts. It is useless to implore them. What one can do is to take things away from them, and I, Khoja Nasreddin will take Guljan from the Emir!"

"He is too powerful. He has thousands of soldiers, thousands of guards and thousands of spies! What can you do against him?"

"I don't know yet what I shall do. But this I do know: he will not have her today! And he will not have her tomorrow! And he will not have her the day after tomorrow! Nor will he ever have or possess her, as true as my name from Bukhara to Baghdad is Khoja Nasreddin! So dry your tears, old man, do not wail in my ears. Don't disturb my thinking."

Khoja Nasreddin spent little time in thinking.

"Tell me, old man, where do you keep your late wife's clothes?"

"Over there, in the chest."

Khoja Nasreddin took the key, disappeared into the house and a few moments later came out dressed as a woman. His face was concealed under a veil of closely woven horse-hair.

"Wait for me, old man and don't attempt to do anything by yourself."

He led his ass out of the barn, saddled him and left Niyaz's house.

6

BEFORE bringing Guljan into the palace garden and introducing her into the Emir's presence Arslan-bek sent for the old women of the harem. He ordered them to dress and adorn her fittingly so that the Emir might delight in the contemplation of her perfections.

The old women immediately set about the familiar task: they washed Guljan's tear-stained face in warm water, clothed her in diaphanous silks, darkened her eyebrows, rouged her cheeks, poured attar of roses on her hair and dyed her finger-nails red. Then they summoned from the harem His Chastity the Chief Eunuch. At one time this man had been famous in all Bukhara for his licentiousness. It was to his knowledge of and experience in these matters that he owed his appointment to this high dignity, having been duly prepared for it by the court surgeon. It was his duty to watch incessantly over the Emir's one hundred and sixty concubines and make sure they were sufficiently alluring to rouse the Emir's passion.

With every passing year this duty became more onerous, for the Emir became more sated and his energy waned. More than once the Chief Eunuch's reward in the morning had consisted of a dozen lashes. This, however, was only a minor punishment for him. A far greater one was having to prepare the lovely concubines before they met the Emir, for then he experienced the most exquisite torment, similar to that which awaits the libertine in hell. It is well known that the libertine in hell is condemned to stand for ever chained to a pillar amid a bevy of naked houris.

When the Chief Eunuch saw Guljan he was startled by her beauty.

"Indeed, she is beautiful!" he exclaimed in his piping voice. "Lead her to the Emir. Take her away! Take her out of my sight!"

And he hurried away, striking his head against the walls, gnashing his teeth and wailing: "O bitterness! O unbearable bitterness!"

"That is a good sign," said the old women. "It means our master will be pleased."

The pale and silent Guljan was led into the palace garden.

The Emir rose, approached and lifted her veil.

All the viziers, dignitaries and sages screened their eyes with the sleeves of their khalats.

For a long time the Emir could not tear his eyes away from the lovely face.

"The usurer has not lied to us," he said in a loud voice. "Give him as reward three times the sum promised."

Guljan was taken away. The Emir had brightened visibly.

"He has found diversion. He is gayer. The nightingale of his heart inclines towards the roses of her countenance," whispered the courtiers among themselves. "In the morning he will be in still better humour. Allah be praised, the storm has passed over without thunder or lightning striking any of us down."

The emboldened court poets stepped forward and in turns extolled the Emir in their verses, comparing his face to the full moon, his stature to the slender cypress and his reign to the Conjunction of two Planets.

At last, and as though suddenly inspired, the chief poet took occasion to recite the poem which had been on the tip of his tongue since the morning of the previous day.

The Emir threw him a handful of small coins, and the king of poets crawled about the carpet to collect them, not forgetting to press his lips to the Emir's slipper.

Then the Emir said with a condescending laugh: "We too have composed a verse:

"When we went out into the garden in the evening

The moon, ashamed of her insignificance, hid behind a cloud,

And all the birds became silent, and the wind was lulled.

There we stood—great, famous, unconquerable, sun-like and mighty."

All the poets fell on their knees crying:

"O such greatness! He has eclipsed Rudaki himself!"

Some of them even lay face down on the carpet as though struck senseless in admiration.

Dancers appeared, followed by buffoons, jugglers and fakirs, and the Emir rewarded them all generously.

"My one regret," he kept saying, "is that I can't command the sun, otherwise I would order it to go down faster today."

And the courtiers responded with obsequious laughter.

7

THE bazaar hummed with activity. These were the busiest trading hours: selling, buying and bartering went on while the sun rose higher and higher. The heat drove the people into the thick, odorous shade of the covered rows. The bright noon rays of the sun cut vertically through the round openings in the reed roofs and seemed to stand like smoky pillars. In their soft radiance brocades sparkled, smooth silks shone and velvets glowed with a gentle secret flame. Turbans, khalats and dyed beards, picked out by the light, gleamed colourfully on all sides. Burnished copper flamed blindingly and in turn was challenged and vanquished by the pure lustre of the noble gold scattered on the leather carpets of the moneychangers.

Khoja Nasreddin reined in his ass before the tea-house from the porch of which one month ago he had appealed to the citizens of Bukhara to help save the potter Niyaz from the Emir's justice. In this short lapse of time Khoja Nasreddin had formed a strong friendship with the jovial, paunchy owner Ali, a straightforward and honest man who could be fully trusted.

Choosing a favourable moment Khoja Nasreddin called out to him:

"Ali!"

The owner looked round. He was bewildered. A man's voice called him yet what he saw was a woman.

"It is I, Ali," said Khoja Nasreddin without lifting his veil. "Do you recognize me? In the name of Allah, don't stare like that. Have you forgotten the spies?"

Glancing round cautiously Ali took him into a back room where he stored firewood and spare kettles. It was damp and cool here, and the noise of the bazaar could be heard only faintly.

"Take my ass, Ali," said Khoja Nasreddin. "Feed him and keep him ready, for I may need him at any moment. And don't say a word about me to anyone."

"But why are you dressed as a woman, Khoja Nasreddin?" asked the other, carefully shutting the door.

"I'm going to the palace."

"You are out of your senses!" cried the tea-house owner. "You'll be putting your head into the tiger's jaws."

"It has to be done, Ali. You will soon learn why. Let us take leave of each other in case. . . . I'm going on dangerous business."

They embraced warmly. Tears came into the teahouse owner's eyes and rolled down his round, red cheeks. He saw Khoja Nasreddin off, after which, stifling the heavy sighs which made his paunch heave, he went out to his customers.

His heart was heavy and torn with apprehension. He was sad and absentminded. His customers had to clink their teapot lids twice and thrice to remind him of their thirst. In spirit he was away at the palace together with his irrepressible friend.

The guards stopped Khoja Nasreddin.

"I have brought incomparable ambergris, musk and attar of roses," Khoja Nasreddin said over and over again, cleverly disguising his voice to make it sound like a woman's. "Let me pass into the harem, O valiant warriors. I shall sell my wares and then share the profit with you."

"Go away, old woman! Go and trade in the bazaar!" the guards replied gruffly.

Thus thwarted of his purpose Khoja Nasreddin became thoughtful and downcast. He had little time left, for the sun had already passed its zenith. He circled the palace walls. Chinese mortar held the stones so closely together that not a chink, not a hole could he discover. As for the orifices of the irrigation ditches, these were guarded by strong cast-iron grilles.

"I *must* get into the palace," Khoja Nasreddin said to himself. "I mean to and I will. If according to heavenly predestination the Emir has seized my betrothed, why should I not be predestined to get her back? I already feel in my heart it will be so."

He went back to the bazaar. He believed that if a man's mind is firmly made up and his courage inexhaustible, then Fate will come to his aid. Among a thousand meetings, conversations and conflicts there is bound to occur one which will create a favourable opportunity and by cleverly exploiting it a man can overcome all the obstacles on the way to his goal, and thus fulfil predestination. Somewhere in the bazaar such an opportunity was awaiting him. He believed this implicitly and set off to find it.

Nothing was lost upon Khoja Nasreddin—not a word, not a face in the noisy crowd of many thousands. His mind, ears and sight were keyed up to that extraordinary pitch when a man easily transcends the limits imposed upon him by nature. In that case victory is his, for his opponents remain in the meantime within their usual human limitations.

At the point where the jewellers' and perfumers' rows crossed, Khoja Nasreddin caught through the noise and buzz of the crowd an insinuating voice saying:

"You say your husband has ceased to love you and no longer shares your bed? There is a remedy for your trouble but for this I must consult Khoja Nasreddin. You have, no doubt, heard that he is here? Find out where he is and let me know. Together we will bring your husband back to you."

Khoja Nasreddin moved closer and saw the pockmarked fortune-telling spy. A woman holding a silver coin stood before him. The fortune-teller had scattered his beans on the rug and was turning the pages of an ancient book.

"But if you fail to find Khoja Nasreddin," he said, "then woe betide you, woman, for your husband will leave you for ever!"

Khoja Nasreddin decided to teach the fortune-teller a lesson. He squatted down in front of the rug.

"Tell me my fortune, O wise seller of other people's destinies."

The man scattered his beans.

"O woman!" he exclaimed suddenly as though stricken with horror. "Woe to you, woman! Death has already raised her black hand over your head!"

Several curious bystanders gathered around them.

"I could help you to parry the blow but I cannot do it alone," the fortune-teller went on. "I must consult Khoja Nasreddin. If you could find him and tell me where he is, then your life would be saved."

"Very good, I will bring Khoja Nasreddin to you."

"You will bring him?" cried the other pleasantly startled. "When?"

"I could bring him this very instant. He is quite near."

"Where is he?"

"Here, quite close."

"But where is he? I don't see him."

"And you a fortune-seller! Can't you guess? Here he is!"

With a swift gesture the woman before him threw back her veil. The fortune-teller recoiled at the sight of Khoja Nasreddin's face.

"Here he is!" repeated Khoja Nasreddin. "What did you want to consult me about? You lie, you are no fortune-teller, but one of the Emir's spies! Don't believe him, O Muslims! He is deceiving you! He is sitting here to try and track down Khoja Nasreddin."

The spy's eyes darted hither and thither but no guard was in sight. Nearly weeping with disappointment he watched Khoja Nasreddin go. Around him the crowd gathered threateningly.

"Emir's spy! Dirty hound!" sounded on all sides.

The fortune-teller's hands trembled as he rolled up his rug. Then he ran back to the palace as fast as his legs could carry him.

8

IN the dirty, dusty, smelly and smoke-filled guard-room, the guards, seated on a well-worn felt which was a breeding ground for fleas, scratched themselves and speculated on the chances of capturing Khoja Nasreddin.

"Three thousand tangas!" they said. "Think of that! Three thousand tangas and the post of chief spy!"

"Someone is sure to be lucky!"

"If only I were that someone," sighed a fat and lazy guard, the stupidest of the lot, who had so far avoided dismissal only because he had mastered the art of swallowing raw eggs whole without damaging the shell. He occasionally entertained the Emir by doing this trick and received small tips from him, although he paid for it afterwards with excruciating pain.

The pock-marked spy burst into the guard-room like a tornado.

"He is here! Khoja Nasreddin is in the bazaar! He is dressed as a woman!"

The guards rushed to the gates snatching up their arms on the way.

"The reward is mine! Do you hear? I saw him first! The reward is mine!"

At sight of the guards the people began hastily to scatter, and in the resulting crush the bazaar became a scene of panic. The guards plunged into the thick of the crowd. The most zealous of them who was in the lead caught hold of a woman and tore off her veil exposing her face to the crowd.

The woman uttered a piercing scream. From another direction came another scream. Then a third woman shrieked as she struggled in the hands of the guards. Then a fourth and a fifth. . . . The whole bazaar was filled with women's screams, wails, shrieks and sobs.

The dumbfounded crowd did not move. Such an outrage had never before been witnessed in Bukhara. Some turned pale, others turned red. Every heart was disturbed. The guards went on with their rough work seizing the women, pushing them about, mauling them, hitting them and tearing off their clothes.

"Help!" cried the women. "Help!"

Yusuf the Blacksmith raised his voice, sternly dominating the crowd:

"Muslims! Why do you hesitate? Isn't it enough that the guards rob us, that we should let them insult our women in full daylight?"

"Help!" cried the women. "Help!"

The crowd growled and stirred. A water-carrier recognized his wife's voice and rushed to her rescue. The guards pushed him away, but two weavers and three coppersmiths came to his aid and threw back the guards. Fighting began.

Gradually everybody joined in. The guards brandished their swords. From all sides they were pelted with pots, trays, pitchers, kettles, horseshoes and pieces of wood. They had no time to dodge. The fighting spread all over the bazaar.

Meanwhile the Emir was peacefully dozing in his palace. Suddenly he jumped up, ran to the window, threw it open and banged it shut again in terror.

Bakhtiyar came running in, pale and his lips trembling.

"What is it?" muttered the Emir. "What is going on out there? Where are the guns? Where is Arslan-bek?"

Arslan-bek rushed in and fell on his face.

"Let the Master order my head to be cut off!"

"What is this? What has happened?"

Without rising Arslan-bek replied:

"O Master! Sun-like and eclipsing—"

"Stop!" The Emir stamped in impatient rage. "Say the rest later! What is going on out there?"

"Khoja Nasreddin! . . . He disguised himself as a woman. It is all his fault, it is all because of Khoja Nasreddin! Order my head to be cut off!"

But the Emir had other worries.

9

ON this particular day Khoja Nasreddin treasured every minute of his time. Therefore he did not loiter in the bazaar, but having smashed the jaw of one guard, broken the teeth of another and flattened the nose of a third, he safely returned to his friend Ali's tea-house. Here in the back room he divested himself of the female clothes and put on the coloured Badakhshan turban and the false beard. Thus disguised he chose a convenient seat from where he could survey the battlefield.

Pressed on all sides by the crowd the guards resisted furiously. A tussle started near the tea-house at Khoja Nasreddin's very feet. He could not resist the temptation of emptying his teapot over the guards and did it so skilfully that the boiling liquid ran down the neck of the fat swallower of eggs. The fellow set up a howl and fell on his back waving his arms and legs in the air. Without deigning to look at him Khoja Nasreddin returned to his meditations. Suddenly he heard an old quavering voice crying:

"Let me pass! Let me pass! In the name of Allah, what is going on here?"

Not far from the tea-house, in the very thick of the fighting, loomed the figure of a white-bearded, hawk-nosed old man mounted on a camel. Judging by his appearance he was an Arab. The end of his turban was tucked in showing him to be a man of learning. He clung to the camel's hump in mortal fear, while all around him the battle raged. Someone was trying to drag him off his camel by the leg and the old man struggled desperately. The din of yells, hoarse shouts and fierce howls was deafening.

In his frantic endeavour to reach safety the old man managed to steer his way to the tea-house. Starting fitfully and glancing over his shoulder he tethered his camel by the side of Khoja Nasreddin's ass and climbed on to the porch.

"For the love of Allah! What is going on in your town?"

"Bazaar," Khoja Nasreddin replied laconically.

"Have you always such bazaars in Bukhara? How can I ever reach the palace through this mob?"

At the word "palace" Khoja Nasreddin realized at once that this meeting with the old man was the opportunity for which he had been waiting and that it would allow him to penetrate into the Emir's harem and rescue Guljan.

But haste, as is well known, is of the devil. Has not the most wise Shaikh Sa'di of Shiraz said: "Only he who is patient will bring the matter to its conclusion. He who is hasty will fail." Therefore Khoja Nasreddin rolled up the carpet of impatience and put it away in the coffer of expectation.

The old man groaned and sighed:

"O almighty Allah! O Refuge of the faithful! How am I to make my way to the palace?"

"Wait here until tomorrow," replied Khoja Nasreddin.

"I cannot!" cried the old man. "I am expected at the palace."

Khoja Nasreddin burst out laughing.

"O worthy and venerable Shaikh! I neither know your calling nor your business, but are you so sure they cannot do without you at the palace until tomorrow? Many worthy people in Bukhara wait weeks before being admitted to the palace. Why do you think an exception will be made for you?"

"Be it known to you," the old man replied haughtily, slightly stung by Khoja Nasreddin's words, "that I am a famous sage, astrologer and physician. I have come from Baghdad on the Emir's invitation to enter his service and help him in the administration of his state."

"Oh!" said Khoja Nasreddin with a respectful bow. "Welcome, O wise Shaikh. I have visited Baghdad on occasion and I know the sages of that town. Tell me your name."

"If you have been to Baghdad you must have heard of the services which I rendered to the Caliph. I saved the life of his favourite son and this was proclaimed throughout the country. Maulana Husain is my name."

"Maulana Husain!" exclaimed Khoja Nasreddin. "Can it be that you are Maulana Husain in person?"

The old man could not repress a satisfied smile at seeing that his fame had spread so far beyond the confines of his native Baghdad.

"Why should you be surprised?" he said. "Yes, I am the famous Maulana Husain in person, the great sage unequalled in wisdom, in the art of reading the stars and in curing sickness. But I am entirely devoid of pride and vanity. Look how simply I converse with you, a person of no consequence."

The old man reached out his hand for a cushion and leaned his elbow on it, preparing to extend his condescension towards his companion by giving him a detailed account of his great wisdom. He hoped that the latter would out of vanity recount to all and sundry his meeting with the famous sage Maulana Husain, extol his wisdom and even exaggerate it in order to arouse in his listeners respect for the sage and thus for himself, for that is the way in which men honoured by the attention of the great always act.

"Thus he will contribute to the greatness of my fame among the common folk," thought Maulana Husain, "which is not to be despised. Talk among the common people will come to the Emir's ears through his spies and informers and will confirm my wisdom. Confirmation from outside is without doubt the best confirmation, and thus in the end I shall be the gainer."

In order to impress his companion the sage began to tell him about the constellations and their interrelation, with many quotations from the great sages of old.

Khoja Nasreddin listened most attentively, trying to memorize every word.

"No!" he said at last. "I am still unable to believe it. Are you really Maulana Husain?"

"Of course!" cried the old man. "Why should this be so strange?"

Khoja Nasreddin drew back as though in apprehension. Then he exclaimed in a voice full of alarm and commiseration:

"O unfortunate one! You are lost!"

The old man choked and dropped his tea-glass. All his haughtiness and importance vanished.

"How; Why? What is the matter?" he demanded anxiously.

"Don't you know that all this trouble is on your account?" Khoja Nasreddin pointed towards the marketplace where the battle had not quite subsided. "It has come to our Emir's ears that when you were leaving Baghdad you publicly vowed you would make your way into the Emir's harem—o woe to you, Maulana Husain! and seduce the Emir's wives."

The old man's jaw dropped, his eyes went blank and he hiccupped with fright.

"I?" he stammered. "I . . . into the harem? . . ."

"You swore by the foot of Allah's throne you would do so. This is what the criers have been announcing today. And the Emir has ordered you to be seized as soon as you set foot in the city. You are to be beheaded on the spot."

The sage uttered a moan of despair. He could not think which of his enemies had thus planned his undoing. He did not doubt the truth of the story. In the course of court intrigues he had more than once used the same means to destroy his enemies and had later derived much satisfaction from seeing their heads exposed on poles.

"And so today," went on Khoja Nasreddin, "the spies reported to the Emir that you had arrived. He gave orders to seize you, and the guards hurried off to the bazaar and began to search for you everywhere. They looked round all the stalls. Trade came to a standstill and there was no peace. By mistake the guards seized a man who resembles you and in their haste they cut off his head. He happened to be a mullah, well known for his virtue and piety, and the people belonging to his mosque were indignant. See what is happening here, and all because of you!"

"O woe is me!" exclaimed the sage in horror *and* despair.

He kept on exclaiming, moaning and wailing, thus proving to Khoja Nasreddin that his stratagem had succeeded.

Meanwhile the fighting had moved on towards the palace gates through which the beaten and badly mauled guards were one by one escaping. They had by that time lost their weapons. The bazaar was still humming and seething but things were becoming quieter.

"I must return to Baghdad!" wailed the sage. "I must return to Baghdad!"

"You will be seized at the city gate," retorted Khoja Nasreddin.

"Woe is me! O calamity! Allah sees I am innocent! Never have I made such an insolent, such an impious vow! My enemies have calumniated me to the Emir! O, help me, kind Muslim!"

This was exactly what Khoja Nasreddin had been waiting for,

because he did not want to rouse the sage's suspicions by offering his aid.

"Help you?" he said. "How can I help you? As a loyal and devoted slave of my master I ought to deliver you into the hands of the guards without delay so as to avoid being accused of complicity."

Hiccupping and trembling the sage gazed imploringly at Khoja Nasreddin.

"Still, you say you are innocent and have been calumniated," the latter hastened to reassure him. "I am inclined to believe you, for at your venerable age you have nothing to do in a harem."

"Quite right!" cried the old man. "But what road of salvation is open to me?"

"There is one," replied Khoja Nasreddin. He led the old man into the dark back room and there handed him the bundle of woman's clothing. "I bought this today for my wife and if you like I can exchange it for your robe and turban. Under a woman's veil you will be safe from spies and guards."

With many signs of joy and gratitude the old man took the clothes and put them on. Khoja Nasreddin put on his white robe, his turban with the tucked-in end and the broad star-spangled belt. Then he helped the old man to climb on to his camel.

"May Allah guard you, O sage! Mind, do not forget to speak in a high voice, like a woman."

The old man set off on his mount at a swift lope.

Khoja Nasreddin's eyes shone. The road to the palace was open.

10

ONCE the serene Emir was calm again and had reassured himself that the fighting in the bazaar was subsiding, he decided to go into the great hall and show himself to the courtiers. He tried to assume a calm but slightly pained expression so that none of the courtiers would dare to think his royal heart was open to fear.

As soon as the Emir appeared, the courtiers kept quite still, fearing lest their eyes and faces should betray the fact that they were well aware of the true state of his feelings.

The Emir was silent, so were the courtiers. At last this awe-inspiring silence was broken by the Emir who said: "What have you to say to us? What is your advice? This is not the first time we have put such questions to you."

Not one raised his head or gave answer. A lightning spasm contorted the Emir's features. How many heads might have been forced at that moment on to the executioner's block? How many flattering tongues might have been silenced for ever, bitten through in the agony of death and protruding from bloodless lips as though reminding the living of their illusory fortunes, their vain, unavailing ambitions, struggles and hopes?

But the heads remained on the shoulders, the tongues remained ready to give immediate flattery, for at that very moment the palace steward appeared and announced:

"Praise to the Centre of the Universe! A stranger has appeared at the palace gates claiming that he is Maulana Husain, a sage from Baghdad. He declares he has important business and must appear at once before the luminous gaze of the Refuge of the Universe."

"Maulana Husain!" cried the Emir eagerly. "Let him pass! Bring him here!"

The sage did not walk in, he rushed in, neglecting even to discard his dusty slippers. He made deep obeisance before the throne.

"Greetings to the great and famous Emir, the Sun and Moon of the Universe, its Welfare and Terror! I have hastened by day and by night to warn the Emir of a terrible danger. Let the Emir say whether he has visited any woman today? Let the Emir, my Master, answer his miserable slave . . . I implore him. . . ."

"A woman?" the Emir repeated in a puzzled voice. "Today? . . . No. . . . We had the intention but have not yet done so."

The sage rose to his feet. His face was pale. He had waited for the answer in the greatest agitation. A deep long-drawn sigh escaped his lips. The colour returned slowly to his cheeks.

"Praise to almighty Allah!" he cried. "Allah has saved luminary of wisdom and grace from being extinguished! Be it known to the great Emir that last night the planets and stars were so disposed as to be most unfavourable for him. And I, wretch that I am, unworthy even to kiss the dust beneath the Emir's footsteps, I have studied, I have calculated the position of the planets. I know that until they assume a favourable and propitious position, the Emir must not touch a woman, otherwise his destruction will be inevitable. Praise be to Allah that I was able to warn him in time."

"Stop, Maulana Husain," the Emir interrupted. "You are speaking of incomprehensible things . . ."

"Praise be to Allah, I am in time!" the sage kept saying. "To the end of my days I shall be proud of having prevented the Emir from touching a woman this day. Thus have I saved the universe from becoming bereaved."

He spoke with such gladness and warmth that the Emir could not fail to believe him.

"When I, worthless ant that I am, was illumined by the rays of the Greatness of the Universe who had deigned to remember my unworthy name, and received the command to come to Bukhara to enter the Emir's service, it was as though I had been plunged into an exquisite sea of ineffable happiness. Needless to say I obeyed the command at once and set out on my journey.

"But first I devoted a few days to preparing the Emir's horoscope. Thus I began immediately to serve him by studying the movement of the planets and stars which influence his destiny. Last night, on looking at the sky, I discovered that both the planets and the stars were threatening the Emir most ominously. The star Ash-Shula, which signifies the sting, stood in bad aspect to the star Al-Qalb, which signifies the heart. Further, I saw the three stars Al-Ghafr, signifying the woman's veil, the two stars Al-Iklil, signifying the crown and the two stars Ash-Sharatan which signify horns.

"All this was on a Tuesday—the day of the planet Mars —and this day, contrary to Thursday, points to the death of great men and is extremely unfavourable to Emirs. Having confronted all these signs I, worthless astrologer though I am, realized that the sting of death threatened the heart of the bearer of a crown if he were to touch the veil of a woman. Thus it was that I came in haste to warn the bearer of the crown. I hastened by day and by night. I drove two camels to death and entered Bukhara on foot."

"O, almighty Allah!" exclaimed the Emir, greatly impressed. "Is it possible that we are threatened by so great a danger? Are you sure you are not mistaken, Maulana Husain?"

"Mistaken? I?" cried the sage. "Let the Emir know that from Baghdad to Bukhara there is none who equals me in wisdom, in the art of calculating the position of the stars or in curing sickness. I could not have made a mistake. Let the Master, the Sun of the Universe, the great Emir, ask his sages whether I have correctly named the stars and interpreted their positions in the horoscope."

In obedience to a sign from the Emir the wry-necked sage

stepped forward.

"Maulana Husain, my incomparable colleague in wisdom, has correctly named the stars which proves his knowledge that no one would dare to dispute. But, continued the sage with what Khoja Nasreddin felt to be a note of malice, "why has the most wise Maulana Husain not mentioned to the great Emir the sixteenth position of the moon and the signs in which this position occurs, for without these designations it would be groundless to affirm that Tuesday—the day of the planet Mars— definitely indicates the death of great men, including crowned heads, for the planet Mars has its house in one sign, its zenith in another, its nadir in a third and its waning in a fourth, in correspondence with which the planet Mars has four different indications and not only one, as the most worthy and most wise Maulana Husain has told us."

The sage fell silent, smiling craftily. The courtiers exchanged approving whispers at what they were pleased to think was the confusion of the newcomer: jealous of their revenues and high position they tried to keep out all outsiders and regarded every newcomer as a dangerous rival.

But when Khoja Nasreddin tackled something he never gave up. Besides he had taken the measure of the sage, the courtiers and the Emir himself. He retorted condescendingly and without the slightest embarrassment:

"My wise and worthy colleague may greatly surpass me in some other branch of knowledge, but as far as stars are concerned, his words reveal his complete ignorance of the teachings of Ibn Bajja, the wisest of the wise, who affirms that the planet Mars, having its house in the signs of the Ram and Scorpio, its zenith in the sign of Capricornus, its nadir in the sign of the Cancer and its waning in the sign of the Libra is nevertheless inherent to Tuesday alone, on which it exercises its influence fatal to crowned heads."

In making this answer Khoja Nasreddin was not in the least afraid of being convicted of ignorance for he well knew that victory in such disputes belongs to him who has the glibbest tongue, and in this few could match him.

He stood waiting for the sage's objections and making ready to answer them as they deserved, but the latter did not take up the challenge and remained silent. He did not dare to continue the dispute for, although he strongly suspected Khoja Nasreddin of ignorance and trickery, he was only too well aware of his own ignorance. And thus his attempt to confound the newcomer came to produce the opposite effect: the courtiers hissed him.

With his eyes he conveyed to them that the opponent was too dangerous to be tackled openly.

These manoeuvres did not escape Khoja Nasreddin's notice.

"Just wait!" he thought. "I'll show you!"

The Emir plunged into deep meditation. Everybody remained motionless, fearing to disturb him.

"If you have correctly named and designated all the stars, Maulana Husain," said the Emir at last, "then indeed your interpretation is correct. What we cannot understand though is why the two Ash-Sharatan stars which denote horns have come into our horoscope? Truly you are just in time, Maulana Husain, for only this morning a young girl was brought into our harem and we were preparing—"

Khoja Nasreddin waved his arms in simulated horror.

"Cast her out of your thoughts, O most serene Emir, cast her out!" he cried, as though forgetting that the Emir should never be addressed otherwise than in the third person. In doing thus he calculated that such infringement of etiquette, apparently caused by strong emotion due to devotion to the Emir and fear for his life, would not only not be held against him, but on the contrary would set him higher in the Emir's regard as a proof of the sincerity of his feelings.

He begged and implored the Emir with such vehemence not to touch the girl so that he, Maulana Husain, should not have to shed floods of tears and assume the black garments of sorrow, that the Emir was touched.

"Calm yourself, calm yourself, Maulana Husain. We are no enemy of our people to leave it bereaved and plunged in sorrow. We promise you to safeguard our precious life by not approaching this girl and in general by not entering the harem at all until the stars become favourable, which you will let us know in good time. Come hither."

Having spoken he made a sign to his narghile-bearer, inhaled deeply and with his own hand passed the golden mouthpiece to the newly arrived sage—a great honour and favour on his part. Kneeling with downcast eyes the sage accepted the Emir's favour while a shudder passed over him—from delight, thought the courtiers who were filled with malicious envy.

"We declare our favour and goodwill towards the sage Maulana Husain," said the Emir, "and appoint him Chief Sage of our kingdom. His erudition and wisdom, as well as his great devotion to our person are an example to all."

The court chronicler whose duty it was to register in panegyric style all the Emir's words and actions so that his greatness should not be lost to posterity (about which the Emir was most anxious) began to scratch with his pen.

"As for you," the Emir went on addressing himself to the courtiers, "on the contrary, we declare our displeasure with you, for in addition to all the unpleasantness caused by Khoja Nasreddin, death itself was threatening your master, yet none of you raised a finger to help! Look at them, Maulana Husain, look at these fools with their silly faces. Do they not exactly resemble asses? Truly no sovereign has ever had such stupid and negligent viziers!"

"The Most Serene Emir is quite right," said Khoja Nasreddin eyeing the silent courtiers as though taking aim for a first blow. "As I see them, the faces of these men do not bear the seal of wisdom."

"Quite right, quite right," approved the Emir greatly pleased. "Quite right—they do not bear the seal of wisdom. You hear that, you blockheads?"

"I should like to add," Khoja Nasreddin continued, "that neither do I see any face bearing the seal of virtue and honesty."

"They are thieves," said the Emir with hearty conviction. "All of them are thieves! They rob us day and night! We are obliged to guard every item in the palace. Each time we check our property something is missing. Only this morning we left our silk sash in the garden, and half an hour later it was gone! . . . Which of them had the time . . . you understand me, Maulana Husain?"

While the Emir was speaking the wry-necked sage lowered his gaze in a particularly sanctimonious manner. At any other time this slight movement would have passed unnoticed, but just then all Khoja Nasreddin's senses were on the alert: he immediately saw how it was.

Confidently he approached the sage, slipped his hand into the bosom of his khalat and extracted a richly embroidered silk sash.

"Was the great Emir deploring the loss of this sash?"

Amazement and terror held the courtiers spell-bound. The new sage was indeed proving himself a dangerous rival, for the first among them to dare oppose him had himself been exposed and crushed. The hearts of many of the sages, poets, dignitaries and viziers were filled with fear.

"By Allah!" cried the Emir. "That is my sash. Indeed, Maulana Husain, you are incomparably wise! Aha!" and he turned triumphantly towards the courtiers showing a face expressing extreme satisfaction. "Aha! Caught in the act, at last! Now you won't dare to steal a single thread from us! We have suffered enough from your depredations! As for this miserable thief who so insolently stole our sash, let all the hairs be plucked from his head, chin and body. Give him a hundred strokes on the soles of his feet. Set him naked on an ass back to front and drive him through the town denouncing him publicly as a thief!"

At a sign from Arslan-bek the executioners seized the sage and hustled him outside where they immediately fell upon him. A few moments later he was pushed back into the hall, naked, hairless, incredibly obscene. It was evident to all that until then his beard and enormous turban had been concealing his lack of intelligence and the seal of depravity which marked his features, and that a man with such a thievish look could only be an abandoned rascal and thief.

"Take him away," ordered the Emir with a grimace of distaste.

The executioners dragged him away. A moment later from outside the window came the sound of yells punctuated by the thwacking of sticks. Finally he was seated naked on an ass facing its tail and driven off to the market-place to the accompaniment of blaring trumpets and beating drums.

The Emir conversed at length with the new sage. The courtiers stood around motionless, which was a veritable torture. The heat mounted and under the khalats their backs itched unbearably.

The Grand Vizier Bakhtiyar, fearing the new sage more than anyone present, tried to think of some plan to enlist the courtiers' aid to destroy his rival. In their turn the courtiers, foreseeing from numerous symptoms the outcome of the contest, cast about in their minds how to betray Bakhtiyar at the decisive moment to their best advantage and thus acquire the confidence and goodwill of the new sage.

The Emir plied Khoja Nasreddin with questions about the Caliph's health, news from Baghdad and events during the journey, which he had to answer as best he could. All went well and the Emir, tired by the exertion of the conversation, had given orders for his couch to be prepared so he might rest, when suddenly there was an uproar of voices and a shriek outside. The palace steward hurried into the hall. His face shone as he announced:

"May it be known to the great Lord that the blasphemer and disturber of the peace, Khoja Nasreddin, has been caught and brought to the palace!"

No sooner had he made this announcement than the carved walnut doors were thrown wide open. There was a triumphant clash of weapons and the guards led in a hawk-nosed, grey-bearded old man dressed in woman's clothes. They threw him down on to the carpet at the foot of the throne.

Khoja Nasreddin froze. The walls of the hall seemed to totter before his eyes, and the faces of the courtiers were shrouded in a greenish mist. . . .

11

THE Baghdad sage, the genuine Maulana Husain, had been caught at the very gates beyond which he could see through his veil the roads leading away in all directions. Each road held the promise of escape from a terrible fate.

But the guards on sentry duty at the gates had challenged him:

"Where are you going to, woman?"

The sage replied in a voice which sounded like the crowing of a hoarse cockerel:

"I am hurrying home to my husband. Let me pass, valiant warriors."

The guards exchanged glances, suspicious of the voice. One of them took hold of the camel's bridle.

"Where do you live?"

"Here, quite close," answered the sage in still shriller tones. The effort made him cough and wheeze.

The guards tore off his veil. Their triumph was unbounded.

"It is he!" they shouted. "It is he! Hold him! Tie him up! Hold him!"

Thereupon they took the old man to the palace, discussing on the way the kind of execution which awaited him and the reward of three thousand tangas which they hoped to collect. Every word they uttered fell like a burning coal upon his heart.

He grovelled at the foot of the throne weeping bitterly and begging for mercy.

"Raise him," ordered the Emir.

The guards set him upon his feet. Arslan-bek stepped out of the crowd of courtiers.

"May the Emir deign to listen to the words of his devoted slave. This man is not Khoja Nasreddin. Khoja Nasreddin is young. He is just over thirty, whereas this man is very old."

The guards were dismayed. The reward was slipping out of their hands. Everybody remained silent and perplexed.

"Why did you disguise yourself as a woman?" asked the Emir in awesome tones.

"I was on my way to the palace of the great and gracious Emir," quavered the old man. "But I met a man, a complete stranger, who told me that even before I had arrived in Bukhara the Emir had given orders to have me beheaded. Overcome by fear I decided to escape in this disguise."

The Emir laughed knowingly.

"You met a man. . . . A stranger. And you immediately believed him?. . . An extraordinary tale! And why were we going to behead you?"

"Because it was alleged that I had publicly sworn to penetrate into the great Emir's harem. . . . But Allah is my witness that I never harboured such thoughts! I am old and feeble, and have long renounced my own harem."

"Penetrate into our harem?" repeated the Emir pursing his lips. The expression on his face clearly showed that his suspicions of the old man were growing. "Who are you and where do you come from?"

"I am Maulana Husain, sage, astrologer and physician, from Baghdad. I have come to Bukhara at the order and wishes of the great Emir."

"Maulana Husain?" repeated the Emir. "You are Maulana Husain! Your name is Maulana Husain! That is a barefaced lie, you miserable old man!" he thundered so loudly that the King of Poets fell on his knees at the wrong moment. "You lie! This is Maulana Husain!"

In obedience to a sign from the Emir Khoja Nasreddin boldly stepped forward and confronted the old man, openly and fearlessly looking him in the face.

The old man recoiled in amazement, but the next moment recovered himself and shouted:

"Aha! Why, this is the very man who met me in the bazaar and told me that the Emir intended to behead me!"

"What is he saying, Maulana Husain?" exclaimed the Emir completely bewildered.

"He is not Maulana Husain!" yelled the old man. "I am Maulana Husain. He is an impostor! He has usurped my name."

Khoja Nasreddin bowed low to the Emir.

"May the great Sovereign pardon me for my bold speech, but the shamelessness of this old man is truly boundless! He says that I have usurped his name. Perhaps he will say that I have also appropriated this robe?"

"Yes, yes!" cried the old man. "It is my robe!"

"Maybe this turban is also yours?" derisively asked Khoja Nasreddin.

"Why, yes! It *is* my turban! You took my robe and my turban in exchange for the woman's clothes."

"So," said Khoja Nasreddin with still greater sarcasm. "And does this belt also happen to be yours?"

"It is mine!" angrily asserted the old man.

Khoja Nasreddin turned towards the throne.

"His Serene Majesty the Emir has seen for himself what kind of a man this fellow is. Today this lying and despicable old man says I have usurped his name, that this robe is his, that this turban is his, and the belt is his. Tomorrow he will say the palace is his and the whole kingdom is his, and the real Emir of Bukhara is not our great and sun-like Sovereign who is now seated on the throne before us but he, this despicable liar! One can expect anything from him! Why has he come to Bukhara? Is it not to enter the Emir's harem as though it were his own?"

"You are right, Maulana Husain," said the Emir.

"Yes, we are convinced. The old man is a suspicious and dangerous character harbouring evil designs. We are of the opinion that his head should immediately be separated from his body."

The old man groaned and fell on his knees, covering his face with his hands.

However, Khoja Nasreddin could not allow the execution of a man innocent of the crimes of which he was accused, even if the man was a court sage who had certainly by his perfidy brought about the destruction of many. So he bowed low before the Emir:

"May the Great Emir deign to hear me. It will never be too late to cut off his head. But first, would it not be as well to learn his true name and real intention in coming to Bukhara? By this we may discover if he has accomplices. Perhaps he is an evil magician wishing to avail himself of the unfavourable position of the stars. If so he would take the dust from under the Great Emir's footsteps, mix it with the brains of a bat, introduce it into the Emir's narghile, and thus bring harm to his health. For the moment, let the Great Emir spare his life and give him to me. He is capable of overcoming ordinary guards by his magic, whereas against me he would be powerless, for in my wisdom I know all the stratagems of magicians and all the means of destroying their magic. I shall lock him up and recite prayers known only to me over the lock. Thus by the power of his magic alone he will be unable to open the lock. Then by slow torture I shall force him to a full confession."

"Well," said the Emir, "what you say is quite reasonable, Maulana Husain. Take him and do what you like with him, but be careful he does not escape."

"I shall answer for him with my head."

Half an hour later Khoja Nasreddin—now the Emir's chief sage and astrologer—retired to his new quarters which had been prepared for him in one of the towers of the palace wall. Behind him, closely guarded and with drooping head came the criminal, the genuine Maulana Husain.

In the tower above Khoja Nasreddin's apartment there was a small round chamber with a barred window. Khoja Nasreddin unlocked the discoloured brass lock with an enormous key and opened the iron-bound door. The guards pushed in the old man and left him without even giving him an armful of straw. Khoja Nasreddin locked the door and for a long time mumbled over the brass lock so fast and so indistinctly that the guards could only catch frequent invocations of the name of Allah.

Khoja Nasreddin was quite pleased with his quarters. The Emir sent him twelve quilts, eight cushions, an assortment of crockery, a basket of white bread-cakes, a jug of honey and many other delicacies from his table. Khoja Nasreddin was very tired and hungry, but before sitting down to his meal, he took six quilts and four cushions and carried them up to his prisoner.

The old man sat huddled in a corner, his eyes flashing like an angry cat's.

"Well, Maulana Husain," Khoja Nasreddin said blandly, "we shall be quite comfortable in this tower: I below, you above—as becomes your years and wisdom. How dusty it is in here! I'm going to tidy it up a little."

He fetched from below a jug of water and a broom. Then he carefully washed the stone floor, spread out the quilts and arranged the cushions. Finally he made another journey downstairs to bring some bread-cakes, honey, halva and pistachios which he honestly divided into two parts under the eyes of his prisoner.

"You will not starve, Maulana Husain," he said. "We shall find a way to get enough food. Here is a narghile and here is the tobacco."

Having arranged everything in the little chamber so that it looked almost better than his own, Khoja Nasreddin left, locking the door behind him.

The old man remained alone. He was utterly bewildered. For a long time he pondered and puzzled but he could not understand what was happening to him. The quilts were soft and the cushions comfortable; neither the bread-cakes, nor the honey, nor yet the tobacco contained any poison. . . . Wearied by the exhausting experiences of the day, the old man settled down to sleep entrusting his ultimate fate to Allah.

Meanwhile the man who was the cause of all his misfortunes sat at the window in the lower chamber watching the twilight slowly deepen into night and meditating on his extraordinary stormy existence and on his beloved who was here, quite close, but as yet knew it not. Cool air stole through the window. The ringing mournful voices of the muezzins spun out like silver threads over the town. Stars shone in the dark sky. They sparkled, blazed and twinkled with a pure, cold and distant fire, and there was the star Al-Qalb, which stood for the heart, and the three stars Al-Ghafr, which designate a maiden's veil, and the two stars Ash-Sharatan, which designate horns, and only the ill-omened star Ash-Shula, which designates the sting of death, was absent from the dark blue heights.

"Glory to him who lives and does not die!"
   Arabian Nights.

1

KHOJA NASREDDIN won the confidence and favour of the Emir and became his most intimate counsellor in all matters. Khoja Nasreddin made decisions, the Emir signed them and the Grand Vizier Bakhtiyar had only to set upon them the seal of chased brass.

"O merciful Allah, things have come to a pass indeed in our state!" he exclaimed as he read the Emir's orders abolishing taxes, allowing the free use of roads and bridges and reducing the bazaar rates. "Before long the Treasury will be exhausted! This new sage—may his entrails rot—has destroyed in one week what I have been building up for ten years!"

One day he ventured to put his doubts before the Emir. The latter replied:

"What do you know, O worthless one, what do you understand? We are grieved no less than you by these orders which empty our Treasury, but what can we do if the stars command it? Take comfort, Bakhtiyar; it is only for a short time until the stars take up a favourable position. Explain this to him, Maulana Husain."

Khoja Nasreddin took the Grand Vizier aside, seated him on cushions and explained at length why the additional tax on blacksmiths, coppersmiths and armourers should be immediately abolished.

"The stars Al-Avva in the sign of Virgo and al-Balda in the sign of Sagittarius are opposed to the stars Sa'd-Bula in the sign of Aquarius," said Khoja Nasreddin. "You understand, worthy and excellent Vizier, that they are opposed and are far from being in conjunction."

"Well, what of it? What if they are opposed?" retorted Bakhtiyar. "They have been opposed before, and it never prevented us from regularly collecting the taxes."

"But you have forgotten the star Al-Dabaran in the sign of the Taurus!" exclaimed Khoja Nasreddin. "O Vizier! Look at the sky and you will see for yourself."

"Why should I look at the sky?" persisted the obstinate vizier. "My duty is to see to the safety and replenishment of the Treasury, and I see that since your arrival at the palace the Treasury's income has dwindled and the inflow of taxes has diminished. Now is the time to collect the taxes from the town's craftsmen. Tell me, why shouldn't we collect them?"

"Why?" cried Khoja Nasreddin. "And here have I been explaining it to you for the last hour. Do you still fail to understand that to each of the signs of the Zodiac there fall two positions of the moon with one third—"

"But I have to collect the taxes!" the vizier again interrupted. "The taxes, don't you understand?"

"Patience," Khoja Nasreddin stopped him. "I have not yet explained that the constellation Ath-Thurayya and the eight stars An-Na'aim. . ."

Here Khoja Nasreddin launched into such confused and long-winded explanations that the Grand Vizier's ears buzzed and his sight dimmed. He got up and tottered out, while Khoja Nasreddin turned to the Emir:

"O Master, though age may have covered his head with silver, it has enriched it only on the outside without turning to gold that which is within. He was unable to absorb my wisdom. He understood nothing, O Master! If only he possessed one thousandth part of the Emir's intelligence which eclipses that of Loqman himself!"

The Emir smiled graciously and smugly. For days Khoja Nasreddin had been at great pains to persuade him that his wisdom was unequalled and in this he had entirely succeeded. So now when he set out to prove anything to the Emir, the latter listened with an air of profound attention and without arguing for fear of disclosing the true depth of his intelligence.

. . . On the following day Bakhtiyar unburdened himself to a group of courtiers:

"This new sage, Maulana Husain, will be the ruin of us all! The day when the taxes are collected is the day when we enrich ourselves by dipping into the great and brimming stream which flows into the Emir's Treasury. But now when the time comes for us to dip, this Maulana Husain thwarts us. He invokes the position of the stars. Has anyone ever heard of the stars, governed as they are by Allah, disposing themselves unfavourably for eminent and noble men, and simultaneously favouring some obscure craftsmen who, I am sure, are at this moment shamelessly devouring their earnings instead of handing them to us! Who has ever heard of such a disposition of the stars? It cannot be written in any book, for a book of that kind would have been immediately burnt and the man who wrote it cursed and executed as the greatest blasphemer, heretic and criminal!"

The courtiers said nothing for they were not sure with whom it was more profitable to side—with Bakhtiyar or the new sage.

"The return of taxes is dwindling every day," Bakhtiyar went on. "What will happen next? This Maulana Husain has hoodwinked the Emir by making him believe that the taxes have been abolished only for a short time and that later they can be re-established and increased. The Emir believes him, but we know that it is easy to abolish a tax but very difficult to impose a new one. A man parts easily with money when he has become accustomed to regard it as belonging to someone else, but once let him spend it on himself and he will want to spend it on himself a second and a third time.

"The Treasury will become impoverished, and we, the Emir's courtiers, will be ruined. Instead of wearing robes of cloth of gold we shall have to wear plain coarse ones. Instead of four wives we shall have to be content with only two. Instead of silver dishes we shall be served on earthen ones, and instead of tender lamb we shall have to eat our pilau with tough beef fit only for dogs and craftsmen. This is what the new sage Maulana Husain has in store for us. He who does not realize this is blind, and woe betide him!" Thus spoke Bakhtiyar in his endeavour to rouse the courtiers against the new sage.

Vain were his efforts. Maulana Husain scored success after success in his new dignity.

He particularly distinguished himself on the "Day of Praise". According to an ancient custom all the viziers, dignitaries, sages and poets competed every month before the Emir in the art of praising him. The winner of the contest received a reward.

Everyone had recited his panegyric, but the Emir still remained unsatisfied.

"You said the same things last time," he said. "We find that you are not sufficiently thorough in your praises. You do not wish to strain your minds, but we shall make you work today. We shall ask you questions which you will have to answer in such a way as to combine praise with verisimilitude. Listen carefully—here is our first question:

if we, the Great Emir of Bukhara, are, as you assert, powerful and invincible, why is it that the rulers of the neighbouring Muslim countries have not yet sent us their ambassadors bringing rich presents and expressions of their full submission to our sovereignty? We await your answers."

The courtiers were lost in perplexity. They mumbled incoherently trying to evade a direct answer. Khoja Nasreddin alone remained perfectly calm. When his turn came he said:

"May my poor words find favour in the hearing of the Great Emir. The answer to our Sovereign's question is an easy one. All the other monarchs ruling in the neighbouring countries are in a constant state of fear and trepidation before the omnipotence of our Lord. This is how they reason: 'If we were to send rich presents to the great, glorious and powerful Emir of Bukhara, he might think that our land is rich, which would tempt him to come with his armies and possess himself of our country. If on the contrary, we were to send him poor presents, he would take offence and send his troops against us. The Emir of Bukhara is great, glorious and powerful, and it is safest not to remind him of our existence.'

"These are the thoughts in the minds of the other sovereigns and the reason why they do not send their envoys with rich presents to Bukhara must be sought in their perpetual state of fear before the omnipotence of our Monarch."

"Hah!" cried the Emir carried away by admiration for Khoja Nasreddin's answer. "That is how the Emir's questions should be answered! Did you hear him? Learn from him, O fools and blockheads! Truly Maulana Husain excels you all in wisdom tenfold. We declare our royal thanks to him."

Immediately the court cook ran up to Khoja Nasreddin and stuffed his mouth full of halva and boiled sweets. Khoja Nasreddin's cheeks bulged, he kept choking and thick sweet saliva ran down his chin.

The Emir asked several other tricky questions, and every time Khoja Nasreddin's answers were the best.

"What is a courtier's first duty?" was one such question, to which Khoja Nasreddin answered thus:

"O great and illustrious Sovereign! The first duty of a courtier is to exercise his backbone daily so as to give it the necessary suppleness without which he cannot worthily express his loyalty and reverence. The courtier's backbone should possess the faculty of bending as well as twisting in all directions, as distinct from the ossified backbone of the common man who does not even know how to bow properly."

"Quite right," cried the delighted Emir. "Quite right! The daily exercise of his backbone! For a second time we declare our royal thanks to the sage Maulana Husain."

Once again Khoja Nasreddin's mouth was crammed with halva and boiled sweets.

On that day many courtiers transferred their allegiance from Bakhtiyar to Khoja Nasreddin.

That evening Bakhtiyar invited Arslan-bek to his house. The new sage was equally dangerous to both of them, and in their desire to destroy him they had temporarily shelved their old enmity.

"It might be a good plan to put something into his pilau," suggested Arslan-bek who was past master at such deeds.

"And after that the Emir would cut off our heads," retorted Bakhtiyar. "No, worthy Arslan-bek, we must proceed in a different manner. We must extol Maulana Husain's wisdom in every possible way until a doubt enters the Emir's heart as to whether the courtiers do not hold Maulana Husain's wisdom above his own. Let us continually praise and extol Maulana Husain, and the day is sure to come when the Emir will become jealous. That day will be the last of Maulana Husain's elevation and the first of his downfall."

But Fate was keeping a kindly watch over Khoja Nasreddin and turned even his blunders to his advantage.

When Bakhtiyar and Arslan-bek by their constant exaggerated praise of the new sage had nearly attained their goal and the Emir had begun to feel the first stirrings of jealousy—secretly as yet—it so happened that Khoja Nasreddin made a blunder.

He was walking with the Emir in the garden, breathing the fragrance of the flowers and enjoying the singing of the birds. The Emir was silent. Khoja Nasreddin felt an undercurrent of hostility in this silence without understanding the reason for it.

"And how is that old man, your prisoner, doing'" the Emir asked. "Have you found out his real name and the reasons why he came to Bukhara?"

Khoja Nasreddin's thoughts were at the moment full of Guljan, so he answered absently:

118

"May the Great Sovereign forgive his humble slave! I have been so far unable to get a word out of the old man. He is as dumb as a fish."

"But have you tried to torture him?"

"Oh yes, gracious Master! The day before yesterday I wrenched his joints. Yesterday I spent the whole day loosening his teeth with hot pincers."

"Loosening teeth is a good torture," approved the Emir. "It is strange though that he keeps silent. Shall I send a skilled and experienced executioner to help you?"

"Oh no, the Great Sovereign need not burden himself with such cares. Tomorrow I shall try a new torture: I shall pierce the old man's tongue and gums with a red-hot bradawl."

"Stay! Stay!" cried the Emir, his face suddenly lighting up with pleasure. "How will he be able to tell you his name if you pierce his tongue with a red-hot bradawl? You never thought of that, Maulana Husain, did you? Now we, the Great Emir, have thought of it at once and have thus prevented you from making a grave mistake. This proves that though you are an incomparable sage, our wisdom greatly exceeds yours, as you have just seen."

Jubilant, his face radiating pleasure the Emir ordered the courtiers to be summoned at once. When they had assembled he announced that on this day he had exceeded Maulana Husain in wisdom by preventing a mistake which the sage had been on the point of making.

The court chronicler painstakingly registered every one of the Emir's words for the benefit of posterity.

From that day the Emir's heart no longer harboured any jealously.

Thus a chance slip permitted Khoja Nasreddin to baffle the crafty machinations of his enemies.

Yet he suffered more and more from the long hours of intolerable suspense. The full moon stood high above the city of Bukhara. The glazed tiles capping the innumerable minarets gleamed softly, while the massive stone foundations were shrouded in blue mist. A light breeze blew gently, cool on the roof-tops but stifling down below where the earth and the sun-baked walls had not had time to cool in the night air. All was plunged in slumber: the palace, the mosques and the hovels. Only the owl disturbed the hot repose of the holy city with its shrill cries.

Khoja Nasreddin sat at the open window. He knew in his heart that Guljan was not asleep either and was thinking of him. Perhaps at this very moment they were both looking at the same minaret without being able to see each other, for they were separated by walls, iron grilles, eunuchs, guards and old women. Khoja Nasreddin had gained admission to the palace but the harem still remained inaccessible and only a lucky chance could lead him to it. Tirelessly he sought such a chance, but in vain! He had even been unable to send Guljan a message. He sat at the window kissing the breeze and saying to it:

"It is so easy for you! Slip for a moment through her window and touch her lips and her ears. Give Guljan my kiss and my message. Tell her I have not forgotten her. Tell her I will come, I will rescue her."

The breeze sped past leaving Khoja Nasreddin alone with his sorrow.

Another day would begin with its usual toil and cares. Again he would have to appear in the great hall and there await the appearance of the Emir, listen to the courtiers' flatteries, see through the crafty intrigues of Bakhtiyar and catch his glances charged with secret venom. Then he would have to prostrate himself before the Emir, and sing his praises, after which there would be long hours alone with him looking with concealed aversion at his bloated and dissipated face, listening attentively to his foolish talk and explaining to him the position of the stars. Khoja Nasreddin was so sick and tired of it all that he had ceased to invent new interpretations and explained everything—the Emir's headache, the drought in the fields and the rise in the price of grain—with the same words and invoking the same constellations.

"The stars Sa'd adh-Dhabih," he would drone, "are opposed to the sign of Aquarius, while the planet Mercury stands now to the left of Scorpio. This explains the Emir's insomnia of last night."

"The stars of Sa'd adh-Dhabih are opposed to the planet Mercury while . . . I must remember this. . . . Say it again, Maulana Husain."

The great Emir had no memory whatsoever.

On the following day the conversation would start all over again.

"The death of the cattle in the hill-country is to be explained by the fact, O Great Emir, that the stars Sa'd adh-Dhabih are in conjunction with Aquarius, while the planet Mercury is opposed to Scorpio."

120

"Then the stars Sa'd adh-Dhabih"—the Emir would say, "I must remember this."

"Almighty Allah, what a fool he is!" thought Khoja Nasreddin wearily. "He is even a greater fool than my former master! I am sick of him. When, o when shall I be able to get out of this palace!"

Meanwhile the Emir would start another topic.

"Peace and contentment are reigning in our state, Maulana Husain. No longer do we hear of that rascal Khoja Nasreddin. Whither has he gone? Why is he silent? Explain this to us?"

"O almighty Sovereign, Centre of the Universe! The stars S'ad adh-Dhabih," Khoja Nasreddin drawled wearily and then went on and on repeating over and over again all he had said so many times before. "And besides, O Great Emir, the rascal Khoja Nasreddin has visited Baghdad and has obviously heard of my wisdom. And when he learnt I had come to Bukhara, he went into concealment overcome by fear and trepidation, knowing how easily I can capture him."

"Capture him? That would be well indeed! But how do you intend to do it?"

"For that I shall await a favourable conjunction of the stars Sa'd adh-Dhabih with the planet Jupiter."

"With the planet Jupiter," repeated the Emir. "I must remember that. Do you know, Maulana, an excellent idea came to us last night. We thought Bakhtiyar ought to be dismissed and you appointed Grand Vizier in his place."

At that he was obliged to prostrate himself before the Emir, extol and thank him, and explain that for the present the stars Sa'd adh-Dhabih were unfavourable to any change of viziers.

"Quickly, quickly away from here!" Khoja Nasreddin thought to himself.

Thus he dragged out a joyless and tedious existence in the palace, while awaiting his chance.

He yearned for the bazaar, the crowds, the tea-houses, the smoky taverns. Gladly would he have exchanged all the Emir's delicacies for a bowl of sheep's-feet broth with onions, hot and peppery, or for the tough scraps of mutton in the cheap bazaar pilau; he would have given his cloth of gold robe for any old rag just to hear simple talk and loud hearty laughter instead of flattery and praise.

But Fate persisted in testing Khoja Nasreddin and failed to send him the long-awaited favourable chance. Meanwhile the Emir constantly renewed his inquiries as to when the stars would at last permit him to lift the veil of the new concubine.

2

ONE day the Emir sent for Khoja Nasreddin at an unusual hour. It was very early, the palace slept, the fountains splashed, the doves cooed and rustled their wings.

"What can he want me for;" wondered Khoja Nasreddin mounting the jasper steps which led to the royal chamber.

He met Bakhtiyar who slipped noiselessly like a shadow out of the bed-chamber. They exchanged greetings without stopping. Khoja Nasreddin stepped warily sensing some trick.

In the bed-chamber he found the Chief Eunuch. His Chastity lay prostrate and piteously groaning before the royal couch. Pieces of a broken gold-mounted palm-wood cane were strewn beside him on the carpet.

Heavy velvet curtains protected the bed-chamber from the fresh morning breeze, the rays of the sun and the twitter of birds. The room was lit by the dull flame of a solid lamp which smoked and smelt like any ordinary earthen lamp.

In a corner a carved incense-burner exhaled a sweet and spicy fragrance which however could not prevail over the smell of sheep's fat. The air in the bed-chamber was so thick that it tickled Khoja Nasreddin's nose and rasped his throat.

The Emir sat with his hairy legs sticking out from under the silk quilt. Khoja Nasreddin noticed that the prince's heels were dark yellow as though he had occasionally held them over his Indian incense-burner.

"Maulana Husain, we are exceedingly distressed," said the Emir. "Our Chief Eunuch, whom you see here, is the cause of it all."

"O Great Sovereign!" cried Khoja Nasreddin, growing cold inside. "Can he have dared?"

"Oh no!" the Emir grimaced and waved his hand. "How could he when with our usual wisdom we had foreseen everything and made sure of everything before appointing him Chief Eunuch. No, no, nothing of the kind. We learnt today that this scoundrel, our Chief Eunuch, forgetful of the great favour which we showed him by appointing him to one of the highest dignities in the state, has been criminally neglecting his duty.

"Taking advantage of the fact that we have not been visiting the concubines, he dared to leave the harem for three days to indulge in the vice of hashish-smoking. Order and peace were disturbed in the harem. Our concubines, left to themselves, have been quarrelling, fighting, scratching each other's faces and pulling out each other's hair. This has caused us considerable loss, for a woman with a scratched face or thin hair is far from perfect in our eyes. Moreover, another matter has plunged us into sorrow: our new concubine has fallen ill and has refused food for the last three days."

Khoja Nasreddin started. The Emir kept him quiet with a gesture.

"Wait, we have not finished speaking. She has fallen ill and may depart this life. Had we visited her just once, her illness, even her death, would not have grieved our heart so much. But you can understand, Maulana Husain, how annoyed we are in the present circumstances. Therefore we have decided," the Emir raised his voice, "in order to avoid any further afflictions and worries to dismiss this vicious hashish-smoking rascal, deprive him of our favour and give him two hundred strokes of the whip. As for you, Maulana Husain, we have, on the contrary, decided to show you our great favour and appoint you to the vacant post of Chief Eunuch of our harem."

Khoja Nasreddin felt his legs weaken, his breath stop in his throat and his entrails grow cold.

The Emir frowned and asked in a voice charged with menace:

"You seem prepared to argue with us, Maulana Husain. Is it that you would prefer vain and passing delights to the great happiness of serving our royal person?"

Khoja Nasreddin managed to recover his equanimity. He said with a low bow:

"May Allah preserve our gracious Monarch. The Emir's favour towards my unworthy person is boundless. The Great Sovereign possesses the magic gift of divining the most secret and innermost desires of his subjects. This allows him to overwhelm them with his ceaseless bounty. Many are the times when I, the unworthy one, have craved to replace this lazy and stupid man who is now grovelling on the carpet and wailing after having received the just punishment which he has brought upon himself. How many times have I nursed this desire without daring to mention it to the Emir. But now that the great Monarch himself—"

"Then why delay?" interrupted the Emir amicably and with

evident pleasure. "We shall summon the physician. He will fetch his knives and you will retire with him to a secluded spot. In the meantime we shall have Bakhtiyar write the order appointing you Chief Eunuch. Hey!" he shouted, clapping his hands.

"Let the monarch lend his ear to my unworthy words," said Khoja Nasreddin hurriedly and glancing uneasily towards the door. "I would at once and gladly accompany the physician to a secluded spot, and it is only the anxiety for the Sovereign's well-being which prevents me from doing so. After this business I would be obliged to spend a long time in bed, and meantime the new concubine might die and the Emir's heart would be shrouded in the dark mists of sorrow, the very thought of which is unbearable and intolerable to his slave. Therefore, I suggest that the concubine be first restored to health, after which I shall put myself into the hands of the physician and prepare myself for the dignity of Chief Eunuch."

"Hm," murmured the Emir, eyeing Nasreddin mistrustfully.

"O Master! She has not taken food for three days."

"Hm," repeated the Emir. Then he turned to the grovelling eunuch: "You, miserable progeny of a spider, answer: is our new concubine very ill and should we fear for her life?"

A cold trickle of sweat ran down Khoja Nasreddin's back as he anxiously awaited the answer.

The eunuch said:

"O gracious Sovereign, she has become thin and pale like the new moon. Her face is like wax and her fingers are cold. The old women say these are very unfavourable symptoms. . . ."

The Emir remained thoughtful. Khoja Nasreddin moved away into the shadows, grateful for the smoky half darkness which reigned in the bedchamber and concealed the paleness of his features.

"Yes!" the Emir said at last. "If that is so, then she may well die, and that would grieve us deeply. But are you sure, Maulana Husain, that you can cure her?"

"The great Sovereign knows there is no physician more skilled than I between Bukhara and Baghdad."

"Go, Maulana, and prepare a potion for her."

"Great Sovereign, I must first determine the nature of her sickness. To do this I must examine her."

"Examine her?" chuckled the Emir. "When you are Chief Eunuch, Maulana Husain, you will have plenty of time to do your examining."

"O Majesty!" Khoja Nasreddin bowed to the ground. "I must—"

"Worthless slave!" cried the Emir. "Do you not know that no mortal can see the faces of our concubines under threat of painful death?"

"I do, O Majesty," replied Khoja Nasreddin, "but I did not mean her face. Never would I dare to glance at her face. It is enough for me to see her hand, for I am sufficiently skilled in my profession to determine any sickness by the colour of the nails."

"Her hand?" repeated the Emir. "Why did you not say so at first and so avoid arousing our anger? Her hand? That, of course, can be done. We shall go with you to the harem; we hope that the sight of a woman's hand will cause us no prejudice."

"The contemplation of her hand cannot cause any prejudice to the great Monarch," Khoja Nasreddin answered. He had come to the conclusion that since he would never be able to see Guljan alone and the presence of a witness was inevitable, it was as well for the witness to be none other than the Emir in person, for thus he would remain unsuspecting.

3

AT last, after so many days of fruitless expectation the doors of the harem opened before Khoja Nasreddin.

The guards moved aside bowing low. Khoja Nasreddin followed the Emir up a stone staircase through a wicket-gate into a beautiful garden. Here among masses of roses, stocks and hyacinths fountains played in basins of white and black marble, over which hung a fine vapour. The morning dew sparkled and shimmered on the flowers and grass.

Khoja Nasreddin's colour kept coming and going. The eunuch threw open doors of carved walnut. A thick aroma of amber, musk and attar of roses was wafted to them from the shady interior. This was the harem—the sad dwelling of the Emir's lovely captives.

Khoja Nasreddin took careful note of all the corners, passages and turnings so as not to lose his way when the decisive moment came, and thus bring destruction upon himself and Guljan.

"To the right," he repeated to himself, "then to the left. Here is a staircase with an old woman on guard. Now again to the right. . . ."

The passages were poorly lit by the blue, green and pink light which filtered through coloured Chinese glass. The eunuch stopped before a low doorway.

"She is here, O Master."

Khoja Nasreddin followed the Emir across the fateful threshold.

The room was small, its walls and floor covered with carpets. In niches stood caskets of mother of pearl filled with bracelets, ear-rings and necklaces, and a large silver mirror hung on the wall. Poor Guljan had never seen such riches even in her dreams! Khoja Nasreddin trembled on catching sight of her tiny pearl-embroidered slippers. She had had the time to wear down the backs! He needed all his will-power to stifle his emotion.

The eunuch pointed to a silk curtain in a corner of the room. Guljan lay there.

"She is asleep," whispered the eunuch.

A tremor ran through Khoja Nasreddin. His beloved was quite close. "Steel yourself, bear up, Khoja Nasreddin!" he admonished himself.

When he approached the curtain, heard the sighs of the sleeping Guljan and saw the slight billowing of the silk at the head of the couch, his throat was constricted as though seized in an iron grip. Tears sprang to his eyes and his breath was arrested.

"Why are you so slow, Maulana Husain?" asked the Emir.

"O Majesty, I am listening to her breathing. I am trying to catch through this curtain the beating of the lady's heart. What is her name?"

"Her name is Guljan," said the Emir.

"Guljan!" softly called Khoja Nasreddin.

The rhythmical swaying of the curtain at the head of the couch stopped suddenly. Guljan had awakened and lay motionless, not quite sure whether she was dreaming or whether she was really hearing the voice of her beloved.

"Guljan!" called Khoja Nasreddin. She uttered a low cry. He said rapidly:

"My name is Maulana Husain. I am the new sage, astrologer and physician come from Baghdad to enter the Emir's service. You understand, Guljan. I am the new sage, astrologer and physician called Maulana Husain."

Turning to the Emir, Khoja Nasreddin added:

"For some reason she was frightened on hearing my voice.

Probably this eunuch has been unkind to her in the absence of the Sovereign."

The Emir glowered at the eunuch who trembled and bowed to the ground without daring to raise his voice in self-justification.

"Guljan, danger threatens you," said Khoja Nasreddin, "but I shall save you and you must trust me, for my art overcomes everything."

"I hear you, Maulana Husain, sage from Baghdad, I know you and trust you. And this I say in the presence of the Monarch whose feet I see through the chink between my curtains."

Keeping in mind that it was imperative for him to preserve a dignified and scholarly bearing in the Emir's presence Khoja Nasreddin said sternly:

"Give me your hand so that I can determine the cause of your sickness by the colour of your finger-nails."

The silk billowed and parted. Khoja Nasreddin gently took Guljan's slender little hand. He could express his feelings only by pressing it. Guljan responded by a slight pressure. He turned her hand over and for a long time attentively studied the palm. "How thin she has grown," he thought with a pang. The Emir peered over his shoulder, breathing heavily into his ear. Khoja Nasreddin showed him the nail on Guljan's little finger and shook his head ominously. Although this particular nail was exactly like the other nails, the Emir discerned something amiss, pursed his lips and gave Khoja Nasreddin a meaning look.

"Where is your pain?" asked Khoja Nasreddin.

"In my heart," she replied with a sigh. "My heart aches from sorrow and longing."

"What is the reason of your sorrow?"

"I am separated from the one I love."

Khoja Nasreddin whispered to the Emir:

"She is sick because she is separated from His Majesty."

The Emir's face lit up with pleasure. He breathed more heavily.

"I am separated from the one I love," said Guljan, "and now I feel that my beloved is here close to me, but I can neither embrace him nor kiss him. Oh when will the day come when he will embrace me and hold me close?"

"Almighty Allah!" exclaimed Khoja Nasreddin in feigned amazement. "What a strong passion His Majesty has aroused in her in such a short time!"

The Emir was beside himself with delight. He could not keep still, but fidgeted about and giggled stupidly behind his hand.

"Guljan!" said Khoja Nasreddin. "Be at rest. He whom you love hears you."

"Yes, yes!" broke in the Emir unable to restrain himself. "He hears you, Guljan! Your beloved hears you!"

Light laughter like the gurgling of water came from behind the curtain. Khoja Nasreddin resumed:

"Danger threatens you, Guljan, but fear not, I, the famous sage, astrologer and physician Maulana Husain, will save you."

"He will save you!" echoed the delighted Emir. "He will save you without fail."

"You hear what the Sovereign says?" went on Khoja Nasreddin. "You must trust me, I shall deliver you from danger. The day of your happiness is near. For the present the Sovereign cannot approach you for I have warned him that the stars command him not to touch a woman's veil. But the stars are altering their position, you understand me, Guljan? Soon they will be in a favourable position and you shall embrace your beloved. The day on which I shall send you a potion will precede the day of your happiness. Do you understand me, Guljan? On receiving the potion you must be prepared."

"Thank you, thank you, Maulana Husain," she replied crying and laughing with joy. "Thank you, incomparable and wise curer of sickness! My beloved is near and I feel our hearts beating in unison."

The Emir and Khoja Nasreddin went out. The Chief Eunuch overtook them at the wicket-gate.

"O Master!" he cried falling on his knees. "Truly the world has never yet seen such a skilled physician! For three days she has been lying without a movement, and now of a sudden she has left her couch, she sings, laughs and dances and has even deigned to box my ears when I approached her."

"There I recognize my Guljan," thought Khoja Nasreddin. "She was always quick with her hands."

At the morning meal the Emir showered favours on all the courtiers. To Khoja Nasreddin he gave two purses: a large one full of silver and a smaller one full of gold.

"What a strong passion we have inspired!" he said chuckling. "You must admit, Maulana, that you have not often witnessed such a passion. How her voice trembled, how she cried and laughed! But it is nothing to what you shall see when you take up your post of Chief Eunuch."

A murmur passed along the rows of bowing courtiers. Bakhtiyar smiled wickedly. Only then did Khoja Nasreddin realize who had suggested to the Emir the idea of appointing him Chief Eunuch.

"She has recovered now," said the Emir, "and there is no reason to put off your appointment. You can retire with the physician. Hey you," and he turned towards the physician, "go and fetch your knives. Bakhtiyar, give me the decree."

Khoja Nasreddin choked over the hot tea and coughed. Bakhtiyar stepped forward with the prepared document, thrilled and joyfully vindictive. A pen was presented to the Emir who signed the order and returned it to Bakhtiyar. The latter hastened to set upon it the chased copper seal. The whole transaction took only a minute.

"The magnitude of your joy seems to have robbed you of speech, O worthy and wise Maulana Husain," said Bakhtiyar with a triumphant smile. "Nevertheless etiquette demands that you express your gratitude to the Emir."

Khoja Nasreddin knelt before the throne.

"At last my earnest wish has been granted," he said. "I deeply deplore the delay which will be caused by the necessity of preparing the potion for the Emir's concubine. We must make sure of the cure otherwise the sickness will re-enter her body."

"Does the preparation of the potion demand so much time?" Bakhtiyar questioned uneasily. "Surely it can be prepared in half an hour. ..."

"Quite right," approved the Emir. "Half an hour is ample time."

"O Master! It depends on the stars Sa'd adh-Dhabih," replied Khoja Nasreddin using the last and most potent argument. "According to their position it will take me from two to five days."

"Five days!" cried Bakhtiyar. "O worthy Maulana Husain, I never heard of a potion taking five days to be prepared."

Khoja Nasreddin addressed himself to the Emir: "Perhaps his Serene Majesty will be pleased to entrust the further treatment of the new concubine not to me but to the Grand Vizier Bakhtiyar. Let him try to cure her. In which case I will not answer for her life."

"What's that, Maulana? What are you saying?" cried the Emir in an alarmed voice. "Bakhtiyar understands nothing of medicine, nor is he too clever, as we told you before when you were offered the post of Grand Vizier."

A slow tremor shook the Grand Vizier's body. He gave Khoja Nasreddin a venomous look.

"Go and prepare the potion," said the Emir. "But five days is too long, Maulana. Can't you get it ready quicker than that? We are anxious to have you take up your new appointment."

"O Great Sovereign, I too am anxious!" cried Khoja Nasreddin. "I shall do my best to be quick."

He took his leave walking backwards and making innumerable bows. Bakhtiyar watched him go and his whole expression showed how furious he was at seeing his enemy and rival depart unharmed.

"Snake! Perfidious hyena!" Khoja Nasreddin thought to himself and gnashed his teeth in anger. "But you've missed your chance, Bakhtiyar. You won't have time to harm me, for now I know what I wanted to know: the entrances, passages and exits of the Emir's harem. Oh my precious Guljan, how clever of you to fall sick in the nick of time to save Khoja Nasreddin from the court physician's knives! Though honestly, you were thinking only of yourself!"

He went back to the tower, at the foot of which the guards were sitting in the shade enjoying a game of dice. One of them who had lost everything was just taking off his boots to stake them. It was very hot, but inside the tower and behind its thick walls there was a cool, damp freshness. Khoja Nasreddin mounted the narrow stone staircase. He passed his own door and went to the upper room to see the Baghdad sage.

The old man had a wild appearance, for during his captivity his hair and beard had grown long and shaggy. His eyes glared from under bushy eye-brows. A flood of vituperation poured out on to Khoja Nasreddin.

"You miserable son of sin, how much longer are you going to keep me locked up? May a stone fall on your head and come out at the soles of your feet! O wretched swindler and imposter! You stole my name, my robe, my turban and my belt! May worms devour you in your life-time and destroy your stomach and liver!"

Khoja Nasreddin was quite accustomed to such outbursts and took no offence.

"Worthy Maulana Husain, I have invented a new torture for you today. It is to squeeze your head with the aid of a looped rope and a stick. The guards are below— you must scream so that they hear you."

The old man approached the barred window and began to shout monotonously:

"Oh almighty Allah! My sufferings are boundless! Oh, do not squeeze my head with the loop and stick! Rather death than such torment!"

"Wait! Wait a minute, Maulana Husain," interrupted Khoja Nasreddin. "You shout too lazily and unconvincingly. Remember, the guards are experts in such matters. If they think you are shamming, they will report you to Arslan-bek, and you will fall into the hands of a real executioner. It is in your own interest to show more zeal. Here, I'll show you how to do it."

He went to the window, took a deep breath and suddenly let out such a yell that the old man stopped his ears and recoiled.

"Child of an infidel brood!" moaned the old man. "Where am I to get such a throat? How can I yell so that it is heard at the other end of the town?"

"It's your only hope, unless you want to fall into the executioner's hands," retorted Khoja Nasreddin.

The old man tried again: he did his best. He screamed and shouted so dismally that the guards at the foot of the tower stopped their game to enjoy listening to him.

His efforts left the old man wheezing and coughing.

"Oh! Oh!" he wailed. "My poor throat! What a strain? Now are you satisfied, you miserable vagabond? May Azrael take you!"

"I am satisfied," Khoja Nasreddin replied. "And here, most wise Maulana Husain, is the reward for your efforts." He produced the purses he had received from the Emir, emptied them on to a tray and divided the money into two equal parts.

The old man went on cursing and grumbling.

"Why do you curse me so?" Khoja Nasreddin asked placidly. "Have I dishonoured the name of Maulana Husain in any way? Have I debased his learning? Do you see this money? The Emir gave it to Maulana Husain, the famous astrologer and physician for curing a girl in his harem."

"You have cured a girl?" The old man nearly choked. "What do you know about diseases? You, an ignorant rogue and swindler!"

"I know nothing about diseases, but I do know something about girls," replied Khoja Nasreddin. "Therefore it is fair to divide the Emir's reward into two parts: one for you—for what you know, and one for me—for what I know. I ought to tell you, Maulana, I did not treat the girl casually, but only after studying the position of the stars. Last night I observed that the stars Sa'd as-Su'ud were in conjunction with the stars Sa'd al-Akhbiya and that Scorpio had turned towards Cancer."

"What?" shouted the old man, and he ran up and down the room in blind fury. "Ignorant fellow, you are only fit to drive asses! You don't even know that the stars Sa'd as-Su'ud cannot come into conjunction with the stars Sa'd al-Akhbiya. They belong to the same constellation! And how can you see the sign Scorpio at this time of year? I spent the whole night looking at the sky. The stars Sa'd-Bula and As-Simak were in conjunction, while Al-Jabha was in the descendant. Do you hear what I say, you blockhead? Scorpio isn't there now! You have mixed it all up. The driver of asses has meddled with things he doesn't understand! You have mistaken the stars Al-Haq'a which are at present opposed to the stars Al-Butayn for Scorpio!"

In an angry desire to expose Khoja Nasreddin's ignorance the old man spoke at length about the true disposition of the stars. His listener was attentively trying to memorize every single word, so as to avoid mistakes when talking to the Emir in the presence of the other sages.

"O ignoramus, son of an ignoramus, grandson and great-grandson of an ignoramus!" stormed the old man. "You don't even know that at present, during the nineteenth mansion of the moon, which is called Ash-Shula and which falls on the sign of the Archer, human destinies are determined only by the stars of this sign and none other. This fact is stated quite clearly in the book by the most wise Shihab al-din Mahmud al-Karaji. . . ."

"Shihab al-din Mahmud al-Karaji," Khoja Nasreddin noted. "Tomorrow in the Emir's presence I shall expose the long-bearded sage for his ignorance of this book. And a salutary awe will fill his mind and heart before the greatness of my learning."

4

IN the house of Jafar the Usurer there stood twelve sealed jars full of gold, but his ambition was to have no less then twenty. Fate had handicapped him by giving him an appearance which exposed the greed and dishonesty of his nature. This served as a warning to trusting and inexperienced simpletons and made it more difficult to inveigle new prey. His jars were being filled therefore at a much slower rate than he liked.

"Ah, if only I could get rid of my deformities," he sighed. "Then men would not run at the sight of me. They would trust me without suspecting duplicity. How much easier it would be to trick them! How much quicker my income would increase!"

When the rumour spread in the town that the Emir's new sage Maulana Husain had shown great skill in curing diseases, Jafar the Usurer filled a basket with rich gifts and presented himself at the palace.

After taking a look at the contents of the basket, Arslan-bek expressed complete willingness to help him.

"You have come at the right moment, worthy Jafar. Our sovereign lord is in a happy mood today and he will hardly refuse your request."

The Emir listened to the usurer, accepted his gift, a golden chessboard framed in ivory, and ordered the sage to be summoned.

"Maulana Husain," he said when Khoja Nasreddin came in and knelt before him, "this man, Jafar the Usurer, our loyal slave, has rendered us some services. We order you at once to cure him of his lameness, hump, blind eye and other defects."

Having spoken the Emir turned away to show he was not going to listen to any argument. Khoja Nasreddin could only bow and retire, followed by the usurer who dragged his hump like a tortoise.

"Let us hurry, O most wise Maulana Husain," he said, not recognizing Khoja Nasreddin behind his false beard. "Let us hurry, for the sun has not set yet and I could be cured before night falls. ... As you have heard, the Emir ordered you to cure me at once."

In his heart Khoja Nasreddin was cursing the usurer, the Emir and himself for too much zeal in advertising his learning. How could he extricate himself from such a difficult business? The usurer kept pulling his sleeve to quicken his pace. The streets were deserted. Khoja Nasreddin's feet sank in the hot dust. As he strode along he kept thinking: "How shall I get out of this?" Suddenly he stopped: "It looks as though the time has come to fulfil my oath." Swiftly he devised a plan and weighed every chance. "Yes," he thought, "the time has come! Usurer, you heartless tormentor of the poor, this very day you shall be drowned."

He turned away so that the usurer should not notice the gleam in his black eyes.

They turned into an alley where the wind was raising little whirlwinds of dust. The usurer opened the wicket-gate of his house. At the far end of the court-yard, behind a low fence which shut off the women's quarters, Khoja Nasreddin saw and heard through the screen of foliage vague movements, low murmurs and laughter. The usurer's wives and concubines were pleasantly excited at the visit of a stranger, for in their captivity they knew no other entertainment. The usurer halted and sternly glanced in their direction—all became quiet.

"I shall set you free today, fair captives," thought Khoja Nasreddin.

The room into which the usurer ushered him had no windows, while the door was secured by three locks and several bolts the secret of which was known only to the master of the house. He had to work for quite a time before he got the door open. It was in here that he kept his jars of gold and slept on the planks which covered up the entrance to the cellar.

"Undress!" ordered Khoja Nasreddin.

The usurer threw off his clothes and in his nakedness looked incredibly repulsive. Khoja Nasreddin shut the door and began his incantations.

Meanwhile Jafar's numerous relations had assembled in the yard. Many of them owed money to him and hoped he would mark the happy occasion by cancelling their debts. Their hopes were ill-founded. On hearing his debtors' voices through the closed door, the usurer was filled with evil glee.

"Today I shall tell them I am letting them off," he thought, "but I shall not give back their receipts. Feeling reassured they will live carelessly. I shall say nothing and secretly keep a record of their debts. Then when ten tangas interest has accumulated on every tanga of their debt and the total is greater than the value of their houses, gardens and vineyards, I shall summon the judge, repudiate my promise, produce the receipts, sell them up, reduce them to beggary and fill another jar with gold!"

"Get up!" said Khoja Nasreddin. "We are going to the pond of the holy Turakhan where you shall bathe in the sacred waters. This is indispensable for the cure."

"The pond of the holy Turakhan!" cried the usurer in alarm. "I was nearly drowned once in its waters. You must realize, O most wise Maulana Husain, that I cannot swim."

"On your way to the pond you must recite prayers without ceasing," said Khoja Nasreddin. "And you must not think of worldly things. You will also take a purse of gold and give a golden piece to every person you meet on the way."

The usurer groaned and sighed but carried out these instructions to the letter. They met all kinds of people, craftsmen and beggars, and to each the usurer gave a gold coin though the effort nearly broke his heart. The relations followed behind. Khoja Nasreddin had purposely invited them to look on as a precaution against possible future accusations of having intentionally drowned the usurer.

The sun was dipping behind the roofs, the trees spread their shade over the pond, mosquitoes sang in the air, Jafar undressed and approached the water.

"It is very deep here," he complained. "You haven't forgotten, Maulana, what I said? I cannot swim."

The relations looked on in silence. The usurer, modestly screening himself with his hands, and shrinking apprehensively, circled the pond in search of a shallow place.

He squatted and holding on to some overhanging bushes put a timid toe into the water.

"It is cold," he grumbled; his eyes bulged uneasily.

"You are wasting time," replied Khoja Nasreddin averting his eyes, for he was steeling his heart against unmerited compassion. Then he called to mind the sufferings of the poor people ruined by Jafar; the parched lips of the sick child; the tears of old Niyaz. His face flamed angrily and he was able to look openly and boldly into the usurer's eyes.

"You are wasting time," he repeated. "Get in if you want to be cured."

The usurer began to move into the water. He moved so slowly that when he was up to the knees in water, his belly was still on the bank. At last he stood up and the water reached to his waist. The weeds stirred and their cold touch tickled him. His shoulders trembled from the cold; he took a step forward and looked back. His eyes were pleading like a dumb animal's, but Khoja Nasreddin would not respond. To let off the usurer now would mean condemning thousands of poor people to further suffering.

The water reached above the usurer's hump but Khoja Nasreddin unrelentingly forced him on.

"Go on. ... Go on. . . . Let the water touch your ears. Otherwise I cannot answer for your cure. Come along now! Be brave, worthy Jafar! Take heart! One more step! Just a little further."

"Ulp!" the usurer gurgled as he disappeared below the surface.

"Ulp!" he uttered again as he reappeared.

"He is drowning! He is drowning!" cried the relations.

A general commotion broke out. Branches and sticks were stretched out to the drowning man. Some wanted to help him out of sheer kindness of heart, others only made a pretence of it. Khoja Nasreddin could easily have told who owed Jafar money and how much. He himself ran about, shouting and fussing more than anybody else.

"Here! Give us your hand, worthy Jafar! Listen, give us your hand!"

All the time he knew perfectly well that the usurer would never stretch out his hand, for the word "give" was enough to paralyse him.

"Give us your hand!" called the relations in chorus. The usurer was sinking and coming up again at ever longer intervals. And there, in those sacred waters he would have ended his life had not a bare-footed water-carrier, with an empty water-skin slung on his back, come running past.

"Well!" he exclaimed catching sight of the drowning man. "If that's not Jafar the Usurer!"

Without hesitating he jumped fully clothed into the water, stretched out his hand and yelled:

"Here! Take hold of my hand!"

The usurer caught hold and was safely dragged out of the water.

While the usurer was recovering stretched out on the bank, his rescuer was volubly explaining to the relations: "You went the wrong way about helping him. You kept shouting 'give' instead of 'take'. Didn't you know the worthy Jafar was once before on the point of drowning in this very pond and was saved by a stranger who was riding past on a grey ass? The stranger used the same means to save Jafar, and I happened to remember. Today that knowledge has come in useful."

As Khoja Nasreddin listened, he bit his lips. So twice he had saved the usurer! Once with his own hands and now through the hands of the water-carrier. "No matter," he thought, "I shall see that he drowns, even if it means spending a year in Bukhara."

Meanwhile the usurer had recovered his breath and whined querulously:

"O Maulana Husain! You said you would cure me but you've nearly drowned me. By Allah, I swear I shall never come within a hundred paces of this pond! What kind of a sage are you if a simple water-carrier has to show you how to save a man from drowning? Give me my khalat and turban. Come on, Maulana, it is growing dark and we must finish what we have begun. And you, water-carrier," said the usurer, rising to his feet, "don't forget your debt becomes due in a week's time. But I want to reward you and therefore I will forgive you half . . . I mean a quarter. . . . No, a tenth of your debt. That is sufficient, for I could easily have saved myself without your help."

"O worthy Jafar," said the water-carrier timidly. "You couldn't have saved yourself without my help. Couldn't you forgive me a quarter of what I owe you?"

"Ha! So you saved me out of self-interest!" cried the usurer. "You weren't so much moved by the feelings of a good Muslim, as by sheer greed! That merits punishment, O water-carrier. I shall not forgive you the smallest part of your debt!"

The crestfallen water-carrier moved away and Khoja Nasreddin looked after him with pity. Then he turned a look of hatred and contempt on Jafar.

"Come on, Maulana Husain," hustled Jafar, "what have you got to whisper about with this greedy water-carrier?"

"Wait," said Khoja Nasreddin. "You have forgotten that you must give a gold coin to everyone you happen to meet. Why haven't you given one to the water-carrier?"

"O woe is me! I shall be ruined!" wailed the usurer. "To think I should be forced to give money to such a despicable and covetous man!" He untied his purse and threw out a coin. "Let that be the last. It is dark now, and we shall not meet anyone on our way back."

But it was not for nothing that Khoja Nasreddin had been whispering with the water-carrier.

They started on their way back. The usurer walked in front, followed by Khoja Nasreddin, and the relations brought up the rear. They had hardly covered fifty paces when out of an alley came a water-carrier—the very same man they had just left on the banks of the pond.

The usurer turned away intending to ignore him, but Khoja Nasreddin reproved him:

"Remember, Jafar: to everyone you meet!"

An agonized groan sounded in the darkness—Jafar was untying his purse.

The water-carrier took the coin and disappeared into the night. Some fifty paces further he again came out to meet them. The usurer paled and began to tremble.

"Maulana," he said plaintively, "this is again the same—"

"To everyone you meet," repeated Khoja Nasreddin relentlessly.

Once more a groan rose in the still air: Jafar was untying his purse.

The same thing happened all along their way. The water-carrier reappeared every fifty paces. He was panting heavily, sweat poured from his face. He could not understand what was happening, but seized the coin, rushed away headlong, doubled and again darted out of the bushes farther up the road.

To save his money the usurer quickened his pace and finally broke into a run. But how could he, lame as he was, outstrip the water-carrier who in his frenzy sped like the wind, hurling himself over the fences? He managed to meet the usurer no less than fifteen times, and at the very last, quite close to the house, he jumped off a roof and barred the way through the gate. On receiving the last coin he dropped exhausted to the ground.

The usurer slipped into the yard followed by Khoja Nasreddin. He threw his empty purse at Khoja Nasreddin's feet shouting furiously:

"Maulana, my cure is too expensive! I have already spent over three thousand tangas on presents, alms and this accursed water-carrier!"

"Calm yourself," replied Khoja Nasreddin. "Within half an hour you shall have your reward. Order a large bonfire to be lit in the middle of the yard."

While the servants were bringing the fuel and lighting the fire Khoja Nasreddin racked his brains trying to think of some way of outwitting the usurer and making him bear the blame for failing to be cured. He thought of several plans only to reject them as unsuitable.

Meanwhile the bonfire had got well under way and the flames rose, fanned by a slight breeze, lighting up the foliage of the vineyard with a crimson glow.

"Undress, Jafar, and walk three times round the fire," said Khoja Nasreddin, He had not hit upon any satisfactory plan yet and was playing for time. He looked preoccupied. The relations watched in silence. The usurer walked round the bonfire like an ape on a chain, swinging his arms which reached nearly to his knees.

Khoja Nasreddin's face cleared. He sighed with relief and threw back his shoulders.

"Give me a blanket," he ordered in resounding tones. "Jafar and all the others, come here."

He placed the relations in a circle and made the usurer sit down on the ground in the centre. Then he addressed them with the following words:

"I am now going to cover Jafar with this blanket and shall recite a prayer. All of you, including Jafar, must close your eyes and repeat the prayer after me. Then, when I remove the blanket Jafar will be found to have been cured. But I must warn you of an extremely important condition: unless it is fulfilled, Jafar cannot be cured. Listen carefully and remember what I tell you."

The relations said nothing, preparing to listen and remember.

"While you are repeating after me the words of the prayer," Khoja Nasreddin went on very loudly and distinctly, "not one of you, and least of all Jafar, must let himself think of a monkey! If any one of you were to think of it, or worse still see it in his imagination— with its tail, its red behind, repulsive face and yellow fangs— then there will be no cure, there cannot be a cure, for the accomplishment of a pious deed is incompatible with thoughts about such an unclean creature as a monkey. Do you understand?"

"We understand," the relations replied.

"Prepare yourself, Jafar, and close your eyes," Khoja Nasreddin said solemnly, covering the usurer with the blanket. "Now you close your eyes," he added, turning to the relations, "and remember the conditions: don't think of the monkey."

Then he chanted the first words of the prayer:

"Wise Allah, the Omniscient, by virtue of the sacred signs of *Alif, Lam, Mim* and *Ra* grant recovery to thy unworthy servant Jafar. . . ."

"Wise Allah, the Omniscient," intoned the discordant chorus of the relations. At this point Khoja Nasreddin noticed a certain confusion and anxiety appear on one of the faces; another relation began to cough, a third stumbled over the words, a fourth shook his head as though trying to drive away some vision. A moment later Jafar himself moved restlessly under the blanket. A monkey, repellent and unutterably disgusting, with a long tail and yellow fangs obtruded upon his mental vision and taunted him, showing at one moment its tongue and another, its round red bottom, parts of the body which are the most indecent for the contemplation of a Muslim.

Khoja Nasreddin continued to recite the prayer in a loud voice. Suddenly he broke off as though listening to something. The relations also fell silent and some of them drew back. Jafar gnashed his teeth under the blanket, for his particular monkey was beginning to indulge in decidedly improper tricks.

"How!" Khoja Nasreddin shouted in a thunderous voice. "Miscreants! Blasphemers! How dare you violate my interdiction! How dare you recite the prayer while thinking of what I expressly forbade you to think of?" He tore off the blanket and turned upon the usurer: "Why did you ask for my help? Now I see you never intended to be cured! You wanted to humiliate me. You were working for my enemies! Take care, Jafar! Tomorrow the Emir will know the whole story. I shall tell him how you recited that prayer while deliberately and with blasphemous intent you thought of a monkey! Beware, Jafar! All of you beware! You will not escape lightly. Surely you know the punishment for blasphemy. . . ."

Since the punishment for blasphemy was always very severe, the relations were numbed, they were terrified. The usurer mumbled incoherently in an attempt to justify himself. Khoja Nasreddin did not stay to listen. He turned on his heel and strode away, banging the gate. Soon the moon rose. The town was bathed in a mellow light. Long into the night there was shouting and quarrelling in the usurer's house. Everybody was arguing heatedly, trying to discover who was the first to think of a monkey.

5

HAVING thus fooled the usurer Khoja Nasreddin started on his way back to the palace.

Bukhara was preparing for sleep after the day's labours. The alleys were cool and dark, and the water sang loudly under the bridges. There was a smell of damp earth and every now and then Khoja Nasreddin's feet slipped in the mud, where some particularly zealous street-waterer had generously sprinkled water on the road so that no gust of the night wind should raise the dust and thus disturb the slumbers of the weary people who had lain down to rest in the courtyards and on the roofs. The gardens were wrapped in darkness and spilled their cool fragrance over the walls. Distant stars winked at Khoja Nasreddin and promised him success.

"Yes!" he grinned to himself. "The world isn't such a bad place after all! At least it isn't for the fellow who has a head and not an empty pot on his shoulders."

On his way he turned into the market-place and saw the bright hospitable lights in the tea-house of his friend Ali. The owner opened the door to him. They embraced and went into a dark room. From the other side of the thin partition came the sound of voices, laughter and the chink of crockery. Ali fastened the door and lit a smoky oil-lamp.

"Everything is ready," he reported in a whisper. "I shall wait for Guljan in the tea-house. The blacksmith Yusuf has prepared a safe hiding-place for her. Your ass is kept saddled day and night. He is well, enjoys a good appetite and has grown very fat."

"Thank you, Ali. I don't know that I shall be ever able to repay you."

"Oh, yes," said Ali. "You're always able to do what you want, Khoja Nasreddin. So don't let us think about gratitude any more. Would you like some tea?"

He went out and came back a moment later bringing the teapot.

They sat down to a whispered conference. Ali produced a man's khalat intended for Guljan and a large white turban which would cover her plaits.

Everything was settled, down to the last detail. Khoja Nasreddin was on the point of leaving when suddenly he heard a familiar voice coming from the other side of the partition. Very slightly he opened the door leading into the tea-house and cocked his ears. The voice belonged to the pock-marked spy. Khoja Nasreddin opened the door wider and looked in.

The pock-marked spy, clad in a rich khalat, turban and false beard, sat surrounded by some men and was holding forth importantly:

"The man who has been passing himself off as Khoja Nasreddin is an impostor. I am the real Khoja Nasreddin! But I have long ago repented of my errors for I realized how evil and impious they were. So now I, the genuine Khoja Nasreddin, advise you to follow my example, and say with me that our great, sun-like Emir is truly Allah's vice-regent on this earth, sufficient proof of which are his unequalled wisdom, piety and clemency. I, the real, the genuine Khoja Nasreddin, say this to you."

"Oho!" said Khoja Nasreddin under his breath, nudging Ali with his elbow. "So this is what they are up to now that they think I have left the town? I shall have to remind them of myself. Ali, I am going to leave my beard, my brocaded khalat and turban in this room. Lend me some old clothes."

Ali handed him a dirty, ragged and flea-infested khalat which had long outworn its service.

"Do you breed fleas?" asked Khoja Nasreddin pulling on the garment. "You must be planning to open a flea-butcher's business, but they will devour you before that, my friend."

Then he went out into the street. The owner of the tea-house returned to his customers, where he impatiently awaited further developments. He did not have long to wait. Khoja Nasreddin appeared coming out of an alley. He walked as wearily as a man who has travelled all day. He climbed the steps leading into the tea-house, seated himself in an ill-lit-corner and asked for tea. Nobody paid the slightest attention to him; all kinds of men travelled along the roads of Bukhara. The pockmarked spy was still holding forth:

"My errors were countless, but now I, Khoja Nasreddin, have repented and have sworn to be ever pious, to carry out all the prescriptions of Islam and to obey the Emir, his viziers, governors and guards. Since I have done this I have acquired peace of mind and happiness, and my worldly goods have multiplied. Formerly I used to be a despised vagabond, whereas now I live in a manner befitting every good Muslim."

A driver with a whip thrust into his belt respectfully offered him a glass of tea.

"I have come to Bukhara from Khokand, O incomparable Khoja Nasreddin. I had heard much of your wisdom but never thought that one day I should meet you, even talk to you. Now I shall tell everyone about my having met you and I shall repeat what you have been telling us."

"That is good," and the pock-marked spy nodded approvingly. "Tell everyone that Khoja Nasreddin has reformed, renounced his errors and has become a pious Muslim and loyal slave of the great Emir. Spread the good news to all you meet."

"I have a question to ask you, O incomparable Khoja Nasreddin," resumed the driver. "I am a pious Muslim and do not wish to break the law even out of ignorance. What I would like to know is what I should do if I happened to be bathing and suddenly heard the muezzin's call to prayer. In what direction should I turn?"

The pock-marked spy smiled condescendingly:

"Of course in the direction of Mecca—"

Out of the dark corner a voice made itself heard:

"In the direction of your clothes. That is the safest way to avoid having to go home naked."

In spite of the respect inspired by the pock-marked spy the company bent their heads to hide their smiles.

The spy looked intently towards Khoja Nasreddin but did not recognize him in the shadows.

"Who is that croaking in the corner?" he inquired haughtily. "Hey you, you beggar, are you trying to match your wits against Khoja Nasreddin's?"

"I am too small a man for that," replied Khoja Nasreddin applying himself to his tea-drinking.

The next to speak was a peasant who asked:

"Tell me, O pious Khoja Nasreddin, when taking part in a funeral procession, what is the best place recommended by Islam—in front or behind the bier?"

The spy raised a finger impressively preparing to give answer, but the voice from the corner forestalled him:

"It does not matter in the least whether you are before or behind the bier so long as you are not in it."

The owner of the tea-house, who was easily moved to gaiety, held on to his paunch with both hands and squatted down laughing uproariously. Nor could the others resist laughing. The man in the corner had a ready tongue and seemed able to hold his own even against Khoja Nasreddin.

The spy, whose anger was mounting, slowly turned his head.

"Hey you, what's your name? I observe that your tongue is running away with you. Take care that you do not have to part with it altogether! I could easily ' crush him with one witty word," he added, turning to his audience, "but at present we are holding pious and salutary converse where wit is out of place. All in good time, and for the moment I shall make no reply to the beggar. As I was saying, I, Khoja Nasreddin, call upon you, O Muslims, to follow my example—respect the mullahs, obey the authorities and prosperity will visit your homes. But above all do not listen to suspicious vagrants who falsely claim to be Khoja Nasreddin, like the one who a short while ago caused all this disturbance and disappeared without a trace on learning that the genuine Khoja Nasreddin had arrived. Catch and hold all such impostors and hand them over to the Emir's guard."

"Quite right!" cried Khoja Nasreddin stepping out of the shadows into the light.

All present immediately recognized him and were dumbfounded by the suddenness of it. The spy paled. Khoja Nasreddin came close up to him, while Ali unobtrusively placed himself behind him ready to pounce upon the spy.

"So you are the real, the genuine Khoja Nasreddin?"

The spy looked over his shoulder in confusion, his cheeks quivered, his eyes darted about. He found enough strength to answer:

"Yes, I am the true, the genuine Khoja Nasreddin. All the others are impostors, and so are you."

"Muslims, what are you waiting for?" yelled Khoja Nasreddin. "He has admitted it himself! Seize him, hold him! Have you not heard the Emir's order and don't you know what to do with Khoja Nasreddin? Seize him, or else you will have to answer for shielding him!"

He tore off the spy's false beard.

All the men in the tea-house recognized the hated pock-marked face with its flat nose and shifty eyes.

"He has admitted it himself!" cried Khoja Nasreddin winking to the right. "Seize Khoja Nasreddin!" And he winked to the left.

Ali, the tea-house owner, was the first to lay hands on the spy. The spy tried to tear himself loose but water-carriers, peasants and artisans joined the fray. For a while all that could be seen was rising and falling fists. Khoja Nasreddin pummeled hardest of all.

"It was a joke!" cried the groaning spy. "O Muslims, it was a joke! I am not Khoja Nasreddin! Let me go!"

"You lie!" Khoja Nasreddin shouted back, working with his fists as a baker works his dough. "You confessed it yourself! We all heard it! O Muslims, we all present here are boundlessly devoted to our Emir and must faithfully carry out his commands. Therefore give this Khoja Nasreddin a good beating, O Muslims! Drag him to the palace and deliver him into the hands of the guard! Beat him to the glory of Allah and of our Emir!"

The crowd dragged the spy towards the palace, beating him soundly on the way with unflagging zeal. Khoja Nasreddin sped him on the way with a well placed kick and returned to the tea-house.

"Ough," he said wiping his perspiring face. "We gave him a fine drubbing this time. He is still getting it by the sound of it."

The noise of excited voices and of the spy's plaintive wails still sounded in the distance. One and all had some debt to settle with him, and on the strength of the Emir's order this was their grand opportunity.

The delighted tea-house owner grinned and stroked his paunch.

"This will be a lesson for him. He will never again set foot in my tea-house."

Khoja Nasreddin changed his clothes in the back room, put on his false beard and once again became Maulana Husain, the Baghdad sage.

When he reached the palace he heard groans issuing from the guard-room. He looked in. The pock-marked spy, swollen, bruised and dishevelled lay on a felt. Arslan-bek stood over him holding a lantern.

"What has happened, worthy Arslan-bek?" Khoja Nasreddin inquired blandly.

"A bad business, Maulana. That rascal Khoja Nasreddin has again returned to the town. He beat up our ablest spy, who on my orders had been giving himself out as Khoja Nasreddin and making virtuous and loyal speeches to counteract the evil influence of the real man. You see the result?"

"Oh! Oh!" groaned the spy raising his bruised and battered face. "Never again shall I mix myself up with this accursed tramp. Next time, I know, he will kill me. I won't be a spy any more. Tomorrow I shall go far away where nobody knows me and take some honest job."

"My friends have certainly been thorough," thought Khoja Nasreddin surveying the spy by the light of the lantern and even feeling a little sorry for him. "Had the palace been two hundred paces farther they would not have brought him in alive. It remains to be seen whether he has learnt his lesson."

At dawn Khoja Nasreddin saw from the window of his tower the pock-marked spy walk out of the palace carrying a small bundle. He was limping and kept feeling with his hands his chest, his shoulders, or his side. Every now and then he squatted down to get his breath. He crossed the market-place that was being slowly lit up by the first cool morning rays, and disappeared in the shadows of the covered rows of stalls.

The darkness of the night had fled before the morning, a morning. pure, transparent, serene—dew washed and threaded with sunlight. Birds twittered, whistled and chirped. Butterflies rose fluttering to bask in the first rays of the sun. A bee settled on the window-sill in front of Khoja Nasreddin and crawled about in search of the honey which it smelt in a jar that stood on the ledge.

The sun was Khoja Nasreddin's old and faithful friend. Now it was rising. Every morning they met, and every morning Khoja Nasreddin experienced the same joy as though he had not seen the sun for a whole year. The sun was rising—a kind, generous deity which shed its favours equally on all, and the whole world unfurled its beauty in welcome, flaming, shining and sparkling in the morning rays; fleecy clouds, glazed bricks on the minarets, wet leaves, water, grass and flowers; even the plain and severe lump of rock, neglected stepchild of nature, acquired a strange beauty to greet the sun, its broken surface glistening and sparkling as though sprinkled with diamond dust.

How could Khoja Nasreddin remain indifferent before the countenance of his beaming friend? A tree shimmered in the bright sunbeams, and Khoja Nasreddin shimmered with it, as though he too were clothed in green foliage. Pigeons on the nearest minaret were cooing and preening their wings, and Khoja Nasreddin felt like preening a wing. A couple of butterflies fluttered before the window, and he wished he could make a third in their delicate play.

Khoja Nasreddin's eyes were bright with happiness, and as he thought of the pock-marked spy, he wished that this particular morning could be the morning of a new clean and decent life for him. But no sooner had he thought this than he realized sadly that too much evil had accumulated in the soul of this man for him to throw it off, and that he would be back at his old tricks as soon as he had fully recovered.

Subsequent events proved that Khoja Nasreddin was not mistaken in his forecast. He knew men too well to make mistakes about them, though he would have been happy to be mistaken and would have welcomed the spiritual rebirth of the spy. However, what is rotten can never again become fresh and blossoming; stench cannot turn into fragrance. Khoja Nasreddin sighed regretfully.

His cherished dream was of a world where men would live like brothers, knowing neither greed, nor envy, nor perfidy, nor anger, but helping each other in time of need and sharing the joy of each as a common joy. Yet as he dreamt of such a happy world he realized bitterly that men lived as they should not, oppressing and enslaving each other and staining their souls with every kind of evil. How long would it take mankind to realize at last the laws of a clean and honest existence?

That some day men would realize these laws Khoja Nasreddin never doubted. He firmly believed that there were more good men than bad in this world; Jafar the Usurer and the pock-marked spy with their rotten souls were but hideous exceptions. He firmly believed that nature had endowed man with good alone, and that all the evil in him was a scum brought from outside into his soul by an unfair and wrongly ordered system of life. He firmly believed that the time would come when men would begin to reshape and cleanse their lives, cleansing their own souls from all evil by this noble labour.

That this was the trend of Khoja Nasreddin's thoughts is proved by the many tales about him which bear the stamp of the temper of his soul. Although there have been many attempts to blacken his memory—out of low envy or sheer malice—they have never succeeded because lies can never triumph over truth. Khoja Nasreddin's memory will always remain noble and pure, like a diamond retaining forever its clear sparkle in spite of all. To this day travellers in Turkey who stop before the modest tomb in Ak-Shehir have a good word for the memory of Khoja Nasreddin, the gay wanderer from Bukhara. In the words of the poet they say:

"He gave his heart to the earth, though he circled the world like the wind—the wind which after his death carried all over the world the fragrance from roses that blossomed in his heart. Beautiful is a life spent in seeing the entire beauty of the world. Beautiful is that life which on departing leaves behind the pure temper of its soul." It is true that some say there is no body under the tombstone of Ak-Shehir and that Khoja Nasreddin erected it on purpose to start the rumour of his death and then' resumed his wanderings. Is this true or is it not? Let us not engage in idle speculation. All we know is that anything could be expected from Khoja Nasreddin.

6

THE early morning hours fled and were soon followed by a sultry and breathless noon.

Everything was ready for the escape. Khoja Nasreddin went up to his prisoner.

"The term of your captivity has come to an end, O most wise Maulana Husain. Tonight I shall leave the palace. I shall leave your door unlocked on one condition; you are not to leave this place for another two days. If you were to leave sooner, you might find me still in the palace and then I should be obliged to accuse you of escaping and hand you over to the executioner. Farewell, Maulana Husain, wise man of Baghdad. Do not think too unkindly of me. I entrust you with the task of divulging the truth to the Emir and of telling him my name. Listen carefully: my name is Khoja Nasreddin."

"What!" exclaimed the old man recoiling. He could not utter a single word. He was dumbfounded by the very sound of the name.

The door creaked as it closed. The echo of Khoja Nasreddin's footsteps died away on the stairs. The old man cautiously approached the door and tried it: it was not locked. He peeped out—there was nobody in sight. He hurriedly slammed the door and bolted it.

"No," he muttered. "I prefer to stay here a whole week rather than have anything more to do with Khoja Nasreddin."

At nightfall, when the first stars gleamed in the greenish sky Khoja Nasreddin, carrying an earthen jug, approached the guards posted at the doors of the Emir's harem. The guards had not seen him coming and carried on their conversation.

"There, another star has fallen," said the fat and lazy consumer of raw eggs. "If, as you say, they fall on the earth, why do people never find them?"

"They probably fall into the sea," the second guard replied.

"Hey you, valiant warriors," interrupted Khoja Nasreddin. "Call the Chief Eunuch. I have brought the medicine for the sick concubine."

The Chief Eunuch appeared, reverently held out both hands for the little jug which contained nothing but chalk diluted in plain water, listened to the detailed instructions about how the drug was to be taken and then went off,

"O most wise Maulana Husain," said the fat guard in a wheedling voice. "You know everything in the world. Your learning is unlimited. Tell us, where do the stars fall from the sky and why do people never find them?"

Khoja Nasreddin could not deny himself a joke.

"Don't you know?" he said with the utmost gravity. "When the stars fall they break up into small silver coins which the beggars pick up. I have known men grow rich in this way."

The guards exchanged glances. Their faces expressed the greatest amazement.

Khoja Nasreddin went his way grinning at their stupidity. He had no inkling how useful his joke was going to prove.

He remained in his tower till midnight. At last all was quiet in the town and in the palace. There was no time to be lost. Summer nights fly on swift wings. Khoja Nasreddin went down and made his way stealthily towards the Emir's harem.

"The guards must be asleep by now," he thought.

Great was his disappointment when on approaching he heard their low voices.

"If only one star would fall here," the fat lazy guard was saying. "We could pick up the silver and become instantly rich."

"I don't feel certain that stars do break up into silver coins," his companion replied.

"But the sage from Baghdad said so," retorted the first. "Of course his learning is great and it's not likely he is mistaken."

"Curse them!" swore Khoja Nasreddin hiding in the shadows. "Why did I tell them about the stars' Now they will wrangle until the morning. Will the escape be delayed?"

Thousands of stars were shining in clear and serene light over Bukhara. One tiny star suddenly dropped and took its fatal flight slantwise across the sky; another rushed after it leaving a burning trail. It was the middle of summer and the time for falling-stags was approaching.

"If they really broke up into silver coins ..." began the second guard.

Suddenly Khoja Nasreddin had an inspiration. He hastily pulled out his purse which was bulging with silver. There was a long interval when no stars fell. At last one fell. A silver coin tinkled on the flagstones. The guards were at first petrified, then they rose staring at each other.

"Did you hear that?" asked the first in a voice that trembled.

"I did," stammered the second.

Khoja Nasreddin threw another coin. It glinted in the moonlight. The lazy guard fell upon it uttering a short cry.

"Have you f-f-found it?" The second guard could scarcely speak. Excitement had nearly struck him dumb.

"G-g-got it!" stammered the fat one through trembling lips, getting up and exhibiting the coin.

Several more stars suddenly shot down together. Khoja Nasreddin started throwing silver by the handful. The silence of the night was shivered by the thin tinkling of the coins. The guards, lost to all reason, dropped their lances and scrambled around on the ground.

"Here!" came the hoarse stifled shout of one. "Here it is!"

The second one crawled silently, then gurgled as he came upon a whole scatter of coins.

Khoja Nasreddin threw another handful and slipped through the wicket gate unhindered.

The rest was easy. Soft Persian rugs stifled the sound of his footsteps. He remembered all the twists and turns. The eunuchs slept.

Guljan welcomed him with a passionate kiss and clung to him trembling.

"Hurry," he whispered.

No one stopped them. One of the eunuchs moved and groaned in his sleep. Khoja Nasreddin bent over him, but the eunuch was not destined to die yet; he smacked his lips and resumed his snoring. The moonlight struggled feebly through the coloured glass.

At the wicket gate Khoja Nasreddin stopped and took a cautious look. The guards were standing on all fours in the middle of the courtyard craning their necks to look up into the sky as they waited for another star to fall. He hurled another handful of coins which fell beyond some trees. The guards rushed towards the sound with a clatter of boots. In their frenzy they saw nothing around them and lunged ahead like bears, panting loudly and shouting incoherently as they broke through the prickly hedge which plucked at their clothes.

On this particular night all the concubines, let alone one, could have been easily stolen from the harem.

"Hurry! Hurry!" Khoja Nasreddin kept saying.

They ran to the tower and up the stairs. Khoja Nasreddin pulled out a rope from under his bedding. He had prepared this beforehand.

"It is very high—I am frightened," Guljan whispered, but he spoke sharply to her and she controlled herself.

Khoja Nasreddin tied a loop round her and removed from the window the iron grille which he had sawn through. Guljan sat on the sill. The height made her shudder.

"Out you go!" Khoja Nasreddin ordered resolutely, giving her a slight push in the back.

She closed her eyes, slid along the smooth stone and hung in the air. She came to herself on reaching the ground. "Run! Run!" came to her from above. Khoja Nasreddin leaned out of the window waving his arms and pulling at the rope. Guljan hurriedly untied herself and ran across the deserted market place.

She did not know that the whole palace was in an uproar. His unpleasant experience had fired the Chief Eunuch with an untimely zeal and he had looked into the new concubine's room in the middle of the night only to find her bed empty. He rushed to the Emir and woke him up. The Emir summoned Arslan-bek, Arslan-bek roused the palace guard: torches flamed, shields and lances clanged.

The Baghdad sage was sent for. The Emir received him with shrill complaints.

"Maulana Husain! What state of affairs is this that we, the Great Emir, have no peace in our own palace from that rascal Khoja Nasreddin! It is unheard of that a concubine should have been stolen out of the Emir's harem!"

"O Great Emir," Bakhtiyar ventured to say. "Perhaps this was not Khoja Nasreddin's doing?"

"Who else?" the Emir shouted in a shrill voice. "In the morning they report to us that he is back in Bukhara, and in the night our concubine disappears. Who else could it have been but he? Look for him. Treble the number of guards everywhere. He cannot have had time to sneak out of the palace. Arslan-bek, do not forget your head is unsafe on your shoulders!"

The search began. The guard ransacked every nook and cranny in the palace. Torches flared all over the place shedding a flickering glare. Khoja Nasreddin exceeded all the other searchers in zeal. He lifted up carpets, probed the marble basins with a stick, shouted and bustled about, inspecting kettles and jugs, and even mouse-holes.

Back in the Emir's bed-chamber he reported:

"Great Sovereign, Khoja Nasreddin must have left the palace."

"Maulana Husain!" the Emir replied wrathfully. "We are astonished at your frivolity. Supposing he has found a hiding-place? Why, he may even penetrate into our bedchamber! Call the guard! Here! Guard!" he shouted, terrified by his own imagination.

Outside a gun boomed. It was intended to intimidate the elusive Khoja Nasreddin. The Emir huddled in a corner and kept on shouting:

"Call the guard! Call the guard!"

His fears were allayed only after Arslan-bek had posted thirty guards at the doors of the bedchamber and ten guards under each of the windows. Then he crept out of his corner and asked plaintively:

"Tell me, Maulana, do you think the rascal is hidden somewhere in our bedchamber?"

"The doors and windows are guarded," Khoja Nasreddin replied. "There are only the two of us in the room. Where could Khoja Nasreddin be?"

"He must not be allowed to get away. He cannot abduct our concubine!" shouted the Emir whose fear was now giving place to rage. His fingers worked jerkily as though he were feeling for Khoja Nasreddin's throat. "O Maulana Husain," he went on. "Our wrath and indignation are unbounded! We have not even visited her, not once. This thought wrings our heart. It is all the fault of your stupid stars, Maulana. If we could we would at once cut off all the stars' heads for this affront! We have given our orders to Arslan-bek. You, Maulana, must do your best to catch the rascal! Remember your appointment to the dignity of Chief Eunuch depends on the success of this business. Tomorrow you shall leave the palace and not return without Khoja Nasreddin."

Khoja Nasreddin made deep obeisance, screwing up his roguish eyes.

7

DURING the remainder of the night Khoja Nasreddin unfolded to the Emir his plans for the capture of Khoja Nasreddin. These plans were exceedingly cunning and the Emir was well pleased.

In the morning, supplied with a purse of gold for expenses, Khoja Nasreddin mounted the steps leading to his tower for the last time. He put away the money in a leather belt and looked around him. He sighed, for he felt suddenly sorry to leave. Many a lonely sleepless night he had spent here and many had been his thoughts. Something of his soul would remain forever behind these grim walls.

He slammed the door and ran lightly down the stairs —towards freedom. Once more the whole world was open to him. Roads, mountain passes and tracks beckoned him to distant travel. Green woods promised him the shelter of their shade on a soft leafy carpet. Rivers waited to quench his thirst with cool water. Birds were ready to welcome him with their best songs. The gay vagabond Khoja Nasreddin had been too long shut up in a golden cage, and the world was missing him.

As he reached the gate he had a shock which smote him to the heart. He stopped. The blood drained from his face. He pressed close to the wall.

A long line of his friends surrounded by numerous guards filed in through the open gates. Their hands were bound and their heads drooped. Here came the old potter Niyaz, the tea-house owner Ali, the blacksmith Yusuf and many others. All those whom he had ever met, with whom he had talked, from whom he had accepted a drink of water or taken a handful of hay for his ass—all were there. Arslan-bek brought up the rear of this sorrowful procession.

By the time Khoja Nasreddin had recovered, the gates were shut and the courtyard was empty. The prisoners had been taken to the dungeons. Khoja Nasreddin hurried away in search of Arslan-bek.

"What has happened, worthy Arslan-bek? Where do these people come from? What crime have they committed?"

"These men are harbourers and accomplices of Khoja Nasreddin," Arslan-bek replied triumphantly. "My spies have tracked them down and today they will be publicly put to a cruel death unless they denounce Khoja Nasreddin. But why are you so pale, Maulana? You seem upset?"

"Pale?" exclaimed Khoja Nasreddin. "I should think so! It means the reward will go to you and not to me."

Khoja Nasreddin was obliged to remain in the palace. He could not do otherwise when innocent men were threatened with death.

At noon troops took up their position in the marketplace, forming a circle three deep round the dais. The crowd had been informed by the criers of the coming executions and waited in silence. The brazen sky shed a scorching heat.

The palace gates opened and out came, in the accustomed order, first the running heralds, then the guards followed by the musicians, the elephants and the courtiers. Finally the Emir's litter appeared advancing slowly. The crowd prostrated itself. The litter was brought up on to the dais.

The Emir seated himself on the throne. The culprits were led out of the gate, greeted by the low rumbling mutter of the crowd. Relatives and friends of the condemned men stood in the front rows to have a better view.

The executioners busied themselves preparing axes, pales and ropes. Theirs was going to be a full day, for one after another sixty men would have to be put to death.

Old Niyaz was the first in this fatal procession. The executioners gripped him by the arms. To his right stood the gallows, to his left— the block, and in front of him a sharp pale stuck out of the ground.

The Grand Vizier Bakhtiyar loudly and solemnly announced:

"In the name of Allah the Merciful and Compassionate, the Ruler of Bukhara and the Sun of the Universe, the Emir of Bukhara having weighed in the balance of justice the crimes committed by sixty of his subjects in harbouring the impious disturber of the peace, sower of discord and miscreant Khoja Nasreddin, has ordered the following:

"The potter Niyaz, as chief harbourer in whose house the above-named vagabond Khoja Nasreddin found shelter for a long time, is to be put to death by having his head separated from his body. As for the other criminals, their first punishment will be the sight of the execution of Niyaz so that they may tremble in the expectation of a still more terrible fate. The form of execution for each of them will be announced separately."

So complete was the silence reigning in the place that every word of Bakhtiyar's carried to the last rows of the crowd.

"And let it be known to all," he proceeded raising his voice, "that henceforth the same treatment will be meted out to anyone giving shelter to Khoja Nasreddin and not one will escape the hands of the executioner. If, however, any one of the condemned men will disclose the whereabouts of this impious blackguard, not only will he obtain his reprieve together with the Emir's reward and a heavenly blessing, but he will also gain pardon for all the others. Potter Niyaz, will you redeem yourself and the others by confessing to the whereabouts of Khoja Nasreddin?"

Niyaz remained silent for a long time without raising his bowed head. Bakhtiyar repeated his question. Niyaz replied:

"No, I cannot tell where he is."

The executioners dragged the old man towards the block. Someone in the crowd cried out. The old man knelt down, stretched out his neck and laid his grey head on the block.

At this moment Khoja Nasreddin elbowed his way through the group of courtiers and stepped forward to face the Emir.

"O gracious Lord!" he said loudly so that the crowd should hear. "Order the execution to be stayed. I shall capture Khoja Nasreddin here and now."

The Emir stared at him in amazement. The crowd stirred. The executioner lowered his axe to his feet in obedience to the Emir's sign.

"O Sovereign!" said Khoja Nasreddin in a loud voice. "Would it be just to execute these insignificant harbourers when the chief harbourer remains unpunished, he in whose house Khoja Nasreddin has been living lately and lives even now, who has fed him, rewarded him and given him every care?"

"You are right," the Emir said ponderously. "If there is such a harbourer, in justice he should be beheaded first. But show me that man, Maulana Husain."

A low murmur ran through the crowd. Those in front repeated the Emir's words to those behind them.

"But if the Great Emir does not wish to execute this chief harbourer, if the Great Emir allows him to live, would it be just in that case to execute the petty harbourers?" Khoja Nasreddin asked.

The Emir, more puzzled than ever, replied:

"If we do not desire to execute the chief harbourer, then of course we shall set the others free. But we fail to understand this, Maulana; what reason can force us to abstain from executing the chief harbourer? Where is he? Show him to us and we will immediately separate his head from his body."

Khoja Nasreddin turned to the crowd:

"You have heard the Emir's words. The ruler of Bukhara has said that if he abstains from executing the chief harbourer whom I shall name immediately, then all the petty harbourers, who are now standing at the execution-block, are to be freed and allowed to return to their families. Have I spoken the truth, O Sovereign?"

"You have spoken the truth, Maulana Husain," the Emir confirmed. "We give our word and so it shall be. But be quick and show us the chief harbourer."

"You hear?" Khoja Nasreddin asked of the crowd. "The Emir gives his word."

He sighed deeply. He felt that thousands of eyes were upon him.

"The chief harbourer . . ."

He faltered and looked around him. Many noticed the distress and mortal anguish in his face. He was taking farewell of his beloved world, the people and the sun.

"Hurry!" cried the Emir impatiently. "Say it quickly, Maulana!"

Khoja Nasreddin said in resonant tones:

"The chief harbourer. . . . 'Tis you, O Emir!"

And with these words he tore off his turban and false beard.

The crowd gasped, swayed and became very still. The Emir's eyes bulged, his lips moved but made no sound. The courtiers stood as though turned to stone.

The silence was brief.

"Khoja Nasreddin! Khoja Nasreddin!" shouted the crowd.

"Khoja Nasreddin!" whispered the courtiers.

"Khoja Nasreddin!" exclaimed Arslan-bek.

At last the monarch himself recovered enough to mumble indistinctly:

"Khoja Nasreddin."

"Yes, in person! Well, Emir, order them to cut off your head for being the chief harbourer! I lived in your palace. I shared your meals, and received rewards from you. I was your chief and closest adviser in all affairs. You are the harbourer, Emir—order them to cut off your head!"

Khoja Nasreddin was seized. His hands were tied. He did not resist. He shouted:

"The Emir promised to free the condemned men! You heard the Emir give his word!"

The crowd murmured and surged forward. The triple chain of

guards had all it could do to hold it back. Louder and louder rose the cries:

"Free the condemned men!"

"The Emir gave his word!"

"Free! . . ."

The noise mounted and grew. The lines of guards began to give way.

Bakhtiyar bent down to the Emir:

"O gracious Lord, they must be freed or the people will revolt."

The Emir nodded.

"The Emir keeps his word!" shouted Bakhtiyar.

The guards opened their ranks. The condemned men immediately disappeared in the crowd.

Khoja Nasreddin was led away to the palace. Many in the crowd wept and called after him:

"Farewell, Khoja Nasreddin! Farewell, our beloved, noble-hearted Khoja Nasreddin! You will live for ever in our hearts!"

He walked holding his head high. His expression was fearless. At the gate he turned round. The crowd gave a mighty roar.

The Emir clambered hastily into his litter. The royal procession started on its way back.

8

THE divan assembled to judge Khoja Nasreddin.

When he entered, hands tied and closely guarded, the courtiers lowered their eyes. They were ashamed to look at one another. The sages frowned and stroked their beards. The Emir turned away, sighing and clearing his throat.

But Khoja Nasreddin's gaze was clear and direct. If his hands had not been tied behind his back, it would have seemed that the culprit was not he, but all these men seated before him.

The genuine Maulana Husain, the Baghdad sage, finally freed from captivity, made his appearance at the assembly together with the other courtiers. Khoja Nasreddin gave him a friendly wink, at which the Baghdad sage started up on his cushions and hissed angrily.

The judgment did not take long. Khoja Nasreddin was condemned to death. It remained only to choose what kind of death.

"O great Sovereign," said Arslan-bek. "In my opinion this criminal should be impaled so as to end his life in the cruellest pain."

Khoja Nasreddin did not turn a hair. He stood smiling happily and lifted up his face towards a sunbeam which shone into the hall through an open top window.

"No!" said the Emir firmly. "The Turkish Sultan has already tried to impale this blasphemer. He evidently knows some way of surviving that kind of execution without harm to himself, otherwise he would never have escaped the Sultan's hands alive."

Bakhtiyar advised that he should be beheaded.

"True, it is one of the easiest deaths," he added, "but it is the surest."

"No!" said the Emir. "The Caliph of Baghdad did behead him, yet he is still alive."

One after another the courtiers rose and suggested either hanging Khoja Nasreddin or skinning him alive. The Emir rejected all these suggestions. He had been watching Khoja Nasreddin. He saw no trace of fear in that face and he took this to be proof of the inadequacy of the suggestions.

The courtiers fell into an embarrassed silence. The Emir was beginning to show signs of impatient anger.

Then the Baghdad sage rose. As this was the first time he was going to speak in the Emir's presence, he had carefully considered his advice so as to exhibit his superior wisdom.

"O great Sovereign of the Universe! If until now this criminal has managed to escape-unharmed every kind of punishment, does it not prove that he is helped by evil forces, by the spirit of darkness whom it is not proper to name here, in the Emir's presence?"

Saying so the sage blew on his shoulders, all those present following suit, except Khoja Nasreddin.

"Having considered and weighed all the information concerning this criminal," resumed the sage, "our great Emir has rejected every suggested way of putting him to death fearing that the forces of evil would once again aid the culprit to evade just retribution. But there exists one more method of execution to which the said criminal Khoja Nasreddin has not yet been subjected, and that is —drowning!"

The Baghdad sage threw back his head and triumphantly surveyed the assembly.

Khoja Nasreddin started slightly. The Emir detected his movement: "Aha! So that was his secret!"

Meanwhile Khoja Nasreddin was thinking:

"It is a good sign that they have started to talk about the forces of evil. It means all hope is not yet lost."

"I know from what I have heard and read," went on the sage, "that there is in Bukhara a holy pond called the pond of Shaikh Turakhan. Naturally the forces of evil dare not approach this pond. From this it follows, O Sovereign, that this criminal should be immersed for a long period of time in the holy waters, after which he will die."

"That is wise advice worthy of a reward!" exclaimed the Emir.

Khoja Nasreddin said reproachfully, addressing himself to the sage:

"O Maulana Husain, did I treat you thus when you were in my power? After this how can one rely on the gratitude of men!"

It was decided that Khoja Nasreddin was to be publicly drowned in the sacred pond of Shaikh Turakhan after sunset. To prevent his escaping on the way he was to be taken thither in a leather sack in which he would be drowned.

. . . The whole day long axes rang by the pond where carpenters were erecting a platform. They knew why the Emir wanted a platform there, but what could they do when a guard stood over each one of them? They worked in silence. Their faces were gloomy and sullen.

When the work was finished, they refused the scanty pay and went away with downcast eyes.

The platform and the bank on which it stood were covered with carpets. The opposite bank was left to the populace.

The spies reported that the town was in a turmoil. As a precaution Arslan-bek posted soldiers and guns round the pond. Fearing that the people might set Khoja Nasreddin free on the way, Arslan-bek had four sacks filled with rags. These false sacks he intended to send openly to the pond along the frequented streets, while the sack containing Khoja Nasreddin was to be taken by lonely alleys. He elaborated his cunning plan by appointing eight guards to accompany each false sack and only three to go with the real one.

"I shall send you a messenger from the pond," Arslan-bek said to the guards. "You must bring the false sacks all at once, one after the other, and the fifth with the criminal in it a little later without attracting attention, when the crowds at the gates are following the false sacks. Do you understand? Remember you answer with your lives."

In the evening a roll of drums in the market-place announced the end of the bazaar. Crowds of people streamed from all sides towards the pond. Soon the Emir arrived with his suite. Torches were lit on the platform and round it. The flames hissed and fluttered in the wind throwing crimson streaks on to the rippling water. The opposite bank was veiled in darkness. The crowd was invisible from the lighted platform but its stirring and breathing could be heard, adding vague and uneasy noises to the gusts of the night wind.

Bakhtiyar read out in a loud voice the Emir's order for Khoja Nasreddin's execution. At this moment the wind fell and the ensuing silence was so complete that shivers ran down the Serene Emir's spine. The wind sighed, and the crowd with its thousands of breasts sighed too.

"Arslan-bek," said the Emir shakily, "why this delay?"

"I have already sent the messenger, O Sovereign."

Suddenly shouts rose out of the darkness and a clash of weapons: fighting had broken out somewhere. The Emir started in alarm. A moment later eight guards entered empty-handed into the circle of light in front of the platform.

"Where is the criminal?" shouted the Emir. "They have got him away from the guards! He has escaped! You have allowed this to happen, Arslan-bek!"

"O Sovereign!" replied Arslan-bek. "Your unworthy slave foresaw it all. The sack was filled with old rags." More sounds of fighting came from the opposite bank. Arslan-bek hastened to reassure the Emir:

"Let them have the sack, O Master. This one is also full of old rags."

The first sack was rescued from the guards by the tea-house owner Ali and his friends, the second by the blacksmiths headed by Yusuf. Then the potters took the third sack. The fourth was allowed to pass unmolested. The guards lifted the sack over the torch-lit water in full sight of the crowd and emptied it. Rags fell out.

The perplexed and baffled crowd remained motionless. This was what Arslan-bek had planned, for he knew that perplexity leads to inaction.

The time had come to deal with the fifth sack. Meanwhile the guards who were bringing it had been delayed on the way and had not made their appearance.

9

WHEN the guards brought him out of the dungeon Khoja Nasreddin said:

"So you are going to carry me on your backs? Pity my ass is not here, he would have died of laughter."

"Hold your tongue! You will be weeping soon yourself!" retorted the guards viciously. They could not forgive him for having given himself up to the Emir and so cheating them out of the reward.

They stretched out the narrow sack and began to push Khoja Nasreddin into it.

"O servants of the devil!" cried Khoja Nasreddin folded up in three. "Couldn't you find a larger sack?"

"Be quiet!" muttered the guards puffing and perspiring freely. "It won't be for long. Don't spread yourself out so, you son of sin, or we'll drive your knees into your belly."

A scuffle ensued which brought the palace servants to the spot. Finally, after a great effort, the guards managed to stuff Khoja Nasreddin into the sack and tie it up with a rope. Inside the sack it was close, dark and smelly. A black fog enveloped Khoja Nasreddin's soul. There seemed to be no hope of escape. He appealed to Fate and to all-powerful Chance:

"O Fate, you who have become as a mother to me, O all-powerful Chance, you who until now have protected your child like a father, where are you? Why don't you hasten to the aid of Khoja Nasreddin? They have tied me up in a vile stinking sack and are taking me to be drowned in a slimy pond! Me, whom the whole world has seen! Me, to whom only the sea could give a fitting grave! Where is justice? Where is truth? No, it can't be true! I don't believe it! Something must happen! A fire, an earthquake, a revolt! O Fate! O almighty Chance!"

Meanwhile, the guards had covered half the distance to the pond and still nothing had happened. They took turns in carrying the sack, replacing each other every two hundred paces. Khoja Nasreddin sadly counted these short stops. They told him the distance covered and how much remained.

He knew that Fate and Chance never come to aid a man who whines and moans instead of acting. It is the man who presses on who reaches his destination. If his legs weaken and give out, then he must crawl on his hands and knees. Then he will be sure of seeing far in the night the bright flame of camp-fires, and the caravan will be going in the right direction, and a spare camel will be found on which the traveller will reach his destination. Whereas one who sits at the roadside and gives way to despair will arouse no compassion in the heartless stones, however much he weeps or laments. He will die of thirst in the desert, his dead body will become the prey of strong-smelling hyenas and his bones will be buried under the hot sands. How many men have died before their time simply because their will to live was not sufficiently strong! Khoja Nasreddin thought such a death shameful for a true man.

"No!" he said to himself, and clenched his teeth repeating: "No, I shall not die today! I don't intend to die!"

But what could he do, folded in three and stuffed into a narrow sack where he had no room to move? His knees and elbows were pressed to his body. Only his tongue was free.

"O valiant warriors," he said from the depths of the sack. "Stop for a moment. I wish to recite a prayer before I die so that Allah may receive my soul in his serene abode."

The guards lowered the sack to the ground.

"Go on, recite your prayer, but we aren't going to let you out. Recite your prayer inside the sack."

"Where are we?" inquired Khoja Nasreddin. "I must know, because you will have to turn me towards the nearest mosque."

"We are near the Karshi gates. There are mosques all round and in all directions. Hurry up and say your prayer. We cannot stay long."

"Thank you, O pious warriors," replied Khoja Nasreddin in sorrowful accents.

What did he expect? He himself did not know: "I shall gain a few minutes. Then we shall see. Something may turn up. . . ."

He began to pray aloud, listening at the same time to the talk of the guards.

"How was it we didn't guess at once that the new astrologer was Khoja Nasreddin?" lamented the guards. "If only we had recognized and caught him we could have had a big reward from the Emir."

Their thoughts ran in accustomed channels, for greed was the very essence of their existence.

Khoja Nasreddin was quick to take advantage of this.

"I must try to get them to leave the sack even for a short while . . . I might then be able to break the rope, or perhaps somebody will pass this way and free me."

"Hurry up with your prayer," said one of the guards kicking the sack. "D'you hear me? We can't wait any longer."

"One more minute, valiant warriors! I have one more request to make to Allah. O almighty, most merciful Allah! Grant that the man who finds the ten thousand tangas which I have buried should take one thousand to the mosque and give it to the mullah, charging him to pray for me for a whole year."

At the mention of ten thousand tangas the guards fell silent. Though Khoja Nasreddin could not see out of his sack he could tell exactly what their faces expressed, how they were exchanging glances and nudging each other.

"Take me up now," he said meekly. "I deliver my spirit into the hands of Allah."

The guards hesitated.

"We shall rest a little longer," one of them said insinuatingly. "O Khoja Nasreddin, do not think that we are heartless and evil men. Duty alone compels us to treat you so harshly. If we were able to live with our families without the Emir's salary we wouldn't hesitate to let you out—"

"What are you saying?" whispered another guard in alarm. "If we were to let him out, the Emir would cut off our heads."

"Hold your tongue," hissed the first guard. "All we want is to get hold of the money."

Khoja Nasreddin could not catch their whispering, but he knew what it was about.

"I hold no grudge against you, O warriors," he said with a sanctimonious sigh. "I am too great a sinner to condemn others. If Allah grants me forgiveness in the other world, I promise to pray for you at the foot of his throne. You say that if it were not for the Emir's salary you would let me out of the sack? Think what you are saying! You would be acting contrary to the Emir's wishes, which is a great sin! No! I do not want you to burden your souls with sin on my account. Pick up the sack and carry me to the pond. Let the will of the Emir and the will of Allah be done!"

The guards exchanged perplexed glances, mentally cursing Khoja Nasreddin's sudden and untimely repentance.

The conversation was joined by the third guard who until then had remained silent, working out a cunning scheme.

"It is distressing to see a man repent of his sins and errors only on the point of death," he said at last, winking at his companions. "No, I am not thus. I repented a long time ago and have been leading a pious life ever since. Yet piety unaccompanied by deeds pleasing to Allah is not enough," he went on while the other two pressed their hands to their mouths to stifle their laughter, for they knew him for an incorrigible gambler with dice and a loose liver. "And so I strengthen my piety with a righteous and pious deed. I am building in my native village a large mosque, for which purpose I even deny myself and my family the necessary food."

One of the other guards could no longer contain himself and moved some distance away choking with laughter.

"I save every copper," continued the man, "yet the building of the mosque advances so slowly that it fills my heart with sorrow. A short while ago I sold my cow. I may have to sell my last pair of boots—I am prepared to walk barefoot if that would help to complete what I have undertaken."

Khoja Nasreddin let out a sob inside his sack. The guards exchanged knowing looks. The scheme was working. They nudged their clever companion to hurry him up.

"If only I could find someone who would give eight or ten thousand tangas to help finish the building of this mosque!" he exclaimed. "I would swear to him that for five, or even ten years his name would daily rise wrapped in fragrant clouds of prayer from under the vaults of the mosque towards the throne of Allah!"

The second guard said:

"O my pious comrade! I have not got ten thousand tangas, but will you accept all my savings—five hundred tangas. Do not reject my modest gift, for I would also like to take part in this pious deed."

"And I," added the third, stuttering and quivering with suppressed mirth, "have three hundred tangas. . . ."

"O righteous man! O most pious man!" cried Khoja Nasreddin with tears in his voice. "Could I but press the hem of your garment to my lips! I am a great sinner, but look upon me with favour and do not reject my gift. I have ten thousand tangas. When through impious deceit I became attached to the person of the Emir, I often received from him purses of gold and silver. I saved ten thousand tangas and hid them away, intending to pick them up when making my escape. As I had meant to go by way of the Karshi gate, I buried this money

164

in the Karshi cemetery under one of the old tombstones."

"In the Karshi cemetery!" cried the guards. "Then it is somewhere near here."

"Yes. We are now at the northern end of the cemetery, and if one goes—"

"We are at the eastern end! Where . . . where is your money buried?"

"It is buried at the western end of the cemetery," said Khoja Nasreddin. "But first swear to me, O pious guard, that my name will indeed be mentioned in the mosque daily for ten years."

"I swear!" cried the guard who was writhing with impatience. "I swear to you by Allah and his Prophet! Now say quickly where is your money buried?"

Khoja Nasreddin took his time. "What if they decide to carry me to the pond first, leaving the search for the money till tomorrow?" he thought. "No, this won't happen. They are consumed with greed and impatience; they will be afraid that someone might forestall them; and finally, they don't trust each other. What place shall I choose to keep them digging as long as possible?"

The guards waited hanging over the sack. Khoja Nasreddin could hear them breathing heavily as though they had come running from afar.

"At the western end of the cemetery there are three old tombstones disposed in a triangle," said Khoja Nasreddin. "Under each of these I have buried three thousand, three hundred and thirty-three tangas and one-third."

"Disposed in a triangle," repeated the guards in chorus like good pupils repeating the words of the Koran after their teacher. "Under each three thousand three hundred and thirty-three tangas and one-third. ..."

They agreed that two of them should go in search of the money leaving the third on guard. At this Khoja Nasreddin might have lost heart had he not possessed the faculty of foreseeing human actions. He knew for certain that the third guard would not remain long at his post. He was not mistaken. Left by himself the guard sighed restlessly, coughed and walked up and down the road with a clatter of weapons. These sounds allowed Khoja Nasreddin to guess his thoughts. The guard was consumed with anxiety over his three thousand, three hundred and thirty-three tangas and one-third. Khoja

Nasreddin waited patiently.

"They are taking a long time," said the guard.

"They are probably burying the money in some other place, and tomorrow you will all come together to fetch it," said Khoja Nasreddin.

These words struck home. The guard breathed noisily, then pretended to yawn.

"I would very much like to hear some edifying story before I die," said Khoja Nasreddin out of his sack. "Perhaps you may remember one and tell it to me, O kind guard!"

"No!" the guard replied angrily. "I know no edifying stories. Besides I am tired. I shall go and stretch myself out on the grass."

But he did not realize that on the hard ground the sound of his footsteps would carry loud and far. At first he walked slowly, then Khoja Nasreddin heard a rapid beat—the guard had broken into a run.

The time for action had come. But in vain Khoja Nasreddin rolled and tumbled about—the rope would not break.

"A passer-by!" prayed Khoja Nasreddin. "O Fate, send me a passer-by!"

And Fate sent him a passer-by.

Fate and favourable Chance always come to the aid of him who is full of determination and struggles to the last (we have mentioned this before but truth does not lose by repetition). Khoja Nasreddin was struggling for his life with all his might and main, and Fate could not refuse her aid.

The passer-by walked slowly. He was lame, as Khoja Nasreddin guessed from the sound of his footsteps, and he was elderly, for he was short of breath.

The sack lay in the middle of the road. The passer-by stopped, looked at it for some time and poked it several times with his foot.

"What can be in this sack? Where has it come from?" muttered the passer-by in a grating voice.

Joy! Khoja Nasreddin recognized the voice of Jafar the Usurer. Now he had no doubts that he would be saved. If only the guards would keep away and not return too soon.

He coughed slightly so as not to alarm the usurer.

"Oho, there is a man inside!" cried Jafar backing away.

"Of course there is a man inside," Khoja Nasreddin replied calmly, disguising his voice. "Why should it be so strange?"

"Strange? Why did you get into the sack?"

"That's my business. Go your way and don't bother me with your questions."

Khoja Nasreddin knew the usurer's curiosity was aroused and that he would not go away.

"It is indeed a most extraordinary thing," said the usurer, "to find a man tied up in a sack and on the road. Were you forced to get into the sack?"

"Forced?" sneered Khoja Nasreddin. "Would I pay six hundred tangas to be forced into a sack?"

"Six hundred tangas? Why did you pay such a sum?"

"O passer-by! I shall tell you the whole story if you promise to go your way after hearing me out, and disturb my peace no more. This sack belongs to an Arab who lives here, in Bukhara. It possesses the magic virtue of curing sickness and deformity. Its owner lends it, but only for large sums and not to all and sundry. I was lame, hump-backed and blind in one eye. I intend to get married and the father of my bride, not wishing to afflict her sight with the contemplation of my deformities, took me to this Arab from whom I have received the loan of the sack for four hours after paying him six hundred tangas.

"As the sack exercises its healing virtues only in the neighbourhood of cemeteries, I came here after sunset, to this old Karshi cemetery. My bride's father, who accompanied me, tied up the sack with a rope and withdrew, for the presence of anybody else may prevent the cure. The Arab who owns the sack warned me that as soon as I remained alone three jinns would appear with great noise and a clanging of their brass wings. They would ask me in human speech in what part of the cemetery were buried ten thousand tangas, in answer to which I was to recite the magic incantation: 'Who has a copper shield has a copper forehead. The owl sits in the place of the falcon. O jinns, you are seeking what you have not hidden, therefore kiss my ass's tail.'

"Everything happened as he had said. The jinns came and asked me where ten thousand tangas were buried; on hearing my answer they became incensed and beat me, while I, bearing in mind the Arab's instructions kept crying: 'Who has a copper shield has a copper forehead. Kiss my ass's tail'. Then the jinns picked up the sack and carried it off. . . . I remember no more. Two hours later I came to my senses in the same place and found myself completely cured. My hump has disappeared, my leg is straight, and my eye can see, of which I have assured myself by looking through a hole which someone before me had made in the sack. Now I am remaining here only because having paid the money it would be a pity to waste it. Of course I have made a mistake. I should have made an agreement with some other man afflicted with the same deformities. Then we could have hired the sack by halves, remaining in it two hours each, and our cure would have cost us only three hundred tangas apiece. But it cannot be helped. Let my money be wasted, the main point is that after all I am cured.

"Now, passer-by, you know the whole story. Keep your word and withdraw. I feel weak after my cure and find speech difficult. Nine people before you have been asking me the same questions and I am weary of repeating the same things over and over again."

The usurer had listened with the deepest attention, interrupting Khoja Nasreddin's recital by exclamations expressing his wonder.

"Listen, O sitter in the sack," said the usurer. "We can both draw some advantage from our meeting. You are sorry that you did not have the foresight to share the hire of the sack with some man similarly afflicted, but it is not too late yet. I happen to be just the man you need. I am hunchbacked, lame in the right foot and blind in one eye. I will gladly give you three hundred tangas to be able to stay in the sack for the remaining two hours."

"Surely you must be mocking me!" replied Khoja Nasreddin. "Such a marvellous coincidence is impossible ! If you are telling me the truth, thank Allah for sending you this happy opportunity. I consent, O passerby, but I warn you that I paid in advance and you too must pay in advance. I give no credit."

"I shall pay in advance," said the usurer untying the sack. "But let us lose no time, for the minutes are passing and now they belong to me."

Khoja Nasreddin covered up his face with his sleeve while he climbed out of the sack. But the usurer did not even look at him; he was hurriedly counting out the money, so jealous was he of the passing minutes. With many a groan he crept into the sack and pulled in his head.

Khoja Nasreddin fastened the rope, then went a short distance away and hid in the shade behind a tree. He was only just in time. From the direction of the cemetery sounded the loud swearing of the guards. Through a breach in the wall he saw first their long shadows, and then they appeared, their copper lances flashing in the moonlight.

10

"HEY you, trickster!" shouted the guards kicking the sack, their weapons clanging and rattling as copper wings might very well have done. "We searched all over the cemetery and have found nothing. Tell us, O son of sin, where are the ten thousand tangas?"

The usurer had learnt his lesson well.

"Who has a copper shield has a copper forehead," he replied from inside the sack. "The owl sits in the place of the falcon. O jinns, you seek where you have not hidden. Therefore kiss my ass's tail."

On hearing such words the guards were roused to fury. "You have tricked us, you stinking cur! And now you call us fools! Look, look—the sack is covered with dust. He must have rolled and tumbled on the road hoping to free himself while we were digging in the cemetery till our hands bled. You'll pay dearly for your trick, O infamous progeny of the fox!"

They belaboured the sack with their fists and in turn trampled it with their iron-bound boots. Meanwhile the usurer, firmly adhering to Khoja Nasreddin's instructions, kept shouting: "Who has a copper shield has a copper forehead!" which drove the guards to still greater fury. They would have liked to finish off the culprit in their own way, but as to their regret they could not, they picked up the sack and set off with it towards the sacred

Khoja Nasreddin left his shelter, washed his face in the irrigation ditch and threw off his khalat, baring his broad chest to the night wind. He felt unutterably light and happy since the dark breath of death had rushed past without scorching him. He found a sheltered spot, spread out his khalat and lay down, putting a stone under his head. He was weary from the confinement of the tight and stuffy sack and needed rest. The wind rustled in the leafy tree-tops. Golden swarms of stars swam in the heavenly ocean. The water gurgled in the ditch. All this was now ten times more precious to Khoja Nasreddin than it had ever been before.

"Yes, there is too much good in the world for me to consent to die even if I were definitely promised a place in Paradise. A man would go mad with boredom up there sitting eternally under the same tree surrounded by the same houris."

So ran his thoughts as he lay under the stars on the warm earth listening keenly to ever flowing, never slumbering life; his heart throbbed in his breast, the owl sent out its night-call from the cemetery, a small creature was making its way stealthily through the bushes—a hedgehog, probably. A spicy fragrance rose from the withering grass; it was alive with mysterious movements, strange rustlings, creepings and crackles.

The world lived and breathed, the wide world equally open to all, extending the same hospitality of its boundless spaces to ant, bird and man, and demanding in return only that they should not misuse this welcome and trust. The host expels with ignominy the guest who at a feast takes advantage of the general gaiety to rob the pockets of the other guests. Such a thief was the infamous usurer who was being expelled from the gay and happy world.

Khoja Nasreddin did not feel in the least sorry for him, for his disappearance would lighten the lot of many thousands of others. What Khoja Nasreddin did regret was that the usurer was not the last and only miscreant on earth. If only one could gather into one sack all the Emirs, dignitaries, mullahs and usurers and drown them together in the sacred pond of Shaikh Turakhan! Then their evil breath would no longer wither the spring blossom on the trees. The clink of their money, their lying sermons and the clash of their swords would no longer drown the twitter of birds. Men would be free to enjoy the beauty of the world and to fulfil their most important duty—to be happy at all times and in all things!

Meanwhile the guards, wishing to make up for the time lost, quickened their pace and finally broke into a run. The usurer shaken and jolted in the sack patiently awaited the end of his extraordinary journey. He heard the clash of arms and the clatter of stones under the guard's feet and wondered why the mighty jinns did not rise into the air instead of running and scraping the earth with their copper wings like young cocks in pursuit of a hen.

At last there sounded in the distance a strange roar like the growl of a mountain torrent which made the usurer think at first that the jinns had brought him into some mountains, perhaps to their retreat Khan-Tengri—the peak of the spirits. But soon he began to distinguish voices and realized that there was a great concourse of people. Judging by the noise there were many thousands here, as in the bazaar—but since when had they started trading at night in

Bukhara?

Suddenly he felt himself being lifted up. Aha, this meant that the jinns had at last decided to rise into the air. How could he have known that the guards were bringing the sack up the steps on to the platform? At the top they let the sack drop. It crashed-on-to the-planks which shook and clattered under its weight. The usurer let out a groan.

"Hey you, jinns!" he broke out. "If you start throwing this sack about like this, you will only maim me instead of curing me!"

He was answered by a savage kick.

"You are going to get your cure fast enough, O son of sin, at the bottom of holy Turakhan's pond!"

The usurer felt a sudden alarm. What had the holy Turakhan's pond to do with this affair? His alarm changed to amazement when close by he heard the voice of his old friend—he could have sworn it was he—Arslan-bek, chief of the palace guard and army. His mind was in a whirl. Where had Arslan-bek suddenly come from? Why was he cursing the jinns for loitering on the way and why did the jinns seem to tremble in fear and servility as they answered him? It was impossible that Arslan-bek was also the chief of the jinns. What should he do? Remain silent or call out to him? As the usurer had received no instructions in this matter he thought it best to keep his own counsel.

Meanwhile the crowd was becoming noisier. One word sounded ever louder and more frequently over the general din. It seemed as though the earth, the air and the wind were charged with this word. It buzzed, roared and thundered, dying away in distant echoes. The usurer held his breath to listen. At last he caught it: "Khoja Nasreddin!" shouted the thousand throats of the crowd. "Khoja Nasreddin! Khoja Nasreddin!"

A sudden silence fell, and in the dead quiet the usurer heard the hissing of the flaming torches, the rustle of the wind and the splashing of the water. Shivers ran down his crooked spine and black terror slowly crept upon him chilling him with its icy breath.

Then another voice made itself heard and the usurer could have sworn that it belonged to the Grand Vizier Bakhtiyar:

"In the name of Allah, the Merciful and Compassionate, by order of the great and sun-like Emir of Bukhara, the criminal defiler of the faith, disturber of the peace and sower of discord Khoja Nasreddin is going to be put to death by means of drowning in a sack."

Hands laid hold of the sack and lifted it up. Now at last the usurer realized his deadly plight.

"Wait! Wait!" he yelled. "What are you going to do to me? Wait! I am not Khoja Nasreddin, I am Jafar the Usurer! Let me go! I am Jafar the Usurer, I am not Khoja Nasreddin! Where are you taking me? I tell you, I am Jafar the Usurer!"

The Emir and his suite silently listened to his wails. Maulana Husain, the Baghdad sage, who was seated nearest to the Emir said ruefully shaking his head:

"The shamelessness of this criminal is immeasurable. Indeed, at one time he called himself Maulana Husain, the sage from Baghdad, and now he tries to make us believe that he is Jafar the Usurer!"

"He must think that there are fools here who would believe him," added Arslan-bek. "Listen how cleverly he disguises his voice."

"Let me go! I am not Khoja Nasreddin, I am Jafar!" wailed the usurer as a couple of guards standing on the edge of the platform swung the sack to and fro in a rhythmic movement. "I am not Khoja Nasreddin! I am . . ."

At this instant Arslan-bek gave the sign and the sack flew out, turning over awkwardly in the air. It landed with a loud splash sending up a shower of spray which glittered in the crimson light of the torches, and then the waters closed heavily over the sinful body and sinful soul of Jafar the Usurer.

A great sigh rose from the crowd and lingered in the night. For a few moments an awe-inspiring silence reigned, when suddenly it was shattered by a wild, heartrending scream. It was the fair Guljan who screamed and struggled in the arms of her old father.

Ali, the tea-house owner, buried his head in his hands. The blacksmith Yusuf shivered as though in a fit of ague.

11

AFTER the execution the Emir left for his palace with his suite.

Fearing that the culprit might be rescued before he was quite dead, Arslan-bek posted guards round the pond with orders to let no one approach it. The pressing crowd wavered, gave way before the guards, then halted in a great black silent mass. Arslan-bek tried to disperse them, but the people moved to another place or hid in the dark, only to return after a while to the same spot.

Great rejoicings began at the palace. The Emir celebrated his victory over his enemy. Gold and silver glittered, kettles boiled, braziers smoked, tambourines throbbed, trumpets roared, drums thundered, rending the air, and so many bonfires lit up the feast that a red glow illumined the palace as though it were on fire.

But the town round the palace was still and bathed in darkness and melancholy quiet.

The Emir distributed gifts with a generous hand. Many were thus favoured on that day. The poets grew hoarse from singing ceaseless praises and their backs ached pleasantly from too frequent stooping to pick up silver and gold coins.

"Call the scribe," ordered the Emir.

The scribe came running and set his reed-pen scratching swiftly.

"From the Great and Splendid and Sun-eclipsing Ruler, Commander and Law-giver of Bukhara, the Emir of Bukhara to the Great, Splendid and Sun-eclipsing Ruler, Commander and Law-giver of Khiva, come roses of greetings and lilies of goodwill. We impart to you, our beloved and royal Brother certain information which may warm your heart in the fire of rapture and deliciously ease your spleen.

"It is that today, on the seventeenth day of the month of Safar, We, the Great Emir of Bukhara, have publicly executed Khoja Nasreddin, the criminal known throughout the world for his impious and ungodly deeds—may the curse of Allah be upon him—by having him drowned in a sack, which drowning took place in Our presence and under Our eyes, for which reason We bear witness to you with Our royal word that the above-mentioned scoundrel, disturber of the peace, defiler of the faith and sower of discord is now no longer among the living and will no longer be able to trouble you, our beloved Brother, with his godless actions."

Similar letters were dictated to the Caliph of Baghdad, the Sultan of Turkey, the Shah of Persia, the Khan of Khokand, the Emir of Afghanistan and many other monarchs of neighbouring and more distant countries. The Grand Vizier Bakhtiyar rolled up the letters, appended seals and handed them to messengers with orders to proceed immediately on their way. That night all eleven gates of Bukhara opened with a loud creaking and screeching of hinges, and along the highways the messengers sped in all directions, scattering the ringing stones and striking sparks from under the hooves of their horses—to Khiva, Tehran, Stambul, Baghdad, Kabul, and many other cities.

. . . In the dead of night, four hours after the execution, Arslan-bek withdrew the guard from round the pond.

"Whoever he may have been, be it the devil himself, he cannot have remained alive after staying four hours under water," said Arslen-bek. "No need to fish him out. Let anyone who wants to do it have his stinking carcase."

As soon as the last guard had disappeared into the night the crowd surged towards the bank shouting noisily. Torches, which had been prepared beforehand and left nearby in the bushes, were lit. The women set up a sorrowful wailing, bemoaning the fate of Khoja Nasreddin.

"We must give him an honest Muslim burial," said old Niyaz. Guljan stood motionless and silent, supporting herself on his shoulder.

The tea-house owner Ali and the blacksmith Yusuf plunged into the water armed with boat-hooks. They prodded about for a long time until at last they caught hold of the sack and dragged it to the bank. When it appeared on the surface—black, shining in the torchlight and entangled with water-weeds—the women wailed still louder, drowning the sounds of revelry which came from the palace.

Dozens of hands took hold of the sack.

"Follow me," said Yusuf, lighting the way with his torch.

The sack was laid on the grass under a spreading tree. The people crowded silently round it. Yusuf produced a knife, carefully slit the sack lengthwise, took a look at the dead man's face and recoiled. He stood as though turned to stone, his eyes bulging, unable to utter a word.

Ali rushed to Yusuf's aid only to be similarly overcome. He squatted down, took a look, yelped and suddenly fell over on his back, his fat paunch turned up to the sky.

"What's the matter?" muttered the crowd. "Let us see! Show us!"

Guljan knelt down weeping, bent over the lifeless body, but as someone stretched a torch towards her, she started back in fear and amazement.

Then men armed with torches crowded in from all sides. The bank was brightly lit up and a great, many voiced cry shook the silence of the night:

"Jafar!"

"It's the usurer Jafar!"

"It's not Khoja Nasreddin! It's Jafar the Usurer!"

After the first moments of stupor and confusion everyone suddenly began to shout, shoving and jostling and climbing over each other's shoulders to see for themselves. Guljan was in such a state that old Niyaz hastened to take her farther away from the bank, fearing for her reason. She cried and laughed, torn between doubt and belief, and struggled to take another look.

"Jafar! Jafar!" resounded the joyous cries which entirely drowned the distant noise of the palace festivities. "It is Jafar the Usurer! It is he! Here is his pouch with the receipts."

Some time passed until one of them recovered sufficiently to ask the crowd at large:

"But where then is Khoja Nasreddin?"

The question was taken up by the crowd which set up the cry:

"Then where is Khoja Nasreddin? Where is our Khoja Nasreddin?"

"He is here!" replied the familiar calm voice, and all turned round to behold in amazement the live Khoja Nasreddin, unaccompanied by any guards, who walked towards them yawning and lazily stretching himself. He had dropped asleep near the cemetery and that was why he was so late in coming.

"I am here," he repeated. "Whoever wants me—come here. O worthy inhabitants of Bukhara, why have you assembled at the pond and what are you doing here?"

"Why? Why are we here?" repeated hundreds of voices. "We came here, O Khoja Nasreddin, to take farewell of thee, to mourn thee and to bury thee."

"Me?" he said. "Mourn me? O noble inhabitants of Bukhara, little do you know Khoja Nasreddin if you think that he ever intends to die! I only lay down for a rest near a cemetery, and already you imagined I was dead!"

That was all he managed to say before the tea-house owner Ali and the blacksmith Yusuf fell upon him with happy shouts and nearly hugged him to death. Niyaz hobbled up but the old man was soon elbowed aside. Khoja Nasreddin found himself the centre of a large crowd where each wished to embrace and welcome him, while he, passing from one embrace to another, strained towards the place where he could hear the impatient and angry voice of Guljan, who was vainly trying to reach him through the press. When at last they

175

came face to face Guljan flung her arms round his neck. Khoja Nasreddin threw back her veil and kissed her in front of the crowd, and not one of those present, even the most zealous upholders of the canons and proprieties, could see anything unseemly in this.

Khoja Nasreddin raised his arm calling for silence and attention.

"You had assembled to mourn me, O inhabitants of Noble Bukhara! Don't you know I am immortal?

"I, Khoja Nasreddin,
Ever free have I been!
And I say, 'tis no lie,
That I never shall die!"

He stood in the glare of the hissing torches, and the crowd took up the refrain which rang and boomed joyously over night-enveloped Bukhara:

"I, Khoja Nasreddin,
Ever free have I been!
And I say, 'tis no lie,
That I never shall die!"

How could the rejoicings in the palace compare with these?

"Tell us," shouted someone, "tell us how you managed to get Jafar the Usurer drowned instead of you?"

"Ah!" suddenly remembered Khoja Nasreddin. "Yusuf, do you remember my oath?"

"I do!" replied Yusuf. "And you have kept it, Khoja Nasreddin!"

"Where is he?" asked Khoja Nasreddin. "Where is the usurer? Have you got his pouch?"

"No, we didn't touch it."

"Ay-ay-ay!" said Khoja Nasreddin reproachfully. "Don't you realize, O inhabitants of Bukhara, most generously provided with nobility of mind but somewhat deficient in commonsense, that if this pouch were to fall into the hands of the usurer's heirs, they would squeeze the debts out of you to the last copper? Give me his pouch."

Scores of jostling and shouting men rushed to obey Khoja Nasreddin's order. They brought the pouch and gave it to him.

He pulled out a receipt at random.

"Saddler Mamed!" he called. "Who is saddler Mamed?"

"I," answered a thin quavering voice. Out of the crowd stepped a little old man with a sparse beard, dressed in a colourful, incredibly ragged khalat.

"You, saddler Mamed, must pay tomorrow five hundred tangas according to this receipt. But I, Khoja Nasreddin, cancel your debt. Use this money for your own needs and buy yourself a new khalit. Yours looks like a ripe cotton-field: the cotton sticks out all over it."

With these words he took up a torch and held the paper in the flame.

Khoja Nasreddin proceeded in the same way with all the other receipts, and the tiny flame of these scraps of paper warmed the men's hearts better than the largest bonfire. Now these men were free for the first time in their lives, for many of them had inherited the debts of their fathers and grandfathers and had been in Jafar's bondage from their early youth for twenty years and more.

When the last receipt had been burnt Khoja Nasreddin flung the pouch far out into the pond.

"Let it lie on the bottom now and forever!" he cried. "And let no one ever hang it over his shoulder. O noble citizens of Bukhara, there is no greater infamy for a man than to carry such a pouch. Whatever may happen to you, even if one of you becomes rich—which is hardly to be hoped for while our sun-like Emir and his watchful viziers live—but if it ever happens and one of you becomes rich, he must never carry such a pouch lest he cover himself and his descendants down to the fourteenth generation with everlasting infamy! He should remember, too, that there is in this world one Khoja Nasreddin who has a heavy hand. You have seen what punishment he has meted out to the usurer Jafar. Now I shall say farewell to you, O citizens of noble Bukhara. The time has come for me to start on a long journey. Guljan, you are coming with me."

"I will go with you wherever you wish," she said.

The inhabitants of Bukhara gave a fitting send-off to Khoja Nasreddin. The caravanserai owners brought for his bride an ass as white as cotton. There was not a single dark mark on its hide and it shone proudly by the side of its grey brother, the old and loyal companion of Khoja Nasreddin's wanderings. The grey ass was not in the least embarrassed by its splendid companion and calmly munched juicy clover, even pushing the white ass away with its muzzle as though to show it that for all its undisputed superiority of colouring the white ass had no services to its credit equal to its own.

The blacksmiths brought up a portable smithy and there and then shod both asses. The saddlers made a gift of two rich saddles: one ornamented with velvet for Khoja Nasreddin, and a silver-mounted one for Guljan. The tea-house owner brought two teapots and two Chinese cups of the finest quality. The armourers gave a sword of famous *gurda* steel, so that Khoja Nasreddin should have a weapon to protect himself against highwaymen. The carpet-makers brought saddle-cloths, the lasso-makers a lasso of horse-hair which when stretched round a sleeping traveller preserves him from the bite of venomous snakes, for the snake does not dare to crawl over its prickly hairs.

Weavers, coppersmiths, tailors and shoe-makers—all brought their gifts. The whole of Bukhara, with the sole exception of the mullahs, dignitaries and men of property, fitted out Khoja Nasreddin for his journey.

The potters stood glumly aloof. They had nothing to give. What would a man do with an earthen pot when he had the copper one given by the coppersmiths?

Suddenly the oldest of the potters, who was more than a hundred years old, raised his voice:

"Who says that we, potters, have given nothing to Khoja Nasreddin? Does not his bride, this fair maiden, belong to the famous and worthy corporation of potters?"

The delighted potters raised a noisy shout. Then they sternly exhorted Guljan to be a loyal and devoted companion to Khoja Nasreddin so as not to betray the fame and honour of her people.

"Dawn is near," said Khoja Nasreddin. "Soon the city gates will be opened. My bride and I must leave unobserved. If you come to watch us go, the guards will think that the whole population of Bukhara is leaving the city to settle elsewhere and will shut the gates letting no one pass. Therefore go back to your homes, O citizens of noble Bukhara, may your slumbers be peaceful and may the black wings of misfortune never cast their shadow over you. Success accompany your deeds! Khoja Nasreddin takes leave of you. For how long? I do not know."

A narrow, barely perceptible streak was breaking through in the east. A slight mist rose from the pond. The crowd began to disperse. Men were putting out the torches and calling out:

"Happy journey, Khoja Nasreddin! Don't forget your native town!"

The leave-taking of the blacksmith Yusuf and the teahouse owner

Ali was particularly touching. Fat Ali could not hold back his tears and they ran down his round red cheeks.

Khoja Nasreddin remained in Niyaz's house until the gates were due to open. As soon as the first muezzin spun out the melancholy ringing thread of his call over the town, Khoja Nasreddin and Guljan started on their way. Old Niyaz went with them to the nearest corner—Khoja Nasreddin would not let him come any further—and the old man stood looking after them through a film of tears until they disappeared round the bend. A gentle morning breeze sprang up and busied itself on the road, carefully wiping out all traces.

Niyaz ran back to the house and hurried on to the roof. From there one could see far beyond the city wall, and he gazed long—straining his old eyes and wiping away the unbidden tears—at the brown, sun-scorched hills among which wound the grey ribbon of the road leading into the distance. He waited so long that anxiety crept into his heart. Could Khoja Nasreddin and Guljan have fallen into the hands of the guards?

But at last he discerned in the distance two specks, a white and a grey one. They gradually receded and dwindled. Soon the grey speck vanished melting into the hillside, but the white speck showed for a long time, disappearing in the dips and folds and coming into sight again. Then it, too, dissolved at last in the rising heat-mist.

The day was beginning and with it came the heat. The old man remained sitting on the roof sadly brooding and heedless of the heat. His grey head trembled and a choking lump came into his throat. He bore Khoja Nasreddin and his daughter no grudge, he wished them lasting happiness, but he was sorry for himself. The house was now empty and there was no one to enliven his lonely old age with happy song and laughter. A hot wind rose, rustling the leaves of the vineyard and whipping up the dust. Its wing struck the pots drying on the roof, and they gave out a thin and plaintive ringing as though grieving for those who had left the house.

A vague noise behind him brought Niyaz to himself. He turned round and saw coming up the stairs one after the other three brothers who lived nearby, big handsome fellows, and all potters. They approached and bowed low with every sign of respect.

"O worthy Niyaz," said the eldest. "Your daughter has left you with Khoja Nasreddin, but you must not grieve and complain, for such is the eternal law of the world. The doe cannot live without the deer. The cow cannot live without the bull and the duck cannot live without the drake. Can then a maiden spend her life without a true and devoted companion? Has not Allah created in couples all that lives on the earth, as he has separated even the shoots of the cotton-bush into male and female?

"However, in order that your old age should not be darkened, O worthy Niyaz, the three of us have decided to tell you this: he who has become related to Khoja Nasreddin has become related to all the inhabitants of Bukhara, and you, O Niyaz, have now become our relative. You know that last year we buried with sorrow and weeping our father and your friend, the most worthy Mamed-Ali, and now at our fireside there is an empty place reserved for the head of the family, and we are deprived of the daily happiness of gazing respectfully at a white beard without which, as also without an infant's cry, a home is half-empty. For a man's soul is only then at peace and contented when he is between the owner of the beard, who has given him life, and the one who lies in the cradle, to whom he himself has given life.

"Therefore, O worthy Niyaz, we beg you to lend your ear to our tears and not refuse our request. Enter our house, take at our hearth the place reserved for the head and be a father to the three of us and a grandfather to our children."

The brothers insisted so much that Niyaz could not refuse. He entered their house and was received with the greatest respect. Thus in his old age he was rewarded for his honest, virtuous life by the greatest reward which a Muslim can obtain on earth. He became Niyaz-baba, that is Grandfather Niyaz, head of a large family in which he had fourteen grandchildren. His eyes were constantly gladdened as they passed from the contemplation of one pair of pink cheeks smeared with the juice of grapes and mulberries, to another no less grubby. From then onwards his ear was never oppressed by silence, so that at times he was somewhat overpowered, and would then retire into his old home to rest and grieve a little for the two so near his heart and now so far away and gone no one knew where.

On market-days he would go to the market-place and question caravan-drivers who come to Bukhara from all the ends of the earth: had they met on the road two travellers—a man on a grey ass and a woman on a white ass without the tiniest dark mark? The drivers creased their sunburnt foreheads and shook their heads: no, they had met no such people.

Khoja Nasreddin had disappeared as usual without trace, only to reappear suddenly where he was least expected.

Last Chapter

which could serve for the beginning of a new book.

"I made seven journeys and about each journey there is an extraordinary tale which troubles the mind."

Sindbad the Sailor.

And he did reappear where he was least expected. He reappeared in Stambul.

This occurred on the third day after the Sultan had received the Emir's letter. Thousands of criers rode through the towns and villages of the Sublime Porte telling the people of Khoja Nasreddin's death. The delighted mullahs read out the Emir's letter in the mosques and gave thanks to Allah twice daily, morning and evening.

The Sultan was feasting in the palace garden, in the cool shade of poplars sprinkled by the moist dust of the fountains. All round him pressed the crowd of viziers, sages, poets and other palace retainers avidly awaiting bounty. Black slaves moved among the groups carrying steaming trays, narghiles and jugs. The Sultan was in a happy and jocose mood.

"Why is it that today, in spite of the heat, there is a delicious lightness and fragrance in the air?" he asked the sages and poets, slyly screwing up his eyes.

To which they, wistfully eyeing the leather purse in his hands, replied:

"The breath of our lustrous Sovereign has permeated the air with a delicious lightness, and the fragrance has spread because the soul of the impious Khoja Nasreddin has at last ceased to exude its vile stench which used to poison the world."

Somewhat apart, watching that order was kept, stood the Chief of the Palace Guard, preserver of peace and piety in Stambul. He differed from his Bukharan colleague Arslan-bek only by a still greater cruelty and an extraordinary leanness. These two qualities were so linked together that the citizens of Stambul had long since noticed it, and every week anxiously inquired from the palace bath-attendants whether the Chief had lost or put on weight: if the news was unfavourable, all the inhabitants who lived in the vicinity of the palace kept to their houses and did not issue forth till the next bath-day unless driven by necessity. So now this awe-inspiring personage stood somewhat apart. His turbaned head stuck out at the end of a long and scraggy neck as though on a pole (many Stambul citizens would have sighed wistfully on hearing this comparison).

All was going well, the festivities were untroubled and there was no premonition of disaster. Nobody noticed the palace steward slip with his accustomed dexterity through the crowd of courtiers towards the Chief of the Palace Guard and whisper into his ear. The Chief started, changed colour and hurriedly followed the steward out. In a few minutes he returned, pale, his mouth working. Elbowing aside the courtiers he made his way to the Sultan's side and bent double before him in a low bow.

"O great Sovereign! ..."

"Well, what is it?" the Sultan asked irritably. "Can't you keep your prison and bastinado news to yourself even on such a day? Well? Speak up!"

"O Serene and Great Sultan, my tongue refuses to speak."

The Sultan frowned, strangely disturbed. The Chief of the Guard added in a low murmur:

"He is in Stambul!"

"Who?" asked the Sultan in a hard voice, though he had immediately understood who was meant.

"Khoja Nasreddin!"

The Chief of the Guard had uttered the name very low but courtiers have sharp ears. A buzzing and babbling spread through the palace grounds:

"Khoja Nasreddin is in Stambul."

"How do you know?" asked the Sultan in a voice suddenly become hoarse. "Who told you? How can this be when we have here the Emir of Bukhara's letter in which he assures us on his royal word that Khoja Nasreddin is no longer among the living?"

The Chief of the Guard made a sign to the palace steward who led up to the Sultan a man with a flat nose on a pock-marked face, and yellow shifty eyes.

"O Sovereign," explained the Chief of the Guard. "This fellow has long served as a spy at the court of the Emir of Bukhara and knows Khoja Nasreddin well. When this man came to Stambul I engaged him in the capacity of spy, which post he occupies at the present moment—"

"Did you see him?" interrupted the Sultan turning to the spy. "Did you see him with your own eyes?"

The spy replied in the affirmative.

"Perhaps you were mistaken?"

The spy denied this. No, he could not have made a mistake. Khoja Nasreddin was accompanied by a woman riding a white ass.

"Why did you not seize him on the spot?" cried the Sultan. "Why didn't you hand him over to the guards?"

"O Serene Sovereign," replied the spy trembling and falling on his knees. "In Bukhara I once fell into the hands of Khoja Nasreddin and only through the mercy of Allah did I escape with my life. This morning when I saw him in the streets of Stambul my sight was dimmed by fear, and when I recovered my senses he was already gone."

"So that's what your spies are like!" exclaimed the Sultan glaring at the bowing Chief of the Guard. "The mere sight of a criminal is enough to frighten them out of their wits!"

He pushed the pock-marked spy contemptuously away with his foot, rose and retired into his apartments, followed by a long file of black slaves.

The viziers, poets and sages pressed towards the exit in an anxiously buzzing crowd. A few minutes later not a soul remained in the garden but the Chief of the Guard. Staring blankly into the emptiness before him he dropped down helplessly on to the marble brim of a fountain. He sat there for a long time listening to the gently splashing and laughing water. He seemed to have suddenly shrunk and shrivelled to such an extent that if the citizens of Stambul could have seen him they would have scattered in all directions, losing their slippers and not bothering to pick them up.

Meanwhile the pock-marked spy sped breathlessly through the hot streets towards the sea. There he found an Arab ship ready to sail. The master of the ship did not doubt for an instant that he was dealing with an escaped convict and demanded an extortionate price. Without stopping to bargain the spy rushed on deck and huddled down in a dark filthy corner. Later, when the slender minarets of Stambul had melted away in the blue mist and a fresh breeze filled the sails, he crept out of his shelter, visited the whole of the ship, closely scrutinising every face, and only then calmed down, reassured that Khoja Nasreddin was not on board.

From then onwards the pock-marked spy spent the rest of his days in constant and ceaseless fear. Whatever town he came to, Baghdad, Cairo, Tehran or Damascus, he never succeeded in staying there in peace longer than three months at a time, for Khoja Nasreddin was sure to appear in that town, and the pock-marked spy, dreading the meeting, fled ever farther. It would be most appropriate here to compare Khoja Nasreddin to a mighty hurricane whose breath ceaselessly chases before it a withered leaf which it sweeps out of the grass and blows out of cracks and crevices. Thus the pock-marked spy was punished for all the evil which he had brought upon others.

On the next day extraordinary and amazing events began to happen in Stambul. . . . But one should not speak of things which one has not witnessed personally and describe lands which one has not seen. So with these words we shall conclude the last chapter of our story. A wise and industrious man could use it for the beginning of a new book on the further adventures of Khoja Nasreddin in Stambul, Baghdad, Tehran, Damascus and many other famous cities.

The End
[72800 words]

A short biography of Leonid Solovyev appears in **Black Sea Sailor**, Stillwoods Edition.